COUSINS II

...DEADLY CONSEQUENCES

*To BARRY
Best Wishes
Always*

By: Libero A. Tremonti

Libero Tremonti

Airleaf
Publishing & Book Selling
airleaf.com

2-20-08

© Copyright 2007, Libero A. Tremonti

All Rights Reserved.

No part of this book may be reproduced, stored in a
retrieval system, or transmitted by any means,
electronic, mechanical, photocopying, recording,
or otherwise, without written permission
from the author.

ISBN: 978-1-60002-466-1

Library of Congress Number: 2007933899

*A special thanks to Connie… my wife and editor
You helped me turn my thoughts
Into a readable story.*

To my sister and brother-in-law…Marie and Joe Dolfi
You know the true meaning of family.

To my cousin and best friend... Vincent Galiffa
The time we spend together…priceless.

TABLE OF CONTENTS:

Chapter 1..1
Chapter 2..9
Chapter 3..15
Chapter 4..25
Chapter 5..33
Chapter 6..41
Chapter 7..55
Chapter 8..65
Chapter 9..73
Chapter 10..80
Chapter 11..88
Chapter 12..94
Chapter 13..103
Chapter 14..110
Chapter 15..117
Chapter 16..124
Chapter 17..131
Chapter 18..143
Chapter 19..152
Chapter 20..158
Chapter 21..164
Chapter 22..168
Chapter 23..178
Chapter 24..187
Chapter 25..197
Chapter 26..208
Chapter 27..215
Chapter 28..221
Chapter 29..230
Chapter 30..239
Chapter 31..249
  Epilogue..258

CHAPTER ONE

It was March and one of those days when it was raining and snowing at the same time. New Jersey often times experiences that kind of weather, with the temperature around thirty-seven degrees and the wind blowing at twenty-five miles an hour. Sonnie and Vince were walking the boardwalk with scarves around their necks and the collars of their top coats turned up and pulled tight. It was one of their favorite places to be when they had a problem or a dilemma to take care of. *'Damn it… It's March. I thought the weather was supposed to be getting better,'* Sonnie thought. They paused for a moment leaning on the ice covered railing. As they looked out over the ocean, the white caps were tranquillizing. *'This is almost as beautiful as my home in Italy but in a different way.'*

In a short time, they revamped J.D.'s organization from top to bottom and made it their own. The sisters from Italy that ran the bakery when J.D. was in charge quit and went back home. All the changes were too fast for them and they didn't trust the new bosses. They liked the old way J.D. did things, which was really their way and they weren't too sure about things to come. Sonnie and Vince agreed to try bringing in Connie and Theresa (their significant others) to handle things for a period of time to see if it would be workable. Things couldn't have gone any better with their new up-to-date ideas and promotions. The business sky-rocketed and sales went through the roof. They rearranged the store so that the customers would have an easier time walking through the bakery making their selections of wonderful goodies to take home. They had murals painted on all the walls of beautiful scenes of the villages where Sonnie and Vince grew up. The girls worked great together and each of their ideas seemed to compliment the other.

    The haircutting salon that Sonnie opened when he came to the U.S. and later brought Vinny in on was doing great. Gina, Sonnie's right hand when he was there, was taking care of the business like a pro and Sonnie gave her free reign over the operation. Gina had great ideas and was redoing the place in a way that Sonnie would have never dreamed of. As most women do when they become in charge and have complete control, she remodeled the whole place to the tune of one hundred-forty thousand dollars and Sonnie didn't blink an eye because he had faith in her and knew she would succeed. Gina kept the over-all look the same as when Sonnie ran it. She made the massage rooms a little more inviting by adding video and CD and DVD players to all the therapy rooms so the patrons could enjoy a movie or listen to their favorite music while they were enjoying their personal treatment. She really brought the place up to par by hiring two new girls, which were twins and retired show girls named Mitsie and Pitsie. Pitsie was to take care of the reception desk. Mitsie was to run the betting parlor, which was upgraded to have all the latest high-tech equipment. Gina also explained to the girls how Sonnie and Vince operated without going into too much detail. Gina trusted them and felt comfortable that they could handle anything that was asked of them. Sonnie and Vince were very pleased with the outcome and now everything and everyone was making the salon a lot of money.

    The like-new car lot which was run by Bull had become a real success in its own way. Bull was selling his cars to all the high rollers in town and making good connections. If you told Bull the kind of car, the year, and the model you wanted… he would find it at the right price. What was good about it… it was all legal. Bull had a good team of employees that would use the internet to locate the cars all over the world and would have them shipped in for the customers. He wanted to expand by putting stores in Philly and Ocean City and Sonnie had to do a lot of talking trying to hold him back until he felt it was right. Sonnie and Vince both agreed that bringing Bull into the organization was one of their best moves. He not only knew how to take care of the dirty work, he had no conscience and found it easy to be the type of enforcer Sonnie and Vince needed. Everything was going so well, it seemed like a dream.

They only had one problem. J.D., their partner, who retired and moved to Vegas. He didn't approve of some of the new ideas, but he realized he was still thinking old school. He missed being the boss and sometimes regretted giving it up to Sonnie and Vince, but deep down inside, he knew he couldn't keep up with the new way things were being done. Besides, the money was rolling in on a regular basis so he couldn't complain but so much. After all, J.D. was living the high life. He did a complete one-hundred-eighty, got away from everything that he had believed in. He sold most all of his stocks, canceled all of his retirement funds and was doing the three evils: drinking, gambling and last but not least... women. Lots and lots of everything and thinking he had clout in Vegas. All he was doing was pissing off all the wrong people. When he ran into a problem, he'd boast by saying 'You don't know who you're fucking with.' Then he would tell them to call back East and check things out. Sonnie and Vince bailed him out of a number of bad situations but knew it wouldn't be too long before his time would run out. They knew they would have to go to Vegas and have a talk with him but that he wouldn't listen to anyone because he thought he was invincible. Why he got that way, no one could say. They let it go too far and now there was nothing they could do but wait.

They decided to get a dog and a drink. Silence between them, Sonnie looked out over the ocean as the sea gulls sailed over the churning tide and the wind blew snow over his receding hair line.

"I wonder how the weather is like back home Vinny."

"I've forgotten what the weather's like there this time of year but it's got to be better than this shit. I bet it's beautiful there now. Remember how much fun we used to have there? Not like over here. People don't give a shit whether you live or die. You could fall out on the street and they just step over you, or piss on you when they walk by. I'd like to shoot half the bastards walking around over here. Sometimes I just want to go off on some of those ignorant bastards."

"Calm down. I only asked how the weather was. Every time you think about that shit, you get all crazy on me, but you're right. These pricks over here don't care about anything except themselves. The bastards don't care anything about family let alone loyalty, they have no conception about what it all means. I wonder how Aldo's getting along," Sonnie continued. "Maybe we ought to give him a call. After all, we never called him to let him know what went down and why Little Aldo hadn't returned home yet. Maybe Maria has gone back to him with some incredible story. You know how convincing that bitch can be. Maybe he thinks we've gone against him and something happened to Little Aldo. We should call him. Take some time off and go for a visit. I think we need to reassure him that we still want to keep doing business, as long as everything is above board. What'da you think, Vinny?"

"Well Sonnie, we've been keeping our end up, as far as Aldo's concerned. I don't think he should be worried about our business agreement. We've been doing business as usual, nothing's changed. As a matter a fact, it's gotten somewhat better. We've doubled what we order from him, sometimes more than double. I don't think that old fucker should have any concerns about our relationship. As a matter a fact, he should be calling us and congratulating us on what we've done for him since we took over. Why should it always be us who makes contact and get things going? You know if we don't get it started... no one does. I get tired of that bullshit. To me, everything should be okay. What puzzles me is just what you said, Little Aldo still being here. Wonder why he's never called his grandfather? Maybe he has and we just don't know what's going on. I'm sure he's been in touch with him, especially the way he's always talking about him."

"Vinny, what'da you saying? You think he's checking us out behind our back, telling Aldo how we're running things and we don't know it? That little prick. Now that you brought it up, what the hell is he doing here? Maybe we should have a talk with that little bastard and find out what the hell's going on."

"Calm down now Sonnie. Don't jump to conclusions. He is having a good time over here. The girls are showing him how it's done in America."

"What the hell did you just say? Besides, now that I think about it, where's he getting all the money he's spending? That little fucker must have an open account somewhere. Look at all the clothes he wears, those tailor made suits, and shoes. He's a shoe freak. I wonder if he's not keeping "you know who" informed about what's going on around here? If he is...I'll kill the little bastard, Don Aldo's grandson or not."

"He wouldn't dare. He knew what the game plan was and he did his part well. I know what I said. I just think we should keep a little closer eye on him and see what's up. We've let him move right in without any questions. Do whatever he wanted and didn't say a damn thing to him. That little fucker didn't hesitate either. Just made himself right at home and we gave him Carte Blanch. I know we appreciated what he did for us......"

"Remember now Vinny," Sonnie interrupted. "He didn't do that for us. He did it for his grandfather. He had their best interest in mind all the time. He didn't even know us before he came over here. He was acting on his grandfather's orders. He did a good job. I can still remember your face when you saw those guys hanging upside down with their throats slit."

"Yea," Vinny replied. "I couldn't believe he got the upper hand on those guys. He's so young if I didn't know any better, I would have thought Tito gave him a few lessons. You remember how spooky that guy was. We should go have a talk with him. Ask him what the hell he's up to. If that little fucker's doing what you said Sonnie, I'll skin him alive myself."

"Take it easy now. We have to be cool about this. We just can't go barging in there and start asking a lot of questions. Besides, he's been hanging out with the girls at the shop and if there was anything unusual going on, I think they would have seen something wasn't right. We need to watch him a while and see what he's up to. Then, if he's doing something under-handed...I'll skin him alive. Better yet, we'll put him in the mixer and turn him into a smoothie or…we could turn him over to Bull."

"Let's get off this boardwalk Vinny, my head's getting cold."

"Yea, what happened? You're starting to get a little thin up there. You used to have more hair than me. Remember what Gramps use to tell all his goombas at the shop don't you? How'd it go…'You're not going bald, you're just gaining face.' I don't know how often you think about him but I think about him on and off quite a bit. I think about the first time I saw him. The way he dressed in those old clothes, needing a hair cut, and he owned a barber shop. You talk about miss judging a person. Boy was I taken back when I started really paying attention to him and how he handled everything. Especially those goofs that hung out at the shop. You talk about loyalty, those guys would do anything he asked without hesitation, no matter what it was. He could tell them to go home and shoot their wives and I think they would have done it."

"I know Vinny, what was weird… he never did anything violent. You know, for every action, there's a reaction. That's what he did. He reacted in a calm manner and everyone and everything just fell into place. The only time I ever seen him really pissed off was when he found out who killed my Mom and Dad. Boy he was pissed that day! He was ready to go over the edge. He was on the way out the door to take care of business… if it wasn't for Mongo and Tito holding him back, he would have tried to handle it himself. I remember Mongo standing in front of him in a protecting way but meaning business. You know how he always had all these little sayings. The one that fit him well was the one he used to tell us all the time, 'power perceived is power achieved.' I wonder if he would approve of our so-called success? The way we went about getting what we've wanted."

"I loved his theory on how to get respect. First he would strike fear into them, then he would show them love by doing something nice like taking care of a problem or doing something to help their family. We thought it was stupid when we were young but like everything else he did, as we got older we realized how smart he really was. So… what do you think we should do?"

"About what Vinny? Oh… you mean the Little Aldo thing?"

"Yea, Vinny nodded. I'm really pissed thinking he might be snooping around behind our backs. All at once I'm starting to get spooked."

"Now let's not jump to conclusions. I think we ought to pack his bags and take the little shit head back to his grandfather. I think if we go to Italy and spend a couple of days there, we'll be able to sense what's going on. Someone will make a mistake or do something to tell us if something's up. I don't think we've gotten so comfortable that we can't tell what's going on around us."

"Good idea, but who's going to take care of everything if both of us go? We're kind of thin in the manpower department. I thought Rando was supposed to bring a couple of guys around to talk to us. What's up with him? He's starting to get a little slacked. It's like he doesn't get it… or he doesn't care. You know like, he had it once then lost it." Vince suggested.

"I've been noticing that. It's like he's in a fog all the time. I think maybe he didn't expect what went down with those guys from Philly. He did know where we were going with that but I guess no one gave him the details about it. After all, he was a plumber before he came to work for us. Probably the most excitement he ever had was a busted pipe or two. What I really liked about him was why you hired him in the first place. He didn't take no shit from anyone. He's a good enforcer. Just what we needed.

"Here's another thing Sonnie. Why doesn't he ever have any chicks with him like he used to? He's so secretive, he never comes around and hangs out with the troops anymore. He don't tell us what he's doing or where he's going when we ask him. He sort of ignores us when we ask him something. Maybe he's got something up his sleeve. Remember Lenny? That fucker went against us after we took him in and taught him the ropes. That's gratitude for ya. You know, Rando doesn't look us in the face anymore. That's one thing I liked about him."

"Vince, what the hell we doing here? We're standing here making things look all fucked up. We keep talking like this and we'll start believing it. We're probably way off base. Let's keep our eyes open, talk to Aldo then set something up… take Little Aldo and go to

7

Italy. Shit Vince, everything can run itself. After all, it's only a week. What can go wrong in a week? Ah….. look at this shit. Some damn pigeon just shit on my coat."

As he takes a napkin and starts wiping his coat, Sonnie can see he was only making the spot worse.

Vince couldn't control himself and burst out laughing.

"I don't think that's so damn funny. I'll never get this shit off of here. If I had my gun I'd shoot that fucker."

"No Sonnie, you know what I think about when I see pigeons? Remember the first time you came to visit me when I was in school in Milan? Remember when we were walking around the square and there were all those pigeons and I screamed?"

"Yea…And that scary old homeless woman came running at you with this stick or something…yelling that you were a communist."

"No shit…Man, that's the first time I was ever scared of anything in my life. She sure was spooky. To make matters worse, she wouldn't even take any money from us afterwards. Kept calling us dirty names. I thought I had a foul mouth at that time but that chick took the prize. What's really sad is that she probably was someone's mother."

They laughed all the way back to the car. Something they hadn't done for a long time. As the ice began melting on the handrails at the boardwalk and the sea gulls circled high above the crashing waves, the two men knew that the time spent here was good for both of them. They would return to discuss business and share their thoughts, past, present and future.

CHAPTER TWO

Sonnie made the call to Aldo in Italy and confirmed the arrangements necessary for himself, Vince, Little Aldo, Connie and Theresa to go for a visit. Sonnie and Vince would do some business there, while the girls would sight-see and do a lot of shopping. Rando would oversee things at the salon and the girls had a back-up crew to handle the things at the bakery.

Everyone arrived at the airport an hour early in case of unforeseen delays. They all checked in and boarded the plane just as the pilot was announcing over the intercom that there was ice on the runway and that there would be a short delay before they could depart.

"Doesn't that just figure? Sonnie grumbled. The more you want to get away from this weather, the worse it gets. I'm starting to get antsy Vinny. This is March…the weather's supposed to be breaking now. I sure hope it's a lot warmer where were going."

"It's the same in Italy as it is here," added Little Aldo. "Maybe a little warmer, no snow."

"That's great! We're supposed to be getting away from this shit, damn it. It's really going to piss me off if it's this bad over there."

Connie rubbed her hand along Sonnie's leg.

"Don't worry Sonnie, I'll keep you warm. First I'll…

"I have a feeling, interrupted Vince. This is going to be more information that we need to know, Connie."

Everyone laughed but Sonnie was not amused.

The plane finally took off after a two hour delay. Once in the air, everything was going well and everyone was laughing, drinking and having a good time, until Vince said something that brought up Rando's name.

"I thought you guys didn't let anyone work for you that did drugs, Little Aldo added." Everyone got quiet and was waiting for what was coming next.

"What are you saying Aldo?" Vince asked.

"Yea, he's into heroin big time. I thought you guys knew he got hooked up with this stripper at one of the clubs, she's the one that got him started. I didn't say anything 'cause he's one of your boys and I thought you knew everything your guys did. I thought you guys were on top of everything. Besides, that's none of my business."

"That's just great! We're 20,000 feet in the air half way across the ocean and you tell us we left some dope-head in charge of everything. That's just fucking great. What do we do now Vince? How can we get this damn plane turned around? We got to do something quick or we won't have anything left when we get back. That prick will stick it all in his arm or up his nose, or give it all away. I bet that hooker-slut got all kinds of ideas for our money. How long you known about this? Who else knows? I can't believe anyone hooked up with us wouldn't tell us. I just talked to that son-of-a-bitch before we left. That bastard has some talking to do. Soon as we land I'm going back. Vince, you can stay and talk with Don Aldo and get things straight for us and I'll go back and get this mess... ah hell, I don't even want to think what's going on."

"Damn Sonnie, calm down. I don't think he would risk doing anything stupid knowing what could happen to him when we get home. Look, I'm going to call Bobby and see what he can find out about Rando. Maybe we're blowing this all out of proportion."

"Look Vince, I... we can't take any chances. We went through a lot to get to where we are. We can't let some dope-head ruin everything for us. We have to get some answers, I mean real quick. It just figures, we think we got everything under control and someone sticks it to us again. I'm getting real tired of this shit."

"I know Sonnie, you don't have to remind me about what we went through. We'll get it all worked out. I'll call Bobby like I suggested... it can't hurt."

'*I wish Petey was around. We wouldn't have to guess where anyone was. He knew everything that was going on before we did,*' Vince mumbled under his breath.

"What did I hear you say Vinny? You wish who was around? Gee, I never thought I would hear that coming out of your mouth."

"You know it's true Sonnie. He was a pain in the ass but a loyal pain in the ass. He could tell you the last time you took a dump. That little fucker aggravated the hell out of us but he would always come through for us. It was like there was ten of him and every time we'd want to do some thing without him, his little ass would show up."

Vince put a call into Bobby but he wasn't home so he dialed Bobby's cell phone and he didn't answer there either. He made a few more calls trying to reach him and left messages for him to call back right away because it was very important. Sonnie was really panicking now. Theresa suggested calling Bull and Vince shot a look at her as if to say keep quiet this doesn't concern you, but then realizes that's not such a bad idea. He smiles at Theresa and called Bull's private number at the dealership. Bull answered and Vince explained what was going on and that he couldn't get a hold of Bobby.

"He's here Vince, I'll let you talk to him."

"Bobby, we're trying to locate Rando. Have you seen him? He doesn't answer any of his phones."

"Right after you guys left, he told me he was going out of town for a while. It didn't sound right to me, so I went to the office and found the safe had been broken into."

"What! "Which one Bobby? Why didn't you call? " Little beads of sweat were appearing on Vinny's forehead.

"The one behind the picture. That's the only one I know about Vince. It looked like he had the combination. That's what I was here talking to Bull about. We were going to try and take care of it with out bothering you'nz on your vacation."

"Forget that for now. I need you to get your ass back to the office and call me as soon as you get there. I need you to check things out for us. Call me as soon as you get there. Don't forget Bobby… this is important. Now put Bull on the phone."

"Don't worry Vince, I'll take care of everything."

"We put Rando in charge and now he's fucking everything up," he told Bull.

Vince asked Bull to watch out for Rando and if he saw him, just to keep his eyes on him and make sure he doesn't flush everything down the toilet. Bull assured Vince that wouldn't happen now that he knew what was going on, he and Bobby would take care of everything. Meanwhile, Sonnie was going nuts babbling out loud and wondering if Bobby was in on it.

"If he's doing drugs, he might just take the damn money from the other safe and piss it all away too. What are we going to do?

After about thirty minutes, Bobby called Vince back.

"Is it Bobby? Sonnie asked. "What's he doing? Where is he? Is the other safe broken into? What's going on? Tell me something Vinny?"

Vince waved his hand as if to tell Sonnie to be quiet so he could hear Bobby who was on the other end of the line.

"Bobby, go into the bathroom, slide back the cabinet on the right side of the wall, and tell me what you see."

All the while this is going on, Sonnie was having a hard time trying to contain himself.

"I don't believe this shit's happening."

Connie tried to calm him down but he was like a Brahma bull in the holding gate just waiting to explode and throw some poor unsuspecting rider half way across the arena floor. Bobby made his way to the bathroom and saw that everything was a total mess.

"Hey Vince, this place is all tore up. It looks like someone tried to beat open the safe but it looks like it's okay."

"That's great Bobby."

"Let me talk to him, Vince." Vince handed the phone to Sonnie.

"Bobby, this is very important. Go check out my house and Vince's condo. See if anything out of place."

"Sonnie, we got everything under control."

"What do you mean, we?"

"As soon as I saw the mess in the office, I told Bull and he suggested sending some of his boys to both places to check them out. They called and said all was secure. They're going to watch both places until you guys say different. I called New York and I have a couple of guys coming down to help me out."

"I didn't want the people in New York to think we don't have enough manpower and can't take care of our own business. That makes us look weak."

"Don't worry Sonnie. These are good friends of mine. They don't have nothing to do with the people I work for. I wouldn't do anything to jeopardize your situation. Besides, I like it here. I'll just tell them that this guy's done some things that don't sit well with my bosses and I know how good they are finding out things. Who knows? It might work out that you'nz like them and want them to stay on. They're not working and looking for a change. They're very loyal and I'd trust them fully."

Sonnie put his hand over the phone.

"I think we put the wrong man in charge," he whispered to Vince.

"I'll remember what you've done for us Bobby. Hunt down that bastard. If you find him, keep him on ice 'til we get back. We'll want to have a long talk with him."

"Do you want me to clean up the mess at the office or wait 'til you guys get back? I could take care of the mess alone and no one would have to know anything."

"Leave it for now Bobby, I'll get back with you. You're doing a good job. Just find that bastard. Call us as soon as you find out something or even if you don't. We can't let this prick...to think what we've done for him. Just find out where he is and you and Bull sit on him 'til we get back. Then we'll handle it."

Sonnie hung up the phone and asked for the stiffest drink on board. '*What the hell did I get us into?* Sonnie thought as he gazed at his reflection on the window. *I'm taking too much for granted. I know better. If I didn't make us take this time to visit Don Aldo, that fucker wouldn't have had the opportunity to rob our ass.*' For a brief moment, Sonnie tried to put himself into his grandfather's shoes and wondered how he might handle the situation but nothing came to him. He looked over at Vince, Theresa, Connie, and Little Aldo but they had all fallen asleep.

'*I can't let nothing happen to them,* Sonnie thought. *They're all I have!*'

CHAPTER THREE

    The flight to Italy was uneventful except for some minor turbulence and having to stay in a holding pattern over Naples for almost an hour. Even though Bobby and Bull seemed to have everything under control, Sonnie was still a nervous wreck about everything going on back home. To make matters worse, the girls' luggage didn't make the flight and they were panicking because the clothes they were wearing were very skimpy and they wanted to make a good impression on everyone. Sonnie and Vince didn't seem to mind what was showing as they knew the girls would make a hit no matter what they were wearing. Actually, the less the better they thought. They were proud of their ladies and wanted to show them off. Little Aldo called his grandfather and Don Aldo was glad that they had arrived safely. He asked why they hadn't let him know when they were to arrive so he could send a car for them. Little Aldo told him that Sonnie and Vince had wanted to rent a car so that they could show the girls where they had grown up and to see what had changed since they had left.

    "Don't worry, I gave them your number and Vince said that he would call as soon as they got settled in. My rental is ready... I'll see you in about an hour."

Don Aldo was disappointed and thought it wasn't the way it should be. He should be seen first but that was the old way and the Don knew times were different now.

As they left the airport crowded into the little compact car they had rented, Sonnie and Vince thought it would be nice to see the old places where they had grown up. Naples is a beautiful city with all the fountains shooting their water into the sky. The bright winter sun made the little crystals look like diamonds in the air. The streets were crowded just like the big cities in the states but it was different in a way. The people seemed happier and the young couples with their arms entwined and smiles on their faces gave you a sense of joy. There were tour buses that took the tourists to various sites but no one seemed to be in a hurry. The pigeons in the square flocked around the fountains cooing for any morsel of food they could find. Even with all the sounds of the city, you could always hear music or someone singing around every corner. The girls saw that it was true what they had heard about Italy, there was always love in the air. The one thing that was the same, everyone either had a cell phone or a cup of coffee in one hand.

As they left the city and drove towards the country where Sonnie and Vince lived, the girls were getting excited. They had heard them talk a lot about how different it was growing up in comparison to living in the states. Connie and Theresa were in ah at the beauty of the mountains and how bright the colors of the countryside were even though it was early spring. They stopped the car several times to take pictures with their cameras and marveled at the landscape. The scenery was like the paintings that they had seen being sold in the square but were much more vivid. They commented how beautiful the little villages were and how they remained untouched by time. The little narrow cobble stone streets, the stone houses with smoke coming from the chimneys and the little yards that were all sectioned off, ready for planting or had already been neatly planted. While driving through the narrow streets, Vince rolled down the front window and told the girls to take a deep breath. Their faces lit up with a big smile as they could smell the aroma of all the wonderful things that were being cooked. They could smell bread baking and sauces being cooked as they passed by each block of houses. They saw little old ladies in front of their houses with aprons around their waist, hair up in a bun and sweeping the steps and sidewalks. It was like a step back in time. *'Boy you don't see much of that in America,'* Theresa thought. It made you forget it was late in the twentieth century. When they got to the marketplace, there were sausages and cheeses hanging in front of store windows. Meat, fish and fresh vegetables sitting on display ready for you to make your pick. Handmade baskets of various sizes hung from nails and around the store for the customer's convenience. There were little old men sitting at tables drinking wine and smoking their cigars. They looked like a painted picture and Connie and Theresa couldn't believe places like this still existed. As they drove on, Sonnie mentioned to Vince that he was a little uncomfortable.

"What now? Why don't you let things rest for a while? We'll handle that prick when we get back to the States. For now, we have to concentrate on the present and what to do with Don Aldo. Making him comfortable with us is our main concern now."

"Well, I wasn't thinking about that son-of-a-bitch. What do you think about going to see Don Aldo first? We'll have plenty of time to renew our feelings. I know he's probably wondering why we're not there. You know Vinny, he's old school and I don't want him to think we're disrespecting him. After all, we came here to make it clear about our alliances to him. We don't need him turning on us. Not now anyway."

"I thought about saying something to you about that but I thought you knew him better than I did," Vince replied. "You think he'll be alright with what we're doing? If you think that's the way to go… let's do it. The only problem I have is… I don't remember how to get there. It's been a long time. Some of the streets look familiar and some I don't even remember."

"I'm the same way. I think we should give him the call. You have his number Vinny? My memories going fast. I can't remember shit anymore. "

"I thought you had it Sonnie."

"We're starting to act like a couple of retards. I guess we'll have to look it up in the phone book if he's even in the book. It's been so long since I looked at anything written in Italian, I wouldn't know what I was looking at. Although…if I look at it long enough maybe it'll come back to me."

"I think I can remember enough Sonnie. Better yet, why don't we surprise him and just show up there?"

"I thought you didn't know how to get there."

"I think with a little time on the road, it'll come back to me. The more I'm driving around, the more familiar it's becoming to me.

After driving around for about thirty minutes, Vince found the compound. As they drove up, they could see the guards walking at the front gates with shotguns. Nothing had changed. Time passed but coming back here was standing still in time. Don Aldo was old and still did things the old way. Little Aldo saw them driving up and ran out to meet them. As they walked through the compound, Connie and Theresa couldn't believe how secure it was. It looked like they were ready for war. It was a little scary to them but in a strange way, they felt safe. *'What the hell's all this? This doesn't look normal to me,'* Connie thought. Don Aldo was glad to see them and the embrace was warm although Sonnie and Vince knew he still might be a little upset with them for taking so long to get in touch with him. A slender middle-aged woman dressed in a bright yellow dress and dark hair down her back combed into a braid showed the girls to their room. Sonnie and Vince sat with Don Aldo in a large room off of the foyer and drank some homemade wine, hoping to find out from him if he was disappointed that they didn't come to see him first when they arrived in Italy.

"I was happy with the way you treated my grandson," Don Aldo said as he nodded and raised his glass. "How you watched over him and made sure nothing happened to him."

"Trust me Don Aldo," Vince replied. "We didn't have to do a thing for him. He moved in and made himself right at home. I don't think you ever have to worry about him taking care of himself. Tell him Sonnie."

Vince settled back in his chair and reached for his wine.

"The way he handled those two thugs…well, I can't explain how surprised we were. You ought to be proud. All the time you spent teaching him everything. He's a good student...he learns well. He'll be very valuable to you someday. Teach him all you can especially what it means to be loyal. You know as well as we do what can happen when people aren't. I don't have to tell you Don Aldo, family's everything. Without them... you're nothing. My grandfather Quadrio used to say '*as the family goes, we go*'."

Don Aldo liked what he was hearing.

"I try to show him how things should be and how he should learn from the people around him. I thought him to take everything he sees and hears into consideration. Take the good and the bad and make it into something he can use. He's still young. All I know are the old ways. The new way, you know the way it is today...it's not the same. The drugs, everyone wanting to be the boss. I'm glad I'm old. I won't have to put up with it much longer. What you say about loyalty cannot be taught. It has to be part of his teachings from birth. Either you have it or you don't. I think he'll be alright with that. Sometimes he's hard headed and doesn't listen. Hey, we were all like that at one time. Hopefully, he'll grow up as we did."

"In a few years," Sonnie added, "He'll be stronger and wiser. How is he with the others? Do they respect him? Do they listen and not make fun of what he says because he's so young? I'm hoping it's not like America here. There, no one has any respect for anybody or anything. In the States it's all about the money... who has it and how much do they have. I hope all the decisions he makes are the right ones. I know if he listens to you Don Aldo and pays attention, he'll become wise beyond his years."

"*Ricordati, ognuno e capace di fare una decisione, ma onorare quella decisione separa l'uomo dal ragazzo.* (Remember anyone can make a decision but to honor that decision separates the man from the boy.) I remember my boys, if only they could have been different. (Sonnie's mind drifted momentarily to when he was young and heard that it was Aldo's sons that killed his parents.) The decisions you and Vincent made, I have no regrets about it. They were my boys but deep down inside, I knew they were rotten. They were destine to destroy themselves and everything in their paths. I never told anyone this but I was ready to take the same action you and Vincent took, but in a different way. I knew it was going to come down to them or me. They were my sons but only in blood. I could see the evil in them. In a way, I'm glad you destroyed them. That way, I wouldn't have a heavy heart."

"My grandfather never taught revenge or never believed in it," Sonnie added. "But when it's your family, things change. He changed... once he found out what happened. I never wanted to hurt him or for him to get hurt. When you made an alliance with him... I'm glad you did what you did Don Aldo. To tell you the truth, I was scared for my grandfather for quite a while after that because I didn't know what your intensions were. I didn't know if your alliance was just a setup back then. Regardless of what you say they were still your sons."

"He was a good man your grandfather. Sometimes misunderstood and a little bull-headed but never the less, we got along. He came along before I did and he had a hard road to get to where he was. That's all in the past Sonnie. Let's talk about happy times and...well tell me about this thing with Maria. You talk about greed. I don't know what got into her. She just went off the deep end. You know, about money and power...she wanted it all. When she came to live here, she was so innocent but as she got older and saw what money and power could do, she changed for the worse. She got hooked up with some of my son's friends and they're the ones that changed her. Together we could have had so much more. Such a beautiful woman. Just like all the women in my family."

"The way she told us when we called here, you were loosing you're memory, didn't know anyone or didn't know what you were doing or saying. You look perfectly alright to me. What was that all about?" Vince asked.

"Here's what happened Vincent. Maria hired this new cook or chef as she called him. Honestly, he couldn't boil water as far as I was concerned. You should have tasted his pasta. How can you mess up pasta? I gave her everything. I felt guilty about what my boys did to her mother and father. When she got older, I just turned everything over to her... don't ask me why. She was very clever. Anyway, it turns out they were drugging me with some kind of poison. It made me...it was like I couldn't... I could think something but couldn't say it. People I knew thought I was going out of my mind. One of my maids was screwing the cook and he told her everything. She called my doctor and told him and he figured out what they were giving me so he gave me the antidote. If he wasn't a life long friend, I don't know what would have happened to me. From then on, we kept quiet. I just sat back and let her think she was in control 'til I could figure out what to do. But once again you guys took care of my problem before I could. Anyway, where is she?"

"That's a good question, Sonnie responded. We thought maybe she came back here and gave you some bullshit story and you took her back. We didn't know if we were going to be welcomed or shot down at the airport. It's been very scary wondering where she was and thinking the worst. You're very important to us. Not only as a business partner but a lifelong friend. We go back a long way and it's important to us that we carry on this relationship this way. You're the closest thing to family I have Don Aldo and I honor and respect you. I don't want that to change."

Just then, Vince's cell phone rang and it was Bobby. He would tell Vince of the progress in finding Rando, which was none. There was no sign of him. All the girls from the salon were out looking for him with no luck. Bobby said Bull said not to worry and that he had all his entourage out looking also. Vince hung up, looked at Sonnie and shook his head no. Sonnie just frowned in dismay.

"Is there a problem?" asked Don Aldo. "Tell me if I can help in anyway."

"It's nothing," replied Vince.

"Our main man," Sonnie informed Aldo. "The one we left in charge has a drug problem. We didn't find it out 'til we were on the plane and half way over here. Little Aldo told us. He's disappeared but not before cleaning out one of our safes. I hope he's having a good time. It'll be his last."

"I hope you make an example of him. You can't afford to let people see how vulnerable you are. That's the biggest mistake people make. They forgive. First thing you know... everyone's pissing on you. It becomes a big problem if you let him get away with this."

"Don't worry Don Aldo, we'll handle it accordingly. He'll wish he'd chosen another way. He was a smart boy but by now the drugs probably changed that."

"From what Little Aldo tells me, you guys take care of business swiftly and without hesitation. So that shouldn't be a problem."

"Isn't that the only way? *Tu sai, le azioni hanno sempre delle conquenze, e se uno sbaglia deve pagare. Se fai le cose per bene, ne sarai ricompensato.* (You know one's actions has a course of consequences and you pay those consequences if one makes the wrong choice. If your actions are right…you reap the rewards.) Right now, Vince and I run our family and we'll handle it our way. There's no other way. We have to show others what we're all about."

"You sound like your grandfather. I only knew him a short while but when I was in the same room or around him, there were nothing but good feelings coming from him. It was like we were always on the same page. I can't explain it. All the other bosses had respect for him and they knew he wasn't to be messed with, even though he didn't associate heavily with any of them. The funny thing was, he never knew that. He always thought by sticking to himself and keeping his business private, was the reason no one messed with him. You don't get respect, you earn it. He did just that by handling his business privately and quickly. Like I said before, he was a little hard headed. He never involved anyone but the people necessary and took care of the problem swiftly and quietly. He was a wise man. He had his own way of doing things, even though he didn't think like we did, it always worked out as if he did. The only thing was, when he got older he got a little too trusting and he wasn't thinking things out properly. I was going to talk with him about that but he had his heart attack."

"Don Aldo, I can remember when I was little, all those guys hanging around the barber shop and no one getting haircuts. It wasn't 'til I was older, I found out what was going on by hiding outside under the window. I learned a lot by hiding out there. I wouldn't want him to give me a shave, especially if I might have done something to piss him off. It was sort of funny. He was always sharpening his razor but never used it. I think it was some sort of a signal. You know, like don't fool around…somebody's going to get hurt. You're right. He was a wise man and the older I got…the smarter he became, if you know what I mean."

"I know it's late and you guys are probably tired and hungry. Can I get them to fix you something? Don Aldo asked. The girls have been taken care of. By the way, you guys have good taste. Are all the women in America… they all look that good? Do they all have those big chummies? I learned that from your grandfather."

"Far from it Don Aldo. We just got lucky. What's good about those two, they don't ask questions. They just go along with everything… well not everything. You know what I mean. It's sort of like the women of the old days. Better seen and not heard. They keep opinions to themselves for now. Who knows when that will change?"

"By the way, my niece is having an engagement party. I've arranged for you and the girls to attend. I think it's just a good reason for everyone to get together. We'll have a great time and it would be something for the girls to see and get familiar with some of our customs. I know they have these things in America, but over here, they're somewhat different. You and Vince should remember. You haven't been away that long that you have forgotten what they were like. Since it will be Sunday, we'll go to church first. The ceremony after, will be here in my main ballroom and then in the square. There will be plenty of food and drink for everyone. I think the girls will enjoy the day. It's more for the young people anyway. I told my wife we shouldn't attend because we had business to take care of but she says otherwise. What a celebration it's going to be."

"We would be honored to attend, Don Aldo. The girls will have to find a place to get the proper clothes to wear. You see, our luggage got here but theirs didn't. Being on vacation they just came casual, not knowing this would be taking place. They would be glad to go shopping. You know how women are when shopping is mentioned."

Vince and Sonnie could see that Aldo was a wise man and they were relieved he didn't mention anything about them not seeing him earlier.

"They will have plenty of time. The ceremony's not 'til two in the afternoon. I'll have someone take them to the village to buy what they need. Then everything's set for tomorrow. Our business can wait. We'll have plenty of time for that. Besides, I don't know why there should be any concerns. I know we haven't talked for a while but the business has been great and sometimes when everything's going well, there isn't much to say. I said to you before...I like the way you operate your organization and so that makes me not worry about there being any misgivings. Our relationship is very comfortable."

Sonnie and Vince turned in for the night, both anticipating what might happen in the next couple of days. Both of them being there with Don Aldo and with what was going on at home thousands of miles away. However, they felt good about what Don Aldo had said to them about their business relationship. They were both relieved that all the misconceptions about Little Aldo weren't coming to be and it was good that he wasn't putting on a front for something else.

Just the thought of Rando taking advantage and making a fool out of them weighted heavily on Sonnie's mind. Sonnie didn't have a restful night, thinking mainly about what Rando had done to the organization. Sonnie knew that he had been taken advantage of and he felt it was his fault because he let friendship come before business. That was the one thing his grandfather preached to him when he was growing up. Sonnie remembered when he was just a young boy and he gave his favorite toy to another boy down the hill from where he lived and the boy never gave it back. That was the first time his grandfather taught him the difference between friendship and trust. Just because you liked and trusted someone, that didn't mean that they think the same way, you do. Vince on the other hand, rested well. He knew that it was only a matter of time before they would have their way with Rando.

CHAPTER FOUR

Sonnie, Vince and the girls woke up to a beautiful morning. The air was brisk but the sun was warm and bright. The houses in the village were painted different colors and as the sun reflected off of them, it would remind you of the beauty of a DiVince masterpiece. Theresa and Connie could see how Sonnie and Vince could fall in love with the quaint villages of their homeland. The breads baking and the aroma of the different dishes cooking, the smells in the morning would awaken your senses. Even though it was early, they could feel the excitement something big was going to happen that day. They all sat down to a wonderful breakfast of fresh bread, salami, egg, sausage and different fruits. They had a choice of regular milk, goat's milk, different fruit juices, coffee and of course wine which was served at all meals. The house was full of energy with people running around everywhere to get things ready for the big event. Even though all this was happening around him, Sonnie felt uneasy. Not because of the excitement but as if something was going to happen. Either there or at home, he couldn't put his finger on it but he felt something was up. Sonnie pulled Vince aside and shared his feelings with him.

"Maybe all this stuff at home has got you going crazy. Maybe your imagination's getting the best of you."

"I can't explain it but every time I feel this way…well something goes wrong. I'm telling you Vinny… I'm usually right. I wouldn't be telling you this if I didn't feel strongly about it. Please Vinny, keep your eyes open. I'm telling you… something's not right."

"Come on Sonnie, try to relax. We're here on vacation. Think about the celebration today and what a good time it's going to be, the singing, the dancing. It'll be like the old times. Think of Gramps with a glass of wine in his hand and that cigar in his mouth, singing only the way he could. Then after he had too much to drink, he would dance balancing his wine glass on his forehead. Remember how he used to make all the old people get up and dance? He was something, wasn't he?"

"Well…maybe you're right Vinny. I'll try to think about today but it's not going to be easy. Do me a favor if you could. Don't take what I say with a grain of salt. I know what I'm saying and what I'm feeling. I wouldn't be worrying you with this stuff if it was just a whim. I just know what I'm talking about."

"All right…if it will make you happy, I'll keep on top of things. I hope you're not driving you and me nuts for nothing. Let me ask you, do you think Little Aldo's up to something?"

"I can't put my finger on it Vinny. It just don't feel right. Casually talk too Little Aldo… see if you think he looks uneasy. See what kind of vibes you get from him. You're real good about that."

After breakfast, they all piled into the car to take ride and see the old house and barbershop where Sonnie and Vince had learned the business. All the way over, Sonnie wondered what kind of condition it was in and who now owned it. Don Aldo had said that he had never thought about seeing the old place or taking care of it. Every now and then, Maria would bring it up but he didn't remember anyone doing anything to it. As they got closer to the house where Sonnie was raised from the age of three by his grandmother and grandfather after the death of his parents, he was starting to get butterflies in his stomach. They could see the old house first. It looked as if someone had been living there and although it had been about ten years since Sonnie had left, the house looked in great condition. It was painted a dark emerald green with white shutters and the little yard in front looked well kept with little spring flowers just starting to break ground.

"What a coincidence," Sonnie remarked of the color of the house. "That's my favorite color."

As they pulled into the driveway and circled around the back of the house where the barbershop use to be, they could see that the place looked the same. It was as if they had stepped back in time ten years even though the barbershop looked smaller than they had remembered. The building had been recently painted with white wash to protect it from the weather and the windows were clean and shiny. Sonnie and Vince were both amazed when they looked through the window and saw all of the pictures still on the walls, just as they had been when Gramps was alive and running the place. Even the picture of the Pope was still there and the two red barber chairs looked brand new, just as they did when Gramps had them.

"Hey Vinny, let's see if my old key still works."

"I'm not believing you still have the key to this place. As a matter of fact, I brought mine just in case you forgot yours."

Theresa pressed against Vince's shoulder.

"Hurry up. I'm anxious to go inside and see what it's like."

"It's spooky how you guys think alike," Connie added. "I've been paying attention to you'nz since we left the airport. You don't realize it but sometimes you finish each other's sentences. Com'on guys try and see if the key works."

Sonnie held out the key to Vince.

"Here... you do the honor."

"No," replied Vince. "You first."

Theresa grabbed the key from Sonnie's hand and while Sonnie and Vince were just standing there, the girls go inside. As they're looking around the place, they noticed that it smelt like someone had recently been there cleaning. Everything was dust free and Gramps's scissors and combs were where they belonged, cleaned and oiled. There were even towels next to the water picture that Gramps used when he would shave one of his goombas. As they slowly walked around the old place, it was like being in a time-warp for Sonnie and Vince. Who would do something like this? Who knew all the little details? The more the four of them looked around, the more they could see that it was quiet obvious that someone was coming there on a regular basis to take care of the place. But who would do this?

"We better go up to the house," Sonnie said. "Who knows what we'll find there?"

As Sonnie locked up the barbershop, the girls had already walked up the path to the house. Vince waited for Sonnie and together they approached the house. Sonnie's key fit the lock just as before and they entered and stood in amazement.

A place for everything and everything in its place. Again, clean and polished… just like Gramps' barbershop. As Sonnie looked around the room where he slept, he noticed something on the night stand next to the bed.

"Hey Vinny, come here. Check this out."

"What is it?"

"Tell me what you think it is."

"It looks like one of those lens covers from the rockets we used to take out those bastards that killed your parents. That's really weird."

"It is. Remember me telling you on the night we did that, Maria showed up and when we left, I told her I had forgot one of the covers. I thought she was behind me so I just kept going but when I turned to look for her, she wasn't there. I started to go back to find her but I saw the light on her scooter coming towards me so I just kept going. I never asked her what happened but I bet she went to get that cover."

"You sure you didn't leave it there?"

"No. I remember burying all that stuff behind the barbershop next to a dead grape vine. I buried it real deep so no one would ever find it."

"Maybe someone dug it up and knew what you did and why you put it there," suggested Connie. "By the way, who's this Maria chick anyway? Is she your old squeeze? Come on Sonnie, you can tell me. I won't get mad."

"What do you think Connie? Theresa asked. We just going to stand here or go back where he buried the stuff and find out if it's still there?"

Cousins II

"Right. Let's go check it out," Connie replied as the two girls stepped out the door into the morning sun.

Sonnie locked the door and the four of them left the house to go behind the barbershop and see if they could find where Sonnie buried the box of evidence. As they walked down the path, they saw a young boy looking around their car.

"Get the hell away from there, yelled Vince."

As the boy turned in surprise, for a split second, his eyes met Vince's and with what looked like a smile on his face, hurried away.

"What the hell was that all about?" Sonnie asked."

"Damn if I know. I wonder if the little bastard took anything."

Sonnie, Vince and the girls finally make their way behind the barbershop. It was all different now. Everything was all overgrown and there were several dead grape vines where their grandfather grew grapes for his homemade wine. Sonnie couldn't remember exactly which one it was and they weren't exactly dressed for digging.

"Let's just forget about it for now," Vince told Sonnie as he wiped the dirt from his shoes. "We'll come back when we're better prepared."

Sonnie just knew that Maria had put the lens cover on the night stand, even if he couldn't convince anyone else that she had. They took one last look around both the barbershop and the house and as they walked to their car, someone pulled into the driveway. A woman got out and they could tell by looking at her that she had worked hard all her life. Her face had age lines and around her eyes were dark circles and wrinkles from squinting. *'She probably needed glasses but couldn't afford them,'* Sonnie thought. Her back was bowed from bending over cleaning and scrubbing floors. The fingers on her little hands were all bent and twisted from arthritis.

"Can I help you?" Sonnie asked.

"Who are you and what are you doing in this house?"

"I used to live here," replied Sonnie. "What's your name and what are you doing here?"

"I come and clean this house once a month."

Sonnie glanced at Vince. "Now, we'll get to the bottom of this." He turned his attention back to the little woman who by now was getting nervous but was standing her ground.

"Who pays you? Tell me her name. How long has this been going on? Tell me where you met the lady who hired you."

"I never seen the person who hired me. I answered an ad on the job-board in the square. I get paid by mail every month but for the last six months or so, I haven't been paid."

"Why do you still come and clean for no pay? That doesn't make sense to me."

"What did you say your name was?" The lady asked Sonnie.

"My name is Sonnie. This was my Grandfather's place."

"I knew Quadrio. The pay was good to have…but now I do it to honor him. He helped my family for many years. Then he had to die. It was a sad day for everyone who knew him. I used to see you when your grandmother would walk you in the square. Where do you live now?"

"I bet he was a real cutie, Connie chuckled."

"He looked like a little angel, the way his grandmother had him dressed. Just perfect every time I would see him."

"Enough about me. I would like for you to keep cleaning this place. I'll pay you. Just tell me how much you charge and when you would like to get it. You have to tell me your name and where you live so I can get the money to you."

"My name is Nammi. I live in the shelter. After your grandfather died, Mother couldn't afford to keep the house. We lived on the street for a while…then she died. A room came up at the shelter so I moved in there. I would still clean this house even if you didn't pay. Your grandfather was a man among men. He was a kind and generous man."

"Sonnie," Vince interrupted. "Can I talk to you for a minute in private?"

The two walked towards the house and spoke with their backs turned to Nammi.

"What is it Vince?"

"She's taken care of this place so long it should be hers. What you going to do with it? Think about. She needs somewhere to live besides that ugly shelter, if it's the same as I remember. It's up to you but if it was me, I'd give her the house. It's not doing you any good living in America. When you ever going to get back here? You got to let it go. I understand how you feel about it but it's just something that's always going to be bothering you."

Sonnie and Vince walked back to where Nammi was waiting with Theresa and Connie.

"Who are you?" Nammi asked looking at Vince.

"Vincent, Sonnie's my cousin."

"I know about you two. Are these your wives?"

"No...they're just our friends."

"They came to another country and you're not married? This new way of thinking...I can't get use to it. It just doesn't seem right. I like the old way better."

"What do you know about me Nammi?" Vince asked.

"You used to like all the girls. For her sake, (pointing at Theresa) I hope you changed." Theresa gave Vince a playful slap on the rear and laughed at Nammi's bold remark.

"Nammi, could you afford to live here and take care of the place if I let you have it?" Sonnie asked. "We can go to the court house and I'll sign the papers today. I need to know someone reliable is taking care of the place where I grew up. If you've taken care of it all these years and you did it out of loyalty and love, that tells me it's you that has to have this house."

"I couldn't afford to pay taxes. I don't make the money. I'm just a house cleaner. I live from day to day. If I don't have a house to clean... I don't eat."

"Okay then, how about moving out of the shelter, living here and taking care of the place for me? I'll send you money every month. You just tell me if anything needs done to the house and it'll be taken care of. What do you say?"

"I would be honored. You would never have to worry about your grandfather's place. I would treat it as my own."

Sonnie reached into his pocket and paid Nammi for the time she cleaned without pay and also gave her enough money to take care of things for a long time. They said their good-by's to Nammi and headed back to Don Aldo's. On the way, they noticed the same young boy again, watching them as they drove by.

"Hey...Isn't that the same kid we saw at the house? What's the little bastard want?"

"Yes it is Vince," Connie agreed. "Why is he looking at you again?"

"Beats the hell out of me. I didn't do anything to the little shithead. Stop the car Sonnie. I'm going to get to the bottom of this."

"We don't have time for that right now," Sonnie reminded him. "If he shows up again, we'll check him out then. We got to get back. We need to get some things straight with Don Aldo."

Cousins II

CHAPTER FIVE

When Sonnie, Vince and the girls arrived back at Don Aldo's Compound, the place was filled with servants and other hired help setting up the villa for the announcement dinner. The main room at the villa was about the size of a large dance hall. The furniture was of the Old Italian style, Antique hand-carved wood with gold-leaf inlay and brass accents, table tops of marble and large sofas and chairs covered in beautifully colored fabrics. There were several large china hutches stocked full with china and crystal that had been handed down from generation to generation. Two large matching servers with four oversized silver candlestick holders and crystal vases for fresh flowers flanked the opposite walls. There were two small water fountains, one at each end of the room with cherub statues spewing water from their mouths. There were about fifty florists bringing in and arranging all the flowers for the day's event. One thousand red, yellow and white roses in baskets, bouquets, and blankets were placed around the room in precise locations. There were carnations of all colors and beautiful ceramic pots of purple orchids everywhere. Connie and Theresa were overwhelmed with the organization of the workers and the sheer beauty of how everything was coming together. They both fantasized about all this happening for them and with a smile, looked at each other knowing what the other was thinking. They knew it was not to be… for now at least. *'Back home something like this would never run this smoothly,'* Connie thought. As they passed one of the tables, they noticed a copy of the menu for the dinner. Connie picked it up and commented to Theresa how it felt like a book. It was beautifully crafted of fine parchment paper and bound together with gold tasseled twine. The front was scripted in gold print announcing the engagement of Paolo and Bernadette. Connie slowly turned to the first page. It started with:

APPETITO (Appetizers)

INSALATA CAPRESE
(Mozzarella, Tomatoes, Basil Salad)

Mozzarella cheese from cow or buffalo milk
Fresh basil
Extra virgin olive oil
Salt and freshly ground pepper

INSALATA di PEPPER ARROSTITI
(Roasted Bell Peppers with Tomatoes)

Red bell peppers
Yellow bell peppers
Ripe plum tomatoes sliced
Sun dried tomatoes in olive oil, drained
Capers, drained
Canned anchovies drained and chopped
Pine nuts
Garlic cloves, thinly sliced

COZZE IN PADELLA ALL-AGLIO
(Sautéed Mussels with Garlic)

Fresh mussels
Lemon slices
Olive oil
Shallots, finely chopped
Garlic cloves, freshly chopped
Chopped fresh parsley
Dried red bell peppers
Sweet paprika

Libero A. Tremonti

BRUSHETTA CASALIMGI
(Tomato and Mozzarella Toasts)

Sfilatini
Dried tomato paste
Mixed herbs
Mozzarella cheese drained
Olive oil
Freshly ground black pepper

PRESCIUTTO CRUDOCON FICHI
(Prosciutto with Figs)

Green and black figs
Paper thin slices of prosciutto
Crusty bread

SOUPS
VELLUTATA di ZUCCHINNI
(Cream of Zucchini Soup)

Olive oil
Butter
Onion, chopped
Zucchini, trimmed and sliced
Dried oregano
Gorgonzola cheese
Light cream
Fresh oregano

ZUPPA ALLA VONGOLE
(Clam and pasta soup)

Olive oil
Large onion, finely chopped
Garlic cloves, crushed
Sugar
Dried mixed herbs
Sub-dried tomato paste
Vegetable stock
Red wine

Small pasta shapes
Clams in natural juice
Flat-leaf parsley

MAIN DISHES
PASTA E BROCCOLI
(Orecchiette with Broccoli)

Broccoli
Orecchiette---small pasta
Garlic, finely chopped
Anchovy, fillets in oil
Olive oil
Salt and freshly ground black pepper

SPAGETTI CON VADKA E CAVIALE
(Spaghetti with Vodka and Caviar)

Olive oil
Scallions, thinly sliced
Vodka
Black and Red Caviar
Spaghetti
Heavy cream
Salt and freshly ground pepper

TAGLIATELLE AL PESTODI NICCOLE
(Tagliatelle with Hazelnut Pesto)

Garlic cloves, crushed
Basil leaves
Shelled hazel nuts
Low fat soft cheese
Dried tagliatelle

POLENTA ALLA GRIGHA
(Boiled Polenta with Gorgonzola)

Polenta, boiled in water, then sliced
Salt Gorgonzola cheese spread lightly on top

Libero A. Tremonti

QUAGLE CON UVA
(Quail with Grapes)

Fresh quail, gutted
Olive oil
Bacon, diced
White wine
Chicken stock, warmed
Green grapes

TRIGLIE CON POMODORO
(Red mullet with tomatoes)

Red mullet
Tomatoes peeled or lg. can of plum tomatoes
Olive oil
Chopped parsley
Lemon slices, cut in half

SPAGHETTI ALLE SARDE
(Sicilian Spaghetti with Sardines)

Sardines, cleaned and boned
Olive oil
Pine nuts
Dill sprigs
Raisins, dried
Fresh bread crumbs
Dried spaghetti

DESSERTS
SALAME AL CHOCCOLATO
(Chocolate roll)

Butter cookies, broken
Plain chocolate broken into squares
Unsalted butter, softened
Amaretto liqueur
Egg yokes
Slivered almonds, lightly toasted Ground almonds

CASSATA SICILIANO

Ricotta cheese
Rind of orange, finely ground
Vanilla sugar
Orange-flavored liqueur
Candied peel
Sponge cake
Freshly squeezed orange juice

TIRAMISU

Eggs, separated
Mascarpone cheese, room temperature
Vanilla sugar
Kahla liqueur
Savoiardi, Italian ladyfingers
Sifted cocoa power

LIQUEURS

AMARO... Mixed with soda and drunk before meals to enhance appetite.

GALLIANO and MARASCHINO...Drunk after meals for pleasure and to cure indigestion.

GRAPPA...For serious drinkers. Not recommended for weenies.

VIN SANTO...Sweet tasting and generally served after dinner with cantucci (bread, olive oil and spices) and biscotti.

While Connie and Theresa were getting ready, Sonnie and Vince were spending time with Don Aldo reassuring their business agreement. Don Aldo was very convincing in showing them that their alliance was not in question. He told them that their commitment to do business was unsurpassed by their loyalty. He was honored that they had continued to do business with him after they had taken over J.D.'s organization. Also, he was impressed at how they made changes in their organization without hurting a lot of people or stepping on

Libero A. Tremonti

anyone's toes. He was sure that they would be able to take care of business the old fashion way but with new ideas. Sonnie and Vince decided to up ante a little by committing to increase their imports by fifteen per cent. Don Aldo was pleased and the three men sealed their new agreement with a glass of wine and a toast.

"Here's to many years of good business and most important, loyalty and honor."

"ENJOY"

CHAPTER SIX

As the ceremony was about to get underway, Paolo and Bernadette made their entrance. Paolo's family was from Northern Italy and so he was a little tall for an Italian. He looked more Swiss that Italian. He was about six-foot tall and his hair was blonde and curly. He had blue eyes and his skin was fair but he always tanned well. Bernadette on the other hand, looked very Italian. She was about five foot six with black hair that hung long down her back. Her eyes were olive shaped and she had that skin that always looked like she had been out in the sun, a nice medium bronze color. She also had an hour glass figure, typical of most Italian women. Paolo stood with his and Bernadette's parents at one end of the room, while Bernadette was ushered in by what was called the society of approval. They were all the senior ladies of the village, all dressed in black with black scarves around their heads. If you made it through them, you were home free. While all this was going on, Sonnie quietly slipped out and called Bobby back in Atlantic City to find out if they had any luck locating Rando and the money that had been taken. When Bobby informed him that it hadn't happened yet and that they were still looking, Sonnie started to get stressed and was pacing the floor. He was feeling the way he had felt earlier, as if something wasn't quite right. He kept telling Vince and the girls to be careful but they just shrugged it off to him being nervous about the way he had been misled by Rando. He had put his trust in him and now he felt that everything was falling apart. He couldn't do anything about it because he was three thousand miles away and wasn't there to oversee everything. Vinny kept telling him that as long as Rando wasn't around, he couldn't do any harm and that they would handle it when they got back home.

The blessing from the church was short and sweet. Don Aldo wanted it that way and it was done. The older Italian women weren't happy and they told Don Aldo of their displeasure to no avail. Smiling, Don Aldo dismissed them respectfully.

"What will be…will be. Give them your blessing."

The food was set up in the main courtyard on tables that seemed to stretch for a hundred yards. Most of the many floral arrangements were moved to the courtyard and made a beautiful presentation.

As the people lined up to eat, Vince turned to Sonnie,

"What do those people in line remind you of?"

"I have no clue…but I have a feeling you're going to tell me anyway."

"Look at them, all in line, just like the Stations of the Cross."

"You're sick Vinny. Only you could come up with some ridiculous shit like that. God's going to get you someday."

Suddenly, a commotion at the far end of the tables caught everyone's attention. It was Paolo's soccer teammates and they were there to celebrate Paolo's engagement. The grandmothers quieted them down pronto and finally got them seated.

It had been a long time since Sonnie and Vince had eaten like that. Connie and Theresa couldn't believe how good everything was and how smoothly the party was going.

As the celebration went on into the early evening, the crowd seemed to grow. People just kept on coming and each time someone would arrive, they would bring more drink. Some brought wine, some beer, and some even brought whiskey. As the night went on, everyone was dancing and having a good time. The soccer team was sitting at a large round table and there must have been at least fifty empty wine bottles stacked behind them but they were still going strong.

Vince and Sonnie spent most of the evening with Don Aldo getting to know the rest of his family, his captains, his soldiers and the wise old men who were always around giving advice and of course, young Aldo who was always at his grandfather's side. Don Aldo kept young Aldo near him, always teaching and making sure he understood. Vince glanced at his watch. It had gotten to be almost ten o'clock so he excused himself and went outside to check on Connie and Theresa but they were nowhere to be found. The look on Vince's face told Sonnie what he feared most. He and Vince made their way around the compound once again. Don Aldo also had his men search everywhere but they also came up empty-handed. None of the guards guarding the compound had seen anything unusual. Don Aldo didn't like the way this was playing out. They kept it quiet so not to ruin the celebration.

Returning to Don Aldo's office, Sonnie was frantic.

"What do we do now? Anyone have a clue to what's going on? Somebody's got to know something. I told you something was going to go wrong!" Sonnie exclaimed. "You just blew me off," he shouted at Vince. "See, sometimes my instincts are justified. Not to say I told you so... but I told you so."

"Okay... you were right. Listen, I hate to bring this up Sonnie, but I wonder...

Before Vince could finish the sentence, Sonnie interrupted.

"I know what you're thinking Vince. Is this Maria's doing? It could very well be. You know she's capable of this type of thing."

"How can I not think it? Look what went on back home, you know... she's going to want revenge. You know how creative that bitch can be. Damn, I should have kept a closer watch on them."

"I'll tell you, if she was here in Italy... anywhere in Italy, I would know it," Don Aldo said with assurance. "Someone inside my organization knows what's going on. Someone's disloyal to me. We have so much security, there has to be a traitor among us. I will do everything in my power and I can assure you this will be resolved. Whoever's doing this is doing it to make me look bad in your eyes. I have an idea it has to do with a bunch of young Turks (in America they would be called wise guys) that want to take over, such as my own flesh and blood wanted to, so many years ago. There's always that threat. It's happened before. I got out of it then and I'll get out of it now. I don't think any harm will come to your girls. They just want to make themselves known and make me look bad."

Sonnie stood up and loosened his tie.

"We can't sit here and not do anything, I'll go crazy waiting. If anything goes wrong… I can't wait for something to happen."

"Maybe Don Aldo's right Sonnie. Maybe we should wait at least 'til morning. See what turns up."

"You can wait Vince. I'm going to do something, I just can't wait around. God forbid if anything happens to them."

Sonnie stormed out of the house, got into the car and headed toward town not knowing where he was going. He was circling the cobblestone streets not even knowing what he was looking for but was hoping to find some sign of the girls. Sonnie was so focused that he didn't notice that someone was following him. Finally, when Sonnie spotted him, he led him into an alley and jammed on the breaks and jumped out of the car. It was the same boy they had seen at Sonnie's grandfather's house. Expecting him to run, Sonnie blocked his path. Instead, the boy just stood there and smiled.

"Where's Vincent?" he asked.

"How do you know his name? Who are you and why the hell you following us around?"

"I know all about Vincent. My mother told me about him."

"What is it you think you know about him? Who's your mother and how does she know him? He hasn't been here for fourteen years."

"That's how old I am. I was born the same year Vincent went away. He left before my mother could see him."

"So what you're telling me is… you're Vincent's son? This doesn't surprise me."

"When can I see him?" the boy asked. "Do you think he'll want to see me? Do you think he'll be mad that I came to him? What should I do Sonnie?"

"I see you know my name too. For now, I don't think you should talk to him. When it's time… I'll help you. Right now we have another problem to take care of and it's very important."

"When I heard you and my father were coming to visit Don Aldo, I started hanging around so I could see what my father looked like. I saw some guys that work for Don Aldo talking to Paolo, his niece's boyfriend. Then I saw Paolo meeting with some of the young Turks in the square one day. I thought it was funny he was talking with them. I know what happened to your friends that came with you."

"You mean you know where they are? Take me to them. No wait… I'll get Vinny and then you can show us where they are."

"No Sonnie, I can't show you where they are. I just know they were taken. I think I know someone that can help. He used to be one of the Turks. I heard he said they were too impatient and wouldn't listen. So he left and is trying to start something on his own without them. His name is Franco."

"You sure know a lot for a kid your age."

"My mother told me, always know what's going on. I was taught to keep my eyes open and my mouth shut. I can go to him and ask if he knows anything."

"Why don't you point him out to us and we'll do the rest. I don't think you should be involved. When we find them, it's not going to be pleasant… especially if they hurt our friends. I don't want to go back to America with that on my hands."

"We'll have to wait 'til tomorrow. I don't know where he is tonight but I know where he works. Why don't I meet with you and my father in the square around eleven in the morning?"

"Be there at nine in the morning, not a minute later. Don't call Vincent your father 'til I have a talk with him."

"I'll listen to you Sonnie, but I want him to know who I am. I told my mother I was going to talk to Vincent but she didn't want me to. She said he would never believe me." Even in the darkness of the alley, Sonnie could still see the look of anguish on the boy's face. "Franco doesn't go to work 'til ten-thirty," he told Sonnie.

We'll still meet at nine and we'll meet him on the way to work. I won't tell Vince you're his son 'til this is all over. I don't want any distractions. You understand?"

"I understand and I'll do as you want but can you promise me you'll tell my father afterwards Sonnie?"

"I told you before... I would be with you and I mean what I say," Sonnie smiled. *'He's just like his old man,'* Sonnie thought.

Back at the compound, Sonnie paced the floor wondering what the reason was for all this bullshit to be happening, *'What's wrong with this picture?'* Sonnie thought. Vince on the other hand, had fallen asleep on one of the big sofas in the room just off the foyer. Someone had covered him with a blanket and his shoes were placed neatly on the floor. He too was worried and when Sonnie left so abruptly he felt all he could do was wait. There was a knock on his door and as he opened it, he saw young Aldo standing there.

"Come in Aldo... what's up? It's late. Why are you still up?"

"I thought I would stop by and let you know, I have all my friends out looking around to see what they can find out. I knocked on Vince's door but there was no answer."

"Could you hear anything? He sounds like a bear when he's sleeping."

"No, it was quiet. I thought he might be here with you. I just want you to know I'll do everything possible to make sure everyone is safe. Then, I'll handle everything."

Sonnie was tired and frustrated and it showed.

"I just want the girls to be returned safely. Whatever happens after that is out of my hands. Whatever help you can give us will be appreciated and if you ever need us for anything... well, you know the rest. I always repay a favor."

"You and Vince took care of me in America. I think after this, we'll be even. I will find out what's going on... I promise. By the way, I miss America. I'm going to have a hard time being back over here. I know this is where I'm supposed to be... with my Grandfather."

"I ran into this young boy tonight while I was driving around and he told me he saw Paolo talking to those people your grandfather called the Turks. Do you think that's possible or do you think this kid's just blowing smoke up my ass? This Paolo seemed like a nice quiet boy when I met him earlier."

"Before I came to America, I caught him nosing around the compound. I asked him about it... he told me he was just getting familiar with the place. He looked kind of nervous when I saw him. What made me wonder about him was, he didn't look at me when we were talking. That made me think something wasn't right. So I followed him and he got on his cell phone as soon as he thought I was out of sight. I thought maybe he was calling Bernadette but she was in the kitchen when I saw her and she didn't have her phone with her. I didn't say anything to my Grandfather because I wasn't sure of Paolo's intentions and I didn't want to jump the gun. If he has something to do with your friends disappearing...well I'll do what's necessary. I'll make everything right for my Grandfather.

Sonnie walked to a small table and opened a small box of cigars and lit one.

"How old are you, Aldo?"

"I'm twenty-three. Why do you want to know that?"

"I was still under my Grandfather's wing when I was twenty-three. Let me tell you something. Even after all these years, he's still teaching me things. You learn everything you can from him, they don't make them like that anymore. Me and Vince are to meet this young boy tomorrow morning at nine in the square. Would you like to be there with us? He's going to take us to someone that he thinks knows something about the kidnapping."

"You say nine in the morning?" Sonnie nodded while blowing smoke rings above his head. "I would like to be with you. I'll be able to tell if this boy is leading you on a wild goose chase. If he is, we'll go have a talk with Paolo. I'll get some answers out of him."

The next morning as Aldo drove Sonnie and Vince to meet the kid, they each were contemplating what was going to happen. When they reached the square where the boy was to meet with them, he wasn't there.

"That's great! The little shit-head's not here... I told him nine sharp. Look around... we may have been set up."

Vince could see the anger in Sonnie's face.

"Don't be so paranoid Sonnie. Maybe he's been held up or something. We'll give him a few minutes and then we'll take matters into our own hands. You know I don't like to depend on anyone else."

It was still early and the tourists were just starting to wander into the square and around the fountain. The men stood with their backs to the car and peered at the streets leading into the square.

"It's been ten minutes now, I'll bet he's not going to show. Let's get on with it."

"What was the name of the guy the kid said he knew?" Aldo asked. "Maybe I know him."

"Aldo you know someone named Franco?" Sonnie asked. "He's supposed to be one of those Turks your grandfather referred to. He was the one that went out on his own because the others wouldn't listen to reason. This boy said, all they wanted to do was force their way into things. It was like they didn't have common sense. They wanted to bully their way into power. Anyway, this Franco seems like he has some common sense about him. We might learn something from him if we can find him."

"Who's this kid Sonnie? Where did you meet him?"

"He's that kid that's been following us all over the place, Vinny. He followed me last night when I left. I pulled into an alley and jumped out of the car to scare him but he smiled at me and starting asking me a million questions. I talked with him for a while and found out he knows a lot about what's going on around here. He knows all about Don Aldo. He knew Little Aldo and that he had came to America. He knew we were coming here. This kid's a ball of information. That's why I was anxious for you to meet him. Let's wait a little longer... what'da you think?"

"What, you soft on this kid or something? He's probably hustling you. You know how these kids are over here. They're sharp as a tack."

"Just wait Vinny... you'll see."

"Okay. Sonnie, enough is enough. It's been thirty minutes now."

"I know. Aldo, do you think you know this Franco? The boy said he went to work at eleven but he didn't say where he worked."

Cousins II

"There's only one Franco I know of. His father has a shoe repair and he works there in the day and runs the streets all night. We can go to his father's place and meet him there."

"I would rather meet him on the way there. That way, no one else will know what's going on."

"There's a little café where we can get something," Aldo added. "From there, we can see all the different directions he has to come to go to his work."

Sitting at a small table in front of the café waiting for Franco to show up, Sonnie couldn't help but wonder what had happened to the kid. He had promised him that he would help him with meeting Vince. Maybe he got scared and was afraid I would change my mind even though I gave him my word. As the men drank coffee and finished up their last biscotti, two Policia cars rushed by with their sirens blaring. Vince called over the waiter and asked if he knew what had happened.

"There was a body found on the edge of town," he told Vince. "Someone said it was a boy. That's all I know."

"Oh shit! I bet they got to the boy before he could tell us about this Franco character. Vince, I hate to tell you this but…"

Suddenly from around the corner, a boy came running toward them calling Sonnie's name. Sonnie turned to Vince with a smile on his face.

"There's that little shit now. He's only forty-five minutes late."

"I don't like it when you got that shitty smile on your face," Vince replied. "What was you going to say before we were interrupted?"

"That's all right. It's not important… We'll talk about it later."

"What's this kid's name anyway, Sonnie?"

"I never asked him Vinny but he's a pretty cool kid."

"Damn… that's not good. You take this kids' word about what… I don't know and you don't even know his name? You've pulled some boners in your time but this takes the cake."

"Just wait… you'll see." Sonnie waved the boy to where they were sitting. "Over here kid. Where the hell you been? I hope you didn't have anything to do with the Polizia. You're not running from them are you?"

"Sonnie, it's Franco."

"What do you mean? You're not telling me it's the guy you wanted us to meet? What the hell went on here? That puts us really in a bind now. I don't know what to do. What about the girls? He might have been our only chance to find them... DAMN IT!!! We don't need this shit now."

Sonnie's cell phone rang and he answered it. Vince could tell by the look on his face and what he was saying that the call was from back home. It must have been bad news because Sonnie had that I want to kill someone look on his face. Aldo, Vince and the boy, waited for Sonnie to finish the call.

"Calm down Sonnie," Vince said while putting his arm around Sonnie's shoulders. "Tell me what's going on? Is it about Rando? What's going on?"

"That fucker shot at a couple of Bull's boys. They almost got him but he spotted them and that's when the shooting started. Bull's afraid he'll skip town now. If he does, we'll never catch up with him. He's lucky he didn't hit anyone. Could you imagine how ugly that could have been?"

"I wouldn't be too concerned about it," Vince replied. "Shit like that always backs up in the toilet. Think about it for a second. Who else does he know? He'll show up begging for forgiveness... I've seen it before. That's when he'll pay for his sins. Hey kid, what's your name?"

"It's Danny, Vince. What did this Rando do? If he betrayed you, don't play with him. Just take care of business."

"Hey, listen to this kid. He's got some balls for his age. How old are you? How do you know my name? Who told you? What's going on here?"

"Remember Vinny," Sonnie said. "I told you, me and the kid talked last night." He turned and looked at the boy. "Danny, do you have any idea who these other Turks are? You know anyone else that might know? We got to do something and fast."

"Sonnie," Danny replied. "There's this old winery that's not used very much anymore. It's owned by one of the guy's families about 20 kilometers away. I heard that's one of their hang-outs."

Aldo leaned forward.

"I know where it is," he said. "I can take you there."

Sonnie shifted his eyes towards Vince. "We have a problem Vince. If we find these guys, what are we going to do to take them down? We have nothing. We can't go barging in there with our fingers up our asses. We have to get something. Hey Aldo… you got any connections? We need some serious fire power."

"Follow me," He replied, as they all made their way over to where Aldo parked his car. When Aldo opens the trunk, Sonnie and Vince were pleasantly surprised. It looked like a gun shop. They heard the door to the car open and as they glanced around the trunk, they saw Danny climbing into the back seat.

"Where the hell do you think you're going kid?" Vince asked walking towards the open door. "Get the hell out of the car. You're too young for this. You don't need to be involved. It'll be better if you stay here. Now get out of the car. Com'on… now."

"I know where this place is Vincent," Danny pleaded. "I've been there a lot of times. I know how to get in there without anyone seeing us."

"How about you, Aldo? Do you know anything about this winery?"

"I've only been there twice Vince. We better let him stay."

"Okay kid, but after you show us the way in, you'll wait in the car 'til we get back. You'll have to listen and stay put."

Vince, Sonnie and Aldo picked their weapons of choice, loaded up and got on the way. It was quiet in the car until Danny broke the silence.

"So what are you guys going to do to this guy Rando? I'll bet it's not going to be pretty. I've heard all about what you guys did when you were about my age. Tell me, how did that feel? Were you scared? What did it look like when that house blew up?"

"Hey kid, I don't know who filled your head with all that shit but they didn't know what they were talking about. Besides, whoever did that to those guys should have got a medal. They deserved it. Where do you hear all this stuff anyway?"

"My mother told me Vince. She knows all about it."

"I think we're getting close," Sonnie interrupted. "We better get ready."

As they pulled up to the old winery, they saw three cars parked in the front and one of them was Paolo's.

"You were right Danny," Sonnie admitted. "You told me he was involved. I didn't want to believe it but I guess it's true. I guess Don Aldo's going to be disappointed but we have no choice."

As they made their way through the secret entrance, Sonnie was becoming a little nervous. He didn't know what the situation was and had always wanted to be aware of what was going down. If they made the wrong choice, the girls could have a serious problem. As they got further into the old winery, they could hear voices but couldn't make out how many there were or if the girls were even there.

The winery was an old building about one city block long and as wide as a football field. This was a small winery by winery standards. It had a basement which was dark and musty and full of huge wine barrels. The barrels could each hold about five hundred gallons of wine. In a separate room was a large wine press where they would crush the grapes. The juices were then piped into a large vat where additives were mixed in before filling the barrels. At that point, the barrels were left while the juices were fermented into wine. When the juices are all drained from the press, it pulverized the stems and skins, into a thick mash which was then flushed into the sewer. Sometimes, the farmers would gather this mash to dry and use to fertilize their grape vines. As Vince, Sonnie and Aldo reached the room where the voices were coming from, they stopped. Without knowing anything about the place they only had one option and that was to go in fast and loud and suffer the consequences later. They kicked in the door and found five of the Turks along with Paolo, playing cards and drinking. One of them reached for a bag but Aldo shot him in the face killing him instantly. The others lay on the floor, one of them crying.

"Where's the girls?" Sonnie yelled as he stuck his gun in the mouth of the boy who was crying.

"We don't know who you mean," Paolo cried out.

Sonnie pulled the trigger and the top of his head splattered all over two of the other Turks.

"Tell them Paolo," one of the other boys yelled out.

"They're down in the basement," Paolo replied.

Sonnie turned and pointed the gun straight at Paolo. "You better not be lying to me."

"I promise Sonnie. That's where they are. We didn't hurt them. Please… believe me. We didn't want to do anything to them. We were going to let them go as soon as we made Don Aldo listen to us and arrange a meeting so we could tell him our demands. We just wanted a piece of the action and he wouldn't even talk to us to hear us out. We think there's enough here for everyone. I figured if I married his niece, we would be able to get his attention that way. This wasn't my idea. I was just going along because they wouldn't listen to me. I told them this wasn't the way to do things."

Sonnie and Vince grabbed Paolo and made him take them to where the girls were while Aldo held the rest of the gang in check. Paolo was right. They were unharmed but were dirty, cold, hungry and scared. When they saw Sonnie and Vince, they both started crying.

"We didn't know if you would ever find us or what was going to happen to us," Theresa said with tears falling down her cheeks.

Vince and the girls made their way out of the winery and to Aldo's car only to find Danny had not stayed with the car as he was instructed to do. Vince wondered where he was and that he had needed him there to be with Connie and Theresa.

"I have to go back inside," he told the girls. "Everything will be alright. I just don't want things to get out of control in there."

"I think we'll be fine as long as you don't take too long. Please hurry."

"I'll be as quick as I can Theresa."

Shivering, Theresa and Connie put their arms around one another.

"What the hell's going on?" Connie asked. "Why did all this happen? What does it mean?"

"I just wonder what's going on in there," replied Theresa. "You know… I've never seen them this way. They look crazy… like they're possessed or something."

"Yea I know," Connie added. They're not the same guys we thought we knew. How can they just change like that? I'm scared, but in a strange way… I feel protected…like nothing can ever hurt us. I guess I'm glad we were with them when something like this happened. This is crazy but, I always knew they would protect us. For now… I'm not going to question what's going on. I'm just glad we're safe and will be going home soon. It's time."

"I know where you're coming from Connie. I sort of feel the same way. I just wish they would hurry up so we can get out of here. I hope no one else shows up. I guess we just have to stay here and wait and see what happens."

CHAPTER SEVEN

Vince made his way back into the winery where Aldo and the Turks were. He could hear them giving the names of the other guys in Don Aldo's organization that were going to join them in the takeover.

"You don't make demands on Don Aldo or try to take over his organization," Aldo told them as he forced them to stand. He lined them up and made them face the wall and shot them execution style, one shot in the back of the head. Without regret, Aldo walked away knowing full well that he had done what had to be done to protect his grandfather. As for Paolo, with his hands tied behind his back, Sonnie took him into the room where the wine press was. Sonnie shoved him into the press and Paolo began crying and begging for his life.

"They were just friends that I hung around with," he pleaded. "I wasn't a part of the gang. What I want is to marry Bernadette and become part of Don Aldo's family. Please don't do this to me. Take me to Don Aldo so I can explain."

"Explain, what's there to explain? We know all about you and the things you've done. Who's to believe what you're saying now? You've changed your story three times since I've been here. Little Aldo had his eye on you for a long time and he knew what you were up to. Maybe if you would have gone to Don Aldo and told him what you wanted, it might have worked out differently. He might have even listened to you. He's a reasonable man. If your demands would have made sense to him, maybe you could have worked something out. It's out of his hands now. When you took something that belonged to me, you didn't take into consideration the consequences. You see... you took something that belongs to me and now you have to pay. This is out of Don Aldo's hands now. No one cares what your plan was. At this point, nothing will make any difference. I protect my people no matter what. Now... you've done something that was unforgivable. I don't let nothing get in the way of that. It's too late for talking. Maybe Don Aldo would have listened to you but you made the mistake of fuck'n with me. There's a difference between a punk and a man. You and your friends are punks. There's no going back. Now it's done my way."

"I just wanted to be something. Come on Sonnie, let me out of here. We can be friends, I promise I'll make this up to you. I know I can convince Don Aldo to see things my way. If he does, we can have a good thing together. Me here, you in America. Please give me another chance."

"If you wanted a friend, you should'a got a dog."

As Sonnie locked Paolo into the press, he could hear him begging for his life. He could hear him confessing his sins and asking God for forgiveness. "Please God, make Sonnie change his mind and let me go," he screamed. Sonnie turned to walk away, but paused for a moment as if to change his mind. He knew that with all that had happened, there was no turning back now. He had saved the girls and that was what was important. With that... he smiled, turned on the press and walked out. He met Vince and they left the winery together, warriors once again. As they were reaching the car, they could see that Aldo was already there with the girls.

"I wonder where that little shit-head Danny went to?" grumbled Vince. "So much for listening to whatever someone tells him."

"Like someone else I know," Sonnie commented. "Does he remind you of anyone Vinny? Take a good look at him, skinny as a rail, hair flopping in his face. Knowing all the ins and outs of everything that's going on around him. I'll tell you Vinny, this kid knows it all. Anything… just ask him. He knew all about us before we even got here. He especially knew all about you. He told me all about you."

"What's going on here? You're starting to piss me off Sonnie. You've been making insinuations all day long. Now tell me what's up. Someone better talk to me."

Suddenly, a crash was heard from around the side of the building and the men prepared themselves for a confrontation. Danny appeared, wiping dirt from his pants and wearing a big smile. "It's okay," he said after seeing Sonnie, Vince and Aldo with their guns pointing at him. "It's just me. I kind of tripped back there. Well actually…I fell off the roof."

The men put away their guns and Danny walked slowly towards the car.

"That was pretty wild," he said. "What I just saw."

"What did you see, Danny? I thought I told you to stay put. You were supposed to stay here in case I needed you here."

"I know Vince, but I was afraid I was going miss something important. Man… you guys are ruthless. There's no other way to put it."

"That's enough. Squeeze in the car so we can get the hell out of here."

On the way back to town, everyone was quiet except Danny. He kept whistling the same tune over and over again.

"I haven't heard that song for ever it seems," Vince interrupted. "How do you know that tune, Danny?"

"My mother taught it to me. She said it was her favorite song. She said she used to sing it all the time and when she would go to this special place with this special guy, they would always play it on the radio. If they were together and walked into a club or a bar, the bartender would play it on the music box."

"Does that bring back any memories Vinny?" Sonnie asked. "Do you remember anyone that liked that song? Think hard now."

"What the hell is this… twenty questions or something? I knew a lot of girls who liked that song. It was real popular when I was young… everyone was singing it. What are you hinting at Sonnie? You're holding something back? Now quit busting my palla's."

"Do you remember a girl you dated at the time you left named Roseanna? She's my Mother," Danny hinted. "She didn't have time to tell you…"

"Just a minute here," Vince interrupted. "You trying to tell me you're my son? That can't be."

Sonnie looked at Vince and smiled. "Hey Vinny, he does look a lot like you." Sonnie turned to Connie in the back seat. "Look at them sitting next to each other Connie, they look just like father and son."

"Go ahead… put your arm around him, honey." Theresa added.

"I don't need any help from you Theresa. I'm not believing this is happening. What am I supposed to do now?"

"You could talk to Danny," she replied. "He'll have all the answers to your questions. I think it's sweet after all these years. I couldn't think of a nicer surprise."

It was a quiet ride back to Don Aldo's. Each of them had their own thoughts running through their minds:

Danny… *'I wonder if Vince likes me, I wonder how he feels about having a son. If he's like all Italians, it's the most important thing in life, having a son. Maybe he already has other children and won't accept me. Maybe he'll think my mother is lying. How will I convince him? At least I got to meet him and find out some things about him. He's a real man, just what I would hoped he would be. Someone that doesn't put up with no bullshit, not cowardly. Takes matters into his own hands and if there's a problem… solves it one way or another, then goes on his way. He doesn't seem to be afraid of anything. I want to be like him. Please God, make him like me.'*

Theresa… *'How could a wonderful time end up like this? Until this, everything was so beautiful. This is not making any sense to me. Why did it have to be so violent? Couldn't they handle it any other way? It was like something I'd read in a book or seen in a movie. I can't believe this is real. I never imagined Vince being like that. I don't like it. I want this all to go away. This changes everything. The way I feel…I don't know. I'm all numb inside, like a part of me died.*

It's kind of sad in a way. I still can't believe what happened. Poor Connie. She was so frightened I hope she'll be alright. I never thought I would be put in this situation. I'm really pissed off at Vincent... Sonnie's no better. When we get home, I'd like to give them a piece of my mind. Well... I don't know if that would be a smart thing to do... after what I saw today.'

Connie... *'What the hell have I gotten myself into? Why am I involved with these kinds of people? I knew Sonnie wasn't on the up and up, but I didn't bargain for almost loosing my life. When we get home... if we get home, I'm going to rethink our relationship. I don't know if I can handle this. I care for Sonnie a lot but I never saw him like this. I'm really scared. If this is the way I'm going to have to live, always scared of what's going to happen next...well... that's not for me. I'm going to have a long talk with Theresa. I'm sure she feels the same way I do. We're going to have to rethink the way things are going and do something about it. We'll just put it to them, tell them the way it is and if they don't like it.... tough shit. What am I thinking? That's too simple. Damn... I'm so confused.'*

Vince... *'What am I going to do if this is really my kid? How will I handle it? Do I take him back home with me? What if he doesn't want to come? I don't need this aggravation or this kid right now, with all the bullshit that's going on back home. I can't wait to get back there so we can straighten it out. Now I got this kid to worry me. Everyone thinks it's cute, having this kid. Maybe it wouldn't be so bad if everything was different. I'm beginning to understand what Sonnie goes through with all this shit piling up on me. How does he do it? Just look at him... he's a wreck. This is the first time this shit's getting to me.'*

Sonnie... *'What the hell is Don Aldo going to think? How will he react to us taking matters into our own hands? We better prepare ourselves for a confrontation. This can't be good. I have a weird feeling he's not going to be to happy. We killed his future nephew. Our only hope is that since Little Aldo was with us and our thoughts were on the same page and if we can convince Don Aldo, there wasn't any other way to handle it. Maybe we should have brought Paolo to him and let him take care of the situation. Too late now. We'll have to deal with it. Sometimes I wonder if I act before I think things out. Gramps always taught me to do that but I just get caught up in the moment and don't take time to think. I'll just tell him we didn't have any other choice. He's a reasonable man...I hope. Ahh... the hell with it, what happens happens. I got enough bullshit to worry about. It's done now and there's nothing anyone can change.'*

Little Aldo...*'We really fixed those bastards. They deserved what they got. I wasn't going to let them hurt my grandfather. I've been hearing about them and what they were up to for a long time. I almost had them before I went to America. Now, they can't do anything to hurt anyone. With the names of the other traitors, we'll be rid of any threats to our family. Don Aldo will be proud of me. I'm glad Sonnie and Vince were here, they're fearless. I wish they would stay in Italy and join in with the family. With them, we would have it all. My grandfather will be happy they were here to help me end this once and for all. Those bastard traitors are the ones I would have chosen to help me when I got older. They're the strongest fighters in the family. I would be dead now and so would Don Aldo and those son of a bitches would be in control. We owe Sonnie and Vince our lives. I'm sure my grandfather will see it that way also.'*

Vince's cell phone rang and when he picked it up, he got some unexpected news.

"We've go to get our asses home," he told Sonnie.

"Now what's going on Vinny? Is there a problem? Talk to me."

"That was Bobby. You'll never believe this shit. Sammy G. and both of his lieutenant's in Philly was taken out yesterday and there was an attempt at the same time in New York on Bobby's boss. That didn't go down... they stopped it. They captured one of the men but he hasn't told them anything yet. He did say, it didn't look like the usual wack job. What he meant by that... I don't know. He said he would tell us all about it later. Someone is trying to take out our competitors. They're trying to kill all the heads of the families to get their power. I told him to hang on and be careful 'til we get there. He said Bull was standing by if we needed him. All we have to do is call and he was all ours. I guess we're stuck with him. What more can I say except now that if we need someone, I'm glad it's him."

Cousins II

"I hope they don't think we had anything to do with that business," Sonnie declared. "I don't want everybody coming down on us. You know, we don't have the manpower we once had. We wouldn't stand a chance. We better get straight with Don Aldo and get the hell out of here and fast. Aldo, do you have any connections at the airport in Naples... someone you can trust? I think we better get our own jet to make sure we get there. That way, we can fly straight through. We might have been on the list but because we weren't there... I guess we dodged a bullet or two. What'da you think, Vinny?"

"You know what I'm thinking Sonnie? That bitch Maria probably sweet talked some of her friends in New York and organized a crew to try and take over. Then, challenge us after she gets the power she needs. You know how that bitch operates. If she gets control of both families, we're in for some big trouble. I think we're safe for now. If it's her, when she gets organized... then she will come after us. When we get back, we've got to hit the streets and find out everything we can about what's going on and who's responsible for all this bullshit. We just have to keep our heads and not act 'til we know what's going on. When we find out all the facts, we'll do what's necessary to survive. We've done it before. We'll hit those bastards before they hit us... we can't sit around and wait. Bobby said he already has some people checking things out in New York and he will fill us in when we get home."

Connie and Theresa were horrified at what they were hearing but tried to act like normal. They both looked at each other and smiled but you could tell it wasn't a happy smile. *'Who was this Maria? Was she a wife or secret lover of one of them and if so, who was covering for whom? It sounded like both of them knew her. Why haven't we heard about her before and how could she be involved in what happened in the winery? Does she know about us and are we in danger?'*

When they got to the compound, Little Aldo went into see Don Aldo first. After about twenty minutes Don Aldo came out to talk to Sonnie and Vince. He told them he understood what they did was necessary and that he might have acted in the same way. He told them that in a strange way, that they had saved him from doing something that in some people's eyes might have made him less respected if he were forced to kill Paolo. So in essence... they saved him again.

"I understand your urgency to get home. My grandson told me of your problems there. I'll call the airport in Naples and have my friend, who I trust with my life, make arrangements for a rapid flight home. I've talked to Aldo and asked if he would like to go back there with you. He told me that if things were different here, he might have gone. He thought I needed him here now. If there's anything else you need... don't hesitate to ask. I admire both of you and you're always welcome in my house. You remind me of my youth. I hope everything goes well. Oh, my grandson said that when he was with you, it was like *Luna Di Cacciatore* (Moon of the hunter). He'll miss the both of you. You've showed him a side of life he would have never seen if he had not went to America."

"Don Aldo," Vince replied. "We're grateful for your understanding. We hope we haven't caused you any despair within your family. Maybe we acted in haste but we're use to not having to confer with anyone before acting."

"I told you, I would have done the same thing. I have no regrets about it Vincent. *Ti considero come uno di famiglia, e uno di famigila ha il mio rispetto, potere, forza, connessioni e innanzi tutto, la mia lealta.* (I consider you family and when you're family you have my respect, power, strength, connections and most of all... my loyalty.) The two of you are reflections of myself. If I were your age...the three of us... there would be no limit as to what we could accomplish."

"There is one favor I would like to ask of you Don Aldo."

"Just ask Vincent and if it's not impossible, I'll take care of it for you."

"I've discovered I have a fourteen year old son here. It happened before I left. I never knew it 'til now. I asked him if he wanted to come to America with me. He's more grown up for fourteen than I was or maybe he just has more common sense than I did at that age. Back then, my only interest was the young ladies... as you see, it got me into trouble. He wants to stay here and make sure his mother is taken care of. If you know anyone that could give him an opportunity, I would appreciate it. I can't tell you what it would mean to me."

"Just tell me his name Vincent and it will be taken care of. I'll watch out for him 'til he gets his schooling and then if he wants... he can come work with me. My grandson will watch over him and make sure everything's alright. His mother will also be taken care of if you want it that way. I know you're anxious to get going, so I'll make the call while you're getting ready. There's plenty to eat if you want to have something before you leave. It's a good ride to the airport and then a long flight. So you and the girls eat. I'll be in touch soon. Let's not go so long without touching base... not only for business. I think I would like to come and visit."

Sonnie and Vince both kissed Don Aldo's hand (a sign of respect) before he left them. Within three hours, Sonnie, Vince, Theresa and Connie were ready to leave for the airport. While packing, Connie and Theresa are trying to figure out what just happened. They never thought they would be the target of revenge. They couldn't understand why they were taken and held hostage. It was something that they had heard happened to other people but never expected it would happen to them. They were thankful Little Aldo was there to help Sonnie and Vince find them, even though they were shocked over what had happened at the winery.

Little Aldo was waiting to take them to the plane. On the way, he thanked them for everything and told them how much he appreciated their help. He wanted them to know that he was ready to come to America at any time if he was needed.

"We know how much you mean to your grandfather and we wouldn't want to interfere with family," Vince pointed out. "However, if anything ever happened that you get a break and are able to come for a visit or whatever, you would be more than welcomed. We are indebted to you for what you did for us."

"Your help to me was just as important. I don't think I could have handled it so quickly and thoroughly if I were alone. Remember... the ones that I would have chosen to help me, were in with the Turks. I guess it was meant to happen this way."

Libero A. Tremonti

On the way to the airport, Little Aldo drove past Danny's house and he was standing on the sidewalk. Aldo stopped the car and Vince got out and gave Danny a hug and told him that he would not be forgotten.

"How soon will it be before you come to visit me in America?" Vince asked.

He took off a medal he had around his neck and put it around Danny's.

"I'm accepting you as my son now. I expect you to act like a man and take care of your family. You know what that means. Don Aldo is going to take care of things while I'm at home in America. If there's anything you need or if anything comes up you can't handle, you go to him and he will see it's taken care of. You have all my phone numbers in America. Don't worry about the time change, just call anytime you want. It doesn't matter when. I want your mother to go to the bank and set up an account. Then, each month I will send money so you won't want for nothing. Don't forget, if there's anything you need…"

"I will make you proud of me, Father. You don't have to worry about me getting mixed up with the wrong people. I've seen what can happen. There are no rewards… only misery and death. As soon as things allow it, I will come to America so I can visit with you. I want to see how wonderful it is to live there. I'm hoping some day to move there. I'll think of you every day and you'll be in my dreams and prayers."

Once again, Vince hugged Danny. This time it was a little harder to let go. When Vince got back into the car, his eyes were tearing. No one said anything on the way to the airport. Just before boarding Don Aldo's private jet, Connie and Theresa gave Little Aldo a hug and told him how much they appreciated what he did for them. Sonnie and Vince told Aldo that he had an open invitation to come back to Atlantic City anytime he wanted. They shook hands and with that, got on the plane for their trip home.

CHAPTER EIGHT

The flight was long and boring. The plane was an old nineteen-fifties two engine, ten passenger with no frills such as televisions or lounge chairs. Just seats on each sides of the plane but at least, they faced each other. The tiny bathroom included a half roll of toilet paper and no paper towels to wipe your hands. There was a small refrigerator tucked in just outside the bathroom with some bottled water and a couple of stale cookies inside but it wasn't turned on. For what it costs, Sonnie and Vince could have bought a ticket to go around the world. The pilots spoke limited English and the Italian that they spoke was different from what Sonnie and Vince understood, so there wasn't much communication there. The pilots were busy arguing with each other and Sonnie couldn't quite make out what they were saying but what little bit he could understand, he didn't like.

"Vince, did you hear what they're arguing about? The pilot's son made the co-pilots daughter pregnant and the co-pilot was telling him that if he didn't make his son pay, he was going to crash the plane. He said she was six months gone and looked disfigured. He wanted to know what his son put inside her. He said he must be part animal."

"Well...that really sucks." Vince replied. "Why would you think this plane ride was going to be any different than the rest of the week? We'll have to keep our eyes on them. I feel real secure now

Libero A. Tremonti

Sonnie. Thanks for telling me that. I hope these guys are like the ones back home, always promising to kill each other but never practicing what they preach."

Vince and Sonnie talked business while keeping both eyes on the fighting pilots. Connie and Theresa were pondering there future with them once they arrived home.

"Connie, what do you think we should do about our dilemma? I can't go on like this."

"What do you mean Theresa?"

"Well, we can't go on looking past what we've been through this week and pretending we don't know what's going on. Besides, they might think we approve of what they're doing. I can't imagine what goes on when we're not around. I can't think straight anymore I'm so upset. I haven't slept and I just keep thinking about what went on at that winery. They went in there and took out those people without hesitation, like it was an everyday thing. Did you see them when they got to the car? They acted like a bunch of kids... as if they did nothing wrong. Laughing and talking about it. My God, they just killed a bunch of people. I'm scared and confused right now. I care a lot for Vincent but I don't want to be any part of that stuff. I've been thinking of just packing up and leaving... not telling anyone."

"I know how you feel. I've thought the same thing. The only thing is, I don't have anywhere to go. My family doesn't get along and I don't want to get in the middle of that. I sure don't want to be involved in anything like what just happened to us, where we live. We might not be as lucky next time. You know, it's different in the states. Johnny Law doesn't look the other way. Don Aldo has the law...well, he is the law in his village. That's why it doesn't matter what anyone in the family does 'cause they can get away with it. You see that shit happen in the movies and you don't give it a second thought. When it's real, it hits you differently. Right now I don't know what to do. I don't know if I can go back to the bakery and act normal. I'm scared. For now, we should just act like we're doing and not let them know we're thinking of anything out of the ordinary."

"I know Vincent will be calling me. What am I going to say? How can I pretend everything's alright? Like you said, it's so scary right now... I don't know which way to turn. Vince always wants to get it on after he's been away but maybe because we were with them, it'll be different. I don't know if I could stand for him to touch me right now. Oh shit, I've just thought of something. How's Sonnie when he gets back from a trip? Is he the same way? What if they need to get laid every time they kill someone? I sure hope that's not the case. That's really depressing to think about."

"I just don't want to think about it, but what you say, does hold some merit. I've heard some doctors on T.V. say the same thing you're saying. Some people just get off when they do something exciting or dangerous. As for Sonnie, he's horny all the time. He's an all-around-the house sort of guy, if you know what I mean. I know he'll be calling me too. This is a real bitch isn't it? How do we act? What do you think we should do?"

"I'll say it's a bitch," Theresa added. "As far as what to do, I haven't a clue."

They settled back in their seats, shut their eyes and just waited for it to be over. What started out as something beautiful, turned ugly. *'How could this happen?* Connie thought. *'Maybe when I open my eyes it will have all been just a bad dream.'* The trip like most seemed to take longer returning than going. For Connie and Theresa, the six hours seemed like twenty.

About a hundred miles from the U. S., they hit a terrible storm with thunder and lighting. At times, the plane seemed to toss around like a kite in a heavy wind. Both Sonnie and Vince were amazed at the poise the pilots had during the storm which lasted about forty-five minutes. However, the storm didn't stop the arguing. They were yelling at each other the whole time. It was unbelievable.

"Listen to those fuckers up there," Sonnie shouted. "We're on the brink of destruction and all they can think about is someone's pregnant daughter. Vince, if we survive this, I'm going to kick their asses when we get off this plane."

"I think I'll help you. You know, they strangely remind me of you-know-who."

"You know Vince, that's the second time you brought him up. I think you miss the little bastard. When we get home I'm going to call that little pain in the ass, so you can tell Petey how much you miss him. I'm getting a little nervous about what we're going to run into when we get back. I hope there's not going to be an all-out-war. If there is… we're sunk. We have to do some heavy duty recruiting when we get back."

"What do you want to do Sonnie? Put up posters with our fingers pointing, saying: **_SONNIE AND VINCE WANTS YOU. BAD PAY, LONG HOURS. NO DEPLOMA NEEDED. INQUIRE AT THE BUS STATION._** That would be real cute but all kidding aside, we do have to get real serious. We need some good help. Someone with a brain…someone that won't be up our asses every five minutes asking us what to do. Do you think there's anyone like that out there? Just someone that's reliable and won't turn on us like the others did. It's ashamed how people abuse a friendship. Maybe that's the problem. Maybe we should find a new way of testing them and not going with first impressions. You know, Gramps never had problems like that."

"I know what you're saying. I wish we could clone ourselves, then our problems would be solved. Hey, that poster idea might work. We could get some old Italian Army uniforms and stand outside all the casinos. I'll bet we'd find a whole bunch of Army misfits. Just what we need. You know Gramps was feared… that's why he didn't have the problems we have. Maybe we have to get a little meaner."

With deafening static, one of the pilots came over the intercom. "Da storm, it'a go away. We gonna be okay now. We go'na put da plane on da ground now… I hope. Ah…you guys have a good'a time. GOD'A BLESS AMERICA." Sonnie and Vince just looked at one another and shook their heads.

Descending out of the clouds at night was beautiful, especially when you could see the strip of Atlantic City all lit up. Sonnie, Vince and the girls were a little tense because landing in the dark with only runway lights was scary enough with pilots that they trusted. Having two jamokes arguing all the while, was down right nerve racking. Upon touch down, a sigh of relief came over the four of them when they heard the screech of the tires hitting the runway. As the plane taxied towards its designated area, Connie and Theresa glanced at each other and took a deep sigh of relief, "*What now*?" They both wondered. When they got out of the plane, there were two limo's there to pick them up. One for Sonnie and Vince and one for Connie and Theresa. Vince explained to the girls that they had some important business to take care of right way and hoped they wouldn't mind going alone. The girls gladly went without question. With the glass up between them and the driver, the girls felt free to talk about their future.

"What do we do?" asked Connie. "I feel like I'm between a rock and a hard place. How can we go on and act normal? I don't feel like I can do it or even if I want to."

"I don't have a clue. Right now I don't think we have an option. We have to go along with anything and everything that comes along until we get a chance to change things. We have to act cool as a cucumber and wait 'til the time is right. I know it will be hard for you Connie, but if we want to get out of this without repercussions, we got to take it slow."

"You don't understand Theresa, I love Sonnie. I've never told him that, but he's got to me good. I feel so different when I'm with him. He just has that charisma…you know, that cool. I always knew he was a little underhanded when it came to business and I never knew what he did, but I never dreamed he was involved in stuff like this. Let's face it Theresa, we're involved with the Mafia. We have to stop denying it. What the hell am I going to do? First, I want to stay and see this through. Then I want to pick up everything and leave like we talked about before, but we can't do that. We never will be able to leave. I'm at my wits end. I think what I need to do, is go away for a while and sort things out but I know that wouldn't work either. I wish my parents were still living. They would solve this for me."

"That's all well and good, but where and what are you going to tell Sonnie? We just came back from a week in Italy. The time we spent with them and the way they acted at the beginning, you would have never thought they were the same two guys. What reason could you give for wanting to go away again… and by yourself? See what I'm getting at? What story could you come up with that might convince Sonnie of that? Especially if he feels the same way as you do. If it's what we think then he's going to want to be with you more then ever now. Has he ever said how he felt about you? Do you think he has any idea you feel the way you do? I never knew you loved him. I have a similar problem with Vince. The difference is... I've told him many times that I was in love with him. In a way, I'm in a worse situation than you are. We've got to get our shit together. We've got to get a plan and stick to it."

Connie took a tissue and wiped back her tears.

"I think they're so wrapped in their problems, Sonnie probably wouldn't even miss me. I could tell him some cock and bull story and he would go for it. Half the time he seems so preoccupied with things going on around him, I don't think he even knows I'm around. What they did in Italy was serious for those families over there. You know they killed the future husband of Don Aldo's niece. I can't imagine that would go over so good with both families. I know if it was in America, there would be hell to pay. "

"I think over there," agreed Theresa. "It's what Don Aldo says. No matter who's involved. He's the law. What about the bakery? You going to leave that for me to take care of by myself? I don't think that's fair. How well do you think I would do without you there?"

"Theresa," Connie added. "You handle most everything anyway. Half the time, I'm only in the way. You make all the important decisions, you handle the inventory, pay all the bills. Come to think of it, why am I there? All I do is make the displays and give the customers a hard time."

"That's what I'm getting at Connie. Who do they ask for soon as they hit the door? They don't even know I'm there. 'Hey, where's Connie?' 'What's she up to?' 'Sure is quiet here without her.' All the wise guys ask for you because you don't go for any of their bullshit. They flirt with you and you give them the cold shoulder and they just love it. There is more to running a business than paying bills and all that boring office crap. What you bring to the business is the most important, communication with the customer. I wish you would give it a little time, so we can come up with some idea of what we can do. I think if we support each other and give it more thought, we can both do what ever… together. I'll help you and you help me… that sort of thing. What do you think?

Theresa checked the built–in cooler in the limo and got out two bottles of water and hands one to Connie.

"What worries me is the way Sonnie's acting," Connie went on to say. "I can tell the way he acts after he gets off the phone with whoever… there's something going on. When we got off the plane and there were two limos there, I realized that they were not coming back with us. I just figured that something very wrong was going on. I have a feeling that there is going to be more of the same things going on here that went on in Italy and I don't want to be any part of that. Even if we don't have anything to do with what Sonnie and Vince are into, we can go down with them and the punishment will be just as harsh as if we did it too. That's what I'm afraid of. Did we really not know what they were or did we just choose to ignore the fact they were in the Mafia? Shit, they are the Mafia. You know, I've heard that once you're in you can't get out. You know… just pick up and leave. I don't know if that applies to their girlfriends, lovers or whatever we are. I'm scared and I'm not afraid to admit it. I just don't know what the hell to do. This is like a nightmare, Theresa. How did we get so involved? I don't know what it was but when I first saw Sonnie in that restaurant by himself, I sort of felt a little sorry for him. I thought he was lonely. I never gave it a thought he might want it that way. Then I had to go over to his table and make a fool out of myself. Then I got you involved and look where it's taken us."

"Connie look, I haven't regretted anything up until now but I think if we run, it would be worse than if we worked out something and then left peacefully. I don't want to be involved in any of that bullshit either, but right now, I think we don't have a choice but to hang out for a while and think of something that will be workable. We just need to be cool and stay out of the way of things. Then with time, we can figure out what to do. When they call us, we just have to put them off in a way that they don't suspect anything's going on. We have to just humor them like we always do. You know… tell them jokes and help them figure out the simple things. How does that sound? Do you know what I'm saying?"

"You make it sound so easy," Connie added. "I know it's not. I don't think it would be fair for me to go and leave you with a lot of explaining to do. You know they'll give you the third degree. Everything's so crazy right now. It's like, I don't know…I'm just going crazy with a million questions and every one of them confusing. I think I'll hang around with my buddy and see what goes from here. Thanks for talking this out with me and helping me get a grip on my emotions. It's good for me to know you feel the same way I do about the circumstances around us. I think with your help, we can figure out something."

The women made a toast with their bottles of water and share a friendly embrace.

"Together we'll be stronger," Theresa toasted. "I'm glad you are going to stay for a while. I need you just as much as you need me. Let's try to look at things in a positive way. We can do this. Every day we'll meet for breakfast and plan out strategies. It will make us stronger. You know they're always preaching about not doing anything without having a plan. Well, we'll make a plan every day and stick to it. That'll be our strength."

The limo came to Connie's apartment first. Connie and Theresa held up their hands and locked little fingers and smiled. The driver took Connie's luggage in and checked out the place as Sonnie instructed, before leaving. Connie locked the door and waved to Theresa from her window as the limo pulled away.

Before the limo reached her apartment, Theresa noticed that a soft rain had begun to fall. Looking out at the familiar buildings and street, a smile came over her face. *'Welcome home,'* she thought. *'God only knows what we're in for.'*

CHAPTER NINE

Sonnie and Vince were contemplating what to do about all the problems they have facing them. Sonnie called Bobby to find out if anything was going on with Rando and the hits on the bosses of the two families.

"Meet me at the office," he told Sonnie. "I'll give you all the details there.

The office is now in a building next to the bakery. The only thing that looked out of place was the painted windows. Sonnie had bought it to use for his office and some extra storage space. The owner of the building had been this Jew that wasn't cooperating with the sale of the place. He had wanted three times what the place was worth and Sonnie wasn't going for that.

"Look," Sonnie told him, "That building has been empty for five years. All the windows in the alley are broken and it's an eye sore to the neighborhood. It's a wonder the city didn't tear it down by now. Meet me there in thirty minutes and bring the papers with you."

The owner showed up with the papers in hand and just knew that he was going to get his asking price but he didn't know who he was dealing with. Let's just say, Sonnie made him a deal he couldn't refuse.

The bakery took off as soon as the girls started running it. It had been renovated and when you walked in you would get the feeling that you were in Italy. Columns on either side of the door as you entered, with murals of the fountains in Rome on one wall and on another, a mural of the village that Sonnie and Vince had grown up. It had been done so well, that you could sense what it was like to be there. The front of the bakery had tables set up like you were at an outside café. Along with the breads and pastries, they now served all the special flavored coffees and espresso. They added a deli with all the different hams and cheeses from around the world. It was now a very popular place to come for lunch and to take home fresh breads and cookies for the family along with that special bottle of imported wine. There was an office in the back of the bakery where the girls could take care of the business end.

Most of the time, Sonnie and Vince would enter their office from the alley. It was well protected with alarms, motion lights and hidden cameras. Nothing went unseen in that alley. Two cameras were also set up in the bakery so that when Sonnie and Vince were in their office, they could see what went on in case the girls needed any help, which was hardly ever. They were a great team and good at handling all situations.

When Sonnie and Vince arrived at the office, they noticed Bobby's car was there already. He was inside and had the coffee going because he knew they would need it. The only other person to have a key to the office was Rando. As the limo pulled up, Bull drove in behind them. He wanted to be there to give his account of what his boys had seen and done for them. When they got inside, they saw the mess that was left by Rando when he robbed the safe and tried to get into the other one with no luck.

"Look at this place Bull! That prick's going to pay for this, he's going to pay real good," Sonnie went on to say with real conviction. "Look… he cleaned us out good. Thank God he didn't get into the other safe. If he had, he would have been sitting real pretty right now. He got about a hundred-thousand from the safe in here. The other one has…"

"I don't need to know your business Sonnie."

Cousins II

"After what you did for us Bull, you need to know everything. We've decided to include you in everything from now on. You've proven to us how committed you could be to this organization. Your loyalty reminds us of the old-timers in Italy. What you say you mean... and that's very important. We need trust and loyalty and you've showed us that. We've misjudged you and we apologize for that. You understand we have to be very careful about what we do and who we trust. You've proved to us in many ways that you should be in our organization. Your patience will benefit all of us."

Bull put his hands on his hips. "I've never thought you guys trusted me one-hundred percent Sonnie. I got to the point where I thought of moving on. Two or three times I wanted to just shut everything down and go back home but something kept me from doing it. I was running out of ways to show you'nz how much I could be trusted."

"We're glad you didn't. It wasn't that we didn't trust you, we were just being stubborn and hard headed," Vince added. "Sonnie and I knew all along, you belonged here with us. Besides... we might need your dogs again, if we ever find that prick Rando. I have a feeling he's going to pay a real hefty price for what he's done to us. He's been real cute the way he's gone about what he did but it takes only one mistake... then he's ours. I wonder how good he sleeps at night? He's probably so fucked up all the time, he doesn't know whether he's coming or going and that will be his downfall."

"Bad news boys, those dogs are gone. They turned on my brother and chewed him pretty bad, so I shot'em and put'em in the same car masher I used for that Desmond cat. I should have seen it coming. They started acting goofy at times, after they chewed up those two brothers. It got to the point they only wanted to eat raw meat. Don't worry... I've got plenty of other ideas what to do with that bastard. I'm thinking of buying some hogs. See what drugs and some bitch can do to you... I always liked Rando. Thought he had a real good head on his shoulders. He would tell me he couldn't believe how anyone could get hooked on drugs. I guess he found out the hard way. We've looked all over the place for him. We looked in all the drug hangouts, talked to all the hookers and even put out a reward...

nothing. That fucker's probably so far away from here and so scared, we'll never find him. We're going to have to get lucky... real lucky. I've got my boys on a twenty-four seven alert to find this son-of-a-bitch. We'll get him. Believe me, if he's around the area we'll get him."

"There's something to what you're saying about him, but I think he'll make a mistake and come back. Who else does he have? Where else could he go, when you're in the fix he's in? He'll get desperate. See how stupid drugs make you? He'll come back wanting forgiveness and when he does... I promise you, that bastard will wish he cut off his nuts and stuffed them up his ass himself."

"I hope you're right Vince," Sonnie added as he poured a second cup of coffee. "Bobby, tell us what you know about the hit on Sammy G. and the attempt on your friends in New York. Does anyone know what went on or what the hell this is all about? We thought everything was good here. We thought everybody was happy with what we all had. All the families were staying to themselves, and handling all their stuff themselves... not interfering in any one else's business."

"You think someone's getting greedy... wanting it all? Me and Vince were thinking the unthinkable. We were thinking Maria had something to do with this. What or who else could it be? Has there been any signs of anybody being disgruntled and wanting a change or someone wanting to take over? You know how they do, they conspire in secret and then one day all hell breaks loose."

"You're really paranoid about this chick Maria, aren't you Sonnie? I hope we meet up with her again. I'll take care of it for you Sonnie... then you won't have this hanging over your head any longer."

"If you knew how dangerous she can be, you would be looking over your shoulder too. You know, she could charm the head off a snake, so you really don't know when her cute little ass is going to show up and put a hurt'n on you. Believe me, I know she's around and I'd bet all the money in the world, she had something to do with this bullshit that's going on now. When we were growing up together going through our problems, I never thought she would turn out the way she did. Once she became Don Aldo's right arm, she took over the whole body. She's the reason I left Italy. She got big into dealing drugs and wanted me to sell for her, even though I was head of a small organization in another village. I couldn't compete, she put the pressure on me so I had to leave. That's when I came to America."

"Remember," Bobby replied. "I told you that it didn't look like the normal type of a hit on those Philly bastards. Well... Sammy G. and his two bodyguards were found in an abandoned gas station with their throats slit from ear to ear. You know Sonnie, wise guys don't operate that way. They... who ever did this, went as far as to go and try to kill a couple family members but didn't have any success. When they went to break into Sammy G.'s house and kill his wife and kids, some off-duty cop was riding by and chased off who ever it was. We've got everybody that's available on standby. The people in New York are all over the streets trying to find out just who's responsible for this shit. A lot of people are worried. The guy they caught committed suicide. The piece of shit had some kind of poison capsule in his mouth. What puzzles the families is that everyone's happy with the set-up. You know... the way everyone's operating, it all checks out. You know... what you said. Everyone's happy the way things are and no one's looking to change anything. Unless someone's lying and you know if they are. We'll find them out eventually. The word is, someone new is trying to move in and they're starting at the top. This poison thing certainly doesn't sound like anything a wise guy would do."

"Have you heard anything here in town?" Sonnie asked. "Did anything out of the ordinary happen besides that fucker Rando ripping us off like he did? What he did was real chicken shit. I can't wait to get my hands on that son-of-a-bitch. That cop in Philly, did he get a description or a plate number of the guys trying to break in Sammy G.'s house?"

"He said those guys looked like foreigners, not our people. You know... like desert rats or something. The police don't see any connection with the murders. The guy the boys caught in New York that committed suicide was a desert rat. That's too much of a coincidence. For the first time in a long time, both New York and

Philly are talking. They're having sit-downs trying to get a clue as to what's going on and trying to see if the two hits are connected. They know we like to handle our problems and hand out the punishment as we see fit. Both organizations are reassuring each other, they didn't call out the hit. They're both saying it wouldn't be in their best interest at this time, to try that sort of thing. Neither side wants to have all-out war. That was in the old days. Once they figured out it wasn't the way we do things, they decided to work with each other, finding a solution to this problem. The people from Philly were wondering if it could have been us but my boss in New York told them he had good sources here and he would have known if the hit came from here."

"Bobby, me and Vince appreciate you looking after things. You and Bull are great to have around. We feel good knowing you guys got our backs. When you told me about Rando... I about shit. Imagine being 40,000 feet in the air and hearing you've just been ripped off. I just about lost it. Vince had to do some quick talking to calm me down. Once we landed and got settled, it wasn't too bad then. Tell me again, how did you find out about this bullshit with Rando?"

"Like I said Sonnie, he was acting weird. Soon as you and Vince left, he said he was going away for a while. I asked him about taking care of things, he said, piss on it. He was tired of all the shit he was having to put up with. He said he was going to take some time off and it didn't matter what happened while he was gone. I asked him if he thought it was the right thing to do, leaving you's guys in the cold. He just looked at me, grabbed a travel bag he had with him and left. I just thought he was bull-shitting me like he always does. When he didn't answer his cell, which I called five times, I went to look for him. When I went by the office, the door was left open so when I went inside, that's when I saw the safe and called you. Sorry I didn't catch on sooner as to what was up. Maybe I could have got the money from him before he left."

Sonnie looked at Vince. "Vinny, I'll bet the money was in that travel bag, he had with him... that prick."

"You did the right thing Bobby." Vince said. "You didn't take chances. The way he was thinking, he could have done anything to get what he wanted. Sonnie said we left the wrong man in charge. I agree with him. What are your plans? You going back to New York now, with all the shit that's going on there? Has your boss asked you to come back? Do they need you back there? We're hoping you're going to stay here with us. We like the way you operate. You seem to think the same way we do."

"I appreciate that Vince," Bobby replied. "Bull and I spent a lot of time together since all this happened. We made some decisions. We figure you guys are the cock of the walk around here. We think it would be that way no matter where you'nz went. We would like to stick around and be in with you guys. I don't care to go back to work in New York. Believe it or not, it's much quieter here, even with all the shit that's going on now. The wise guys there...well, I get tired of all their shit. The same old thing everyday. How someday they're going to wack somebody, take over, and do things their way. I don't like that, planning behind someone's back. Someday, someone's really going to do something stupid and all hell's going to break loose. Not for me... I don't want any part of it. So I would be grateful to stay here and work for you and Sonnie. Besides, I can still get those two friends of mine to come down if you want."

"That's good news, we needed some after the last week. It's been a real pisser. I thought you already told them to come, but since you didn't, let's see what goes down and we'll go from there. If it's not going to cause any problem with your boss, we'd be glad to have you stay."

"Hey...tell them about our trip Vince," Sonnie smiled.

Vince shook his head and smiled back. "Anybody hungry? Let's go find something to eat and we'll tell you guys all about it."

CHAPTER TEN

They found this quiet little place right off the strip and sat down for a nice peaceful dinner. Sonnie and Vince were a little beat from the trip back, so they appreciated the quiet. Bobby and Bull ordered a drink while Sonnie and Vince just wanted coffee before they ordered. As they were looking over the menu, they heard this loud commotion coming from across the room. Vince looked at Sonnie. It couldn't be... it was.

"Hey!!! Where you's guys been? I've went by the bakery and it was closed. It all looks different in there. Who changed it? I didn't know if you's guys still owned it or what. I was starting to get nervous when I couldn't find you. I've been looking everywhere! It's all different now. Where's the office? I don't know where anything is. I went by the Clip Joint... no one would tell me where you'nz were. I've been here two days and no one's around. I had to stay in the bus station. I looked for Rando... I couldn't find him. Bobby, where were you? Did you's guys order yet? I'm hungry. I'll pull up this chair and join the party. So tell me... what's happening? Aren't you glad to see me? Why isn't anybody saying anything?"

Vince looked at Sonnie with amazement and shock on his face.

"You've got to be shitting me," he exclaimed.

"Hey Vinny," Sonnie replied, pointing the menu towards Petey. "You got your wish."

Cousins II

"What the hell you talking about?" Vince frowned.

"You been thinking about him all the time we were away. Go ahead, tell the little shit how much you missed him. Tell him how much we needed him. I always said, be careful what you wish for... you just might get it."

While Sonnie and Vince were in disbelief, Bull and Bobby were laughing so hard, tears were running down their faces. Petey sat down and motioned the waitress to bring him a coffee.

"What the hell you doing here?" Sonnie asked. "Why did you have to stay in the bus station? What the hell did you do now? I thought we were rid of your scrawny little ass forever. You had everything going for you. Tell me, how did you fuck it up this time? Tell me the truth now, what did you do? Are your running from those Jamaicans, 'cause if you are, you can't hide from them, so you better tell me everything and I want the truth or I'll hand you over to them myself. Vince, just when you thought it couldn't get any more bizarre... it does. My stress level was already off the charts, now this. Okay guys, you can stop laughing now. It's not funny anymore. Com'on out with the bad news."

"You don't understand," Petey uttered, sipping his coffee and holding his cup with both hands. "Right away you think it's my fault. "Just because I've been a fuck-up before, doesn't mean I can't change. I'll have you know, I'm not responsible for what happened."

"I knew it Vinny, he's the problem." Sonnie turned his glance back to Petey. "I can't believe it... you blew everything. That's just like you. You just can't stop trying to hustle people. Don't you understand... you're not smart enough to succeed at that? Everyone has you figured out before you make your play."

"Hold on Sonnie," Vince interrupted. "Let him finish. This ought to be good. Let's see how he gets out of this." "Okay," he warned Petey. "Start at the beginning and don't leave anything out."

"Well Vince, it all started out when we went on a safari in Africa. It was really cool, guys. We got to see all the wild beasts. It was supposed to last fifteen days but while we were there, my wife caught some kind of disease and her skin started rotting. It was discusting. We had to go back home. She died about three weeks after we got back. They blamed me 'cause I was the one that wanted to go. So they kicked me and Jumbo out of the family… so here I am."

"Wait… what's this Jumbo?" asked Bull as he tried to compose himself.

"While we were there I helped this native that was being beaten up by three of the chief's sons. So they gave him to me. They said if I wanted him to live so bad… take him. What could I do?"

"So where is he now?" Bobby asked.

"He's down at the bus station."

"What the hell you thinking… leaving him there? You haven't changed one bit. He's probably dead by now."

"I don't think so Bobby. He can take care of himself pretty good. He's taught me a few tricks I didn't know."

"That can't be but so hard," Sonnie added. "Don't you think you should check on him? If he can't speak English, he'll be in a fix. Those druggies down there will steal him blind."

"Trust me Sonnie, that's one of the reasons they were going to kill him. He stole and hustled everyone in the village. He would steal from one person and sell it to someone else. Then go to the person he stole it from and tell them where it was. Then there would be a fight. After a while, they caught on to what he was doing so they tied a dog to him. Not just any dog, but one that barked all the time. That way, they always knew where he was. When I asked them why they were beating him to death, the chief told me Jumbo poisoned the dog and they had enough. So that's when I came to the rescue."

"So what you going to do with him if he can't speak English?"

"But he can. Everyone there could. That wasn't the only reason they didn't like him."

Sonnie leaned back in his chair and folded his arms.

"Here we go. I knew there had to be something else. That was too easy. So what is it?"

"Sonnie, you're going to get a kick out of this. He's a midget. I mean a little fucker too. I think he said he was three foot-nine and he's got this big afro like back in the sixties. I don't think he ever washes that shit. It's nasty."

"What!! A midget named Jumbo with a big dirty head of hair. Get the fuck out of here. You're the only asshole I know that could get yourself involved in shit like that. Every time I think you're doing something good…ah shit, what's the use? Com'on now, tell us this bullshit can't be true. You got to be jerking our chain."

"No shit guys, he's down the bus station. See, everyone in the village was over six feet tall, even the women. I mean they're some tall fuckers. There's one dude that's seven foot six. I tried to get him to come with me to the states. I figured me you and Vinny could get him in the N B A. We'll go get him right after we eat."

"You're a real sensitive guy, Petey. You buying?"

"That's another problem I have Vincent. When they told me to leave and I wasn't a member of the family anymore, they took everything I had, gave me enough money to get here and that was it. So now I'm stuck with this little fucker, a dead wife, no money and no place to stay. Hey Sonnie….."

"Don't even think it," Sonnie interrupted. "You want to stay at my place, you and that short hustler with dirty, nasty hair? Don't even think it. I've already been ripped off, I don't need that again. Bobby, take him down the bus station and pick up this Jumbo character and come back. We'll wait and order when you get back."

"What'da you mean you got ripped off Sonnie? Tell me what's going on. How'd it happen? Who did this to you? Tell me and I'll take care of it. Is it someone I know? What did he take? Tell me Sonnie, who did this to you and Vince? I'm serious. Even though I don't live here, I still got my connections. Just give me the word and I'll get on the street and find who ever did this to you'se guys."

"What'da you think Vinny, should we trust this bull-shitter and tell him what's going on? I'll tell you what Petey, go get that midget and we'll talk it over while you're gone. Maybe when you get back, we'll have an answer for you."

"Wait… you mean Bull and Bobby already know before me? What's going on? Everything's changed around here. I don't want to be left out."

"Your ass don't live here anymore so how could we tell you anything? Even if you were here, I don't think you should know about this. You wouldn't believe this person did this to us. We can't believe it ourselves. So take off and as soon as you get back, we'll talk. Ya know... I don't care if I see you once a year, you still piss me off. The bad thing is... I know you're going to do it and I still let it happen."

Petey leaned forward, "Sonnie you seem a little tense but I'll tell you anyway. How did you like the story I just made up about the midget? Wasn't that great? I just thought it up as I was coming in the door to surprise you guys. It just came to me. I thought it was great. You should have seen the look on your face when I told you he was only three-foot-nine inches tall with a big afro. I would pay a million dollars to see your face look like that again."

As Sonnie looked at Vince in total disbelief, a smile crept over his face. Bull and Bobby were laughing so loud that the other people in the restaurant were beginning to stare.

"I told you Vince he was shitting us. You little bastard, I have to admit, you had me going for a while."

"What do you mean for a while? I think he sold you... well us, pretty good." admitted Vince.

"So tell us the truth now you little shit-head," Sonnie demanded. "What are you doing here? Is everything okay with you... you still married? I guess they haven't found out the truth about you yet or you would be dead by now."

"You mad Sonnie? I thought I was pretty convincing. Everything's cool with me. My wife's in New York for a week shopping. I hate that so I thought I would come for a visit. I'm staying at the plaza in a suite there. The girls told me you guys were in Italy and would be back today. Oh by the way, she's shopping for maternity clothes."

"I don't know whether to congratulate you or try to slap some sense into you," Bobby added. "You're having a baby at you're age. What're you nuts?"

"Bobby, there's nothing else to do there. Everybody has tons of kids. They're running around everywhere. So tell me who ripped you guys off. Let me help. I still know a lot of seedy characters around here. I know I'll be able to find out something. So Sonnie, you're not still mad about that story I made up are you?"

"In the back of my mind I had a feeling you were bullshitting me," Sonnie admitted half embarrassed. "I'll have to say, it was pretty good. Bull and Bobby looked everywhere and used all their resources and couldn't come up with anything. We don't know anything else to do or anywhere else to look. The girls at the shop couldn't find out anything and you know they know everybody."

"Well... tell me what happened," Petey replied with eyes glaring.

"Go ahead Vinny... tell him. I'm tired of talking about it. I'm about half crazy over this thing anyway."

"It's Rando. He got mixed up with some dancer... got on the needle. Then took some money...a lot of money and skipped out. Now we can't find him. When we do, well you know what has to happen. That prick's got a lot of balls to just take our money like that. We trusted him, so that when we heard what he done, we were literally in shock."

Petey shook his head in disbelief. "I can't believe he would do something like that. I always thought he had it all together. See what a bitch and drugs can do to you. It just don't make no sense... why he would go against you guys. I can't believe it. If you want, I'll get in touch with some of my old contacts and see if they know anything."

"Petey," Bull explained, "we've left no stone unturned. We've looked high and low for that son-of-a-bitch. He must have left town or something. We've had shit for luck."

"No offense Bull, but you wouldn't lower yourself to know some of the people I know. You only looked in the toilet, I look under the shithouse. If you don't mind, I'll stay as long as it takes and help out. It'll be like old times. What'da you say, Sonnie...Vince?"

"First of all, you've been gone from here for over a year. Before that, you were back and forth and out of touch with all your cronies. I bet they don't even remember you. You know, out of sight out of mind."

"Sonnie, how do you think I found out where you were having dinner? I know you bought the building next to the bakery and moved the office in the back of it. Connie and Theresa remodeled the bakery and now it's doing better than ever. I know about the boys in Philly and the attempt on your boss, Bobby. We have to talk about all that later. Just because I live hundreds of miles away, don't mean I lost contact with people. I still keep in touch with everyone just like I do with you. If you want me to, I'll get working on this soon as I can. I still know who does what in this town and where all the low-life's live. Anyway…I still have all my contacts in place. All I have to do is call. You see, they know who I'm in cahoots with and they're scared of the penalty if they don't give me what I want."

"What'da you think Vince?"

"Not to interrupt Sonnie. I think you should let him look around. What can it hurt? I'll stay with him in case he needs someone to be convincing," Bull suggested.

"Vince…What do you think? I don't know about Bull going with him. I don't think he has the temperament to put up with the shit he'll put him through. I think, if we let you do this Petey, you've got to promise to keep in contact with us. I can't express how serious the consequences could be if you don't. Now you've got to promise us and I mean it."

"Let's do it Petey," Vince smiled. "One thing and this applies to you too Bobby, if anything looks funny, get the hell away from it. You have to promise to call and keep us informed about what's going on. Remember that fucker Lenny? Don't be like him. He wouldn't call for days. He'd drive us nuts, then when he did call, he wouldn't tell us shit. You see where it got him? There's a lesson to be learned there. Petey, you finally got your life together, don't take anything for granted. You don't have to do this. We'll find him eventually… he'll turn up. Then we'll deal with him in a way he won't forget."

"Look," Petey began to plead. "I miss the old days but look guys, sometimes I won't be in a position to call. You've got to understand that. Besides, I know these guys and I trust that they won't betray me. I love my life for the first time and I'm not going to do anything, not intentionally, to screw it up. It's time I get serious for a change. I know it's hard for you'nz to comprehend that, but it's possible. I can pull this thing off. I'll do everything I can to show you'nz that I can do this without screwing it up. That was the old

Petey. I got my shit together now and I'm not about to piss away everything I have. Besides, I owe you'nz... big time."

"The old days are gone Petey," Vince reminded him. "In a short time, everything's changed out there. Those bastards are ruthless now. They won't stop at nothing. We don't have any clue what happened in Philly. It looks like a new element has come into play here. By that, I mean it appears that outsiders are trying to take over the families. How they think they can get away with something like that, I have no clue. They don't know what they're up against. That's something else we have to address. We have to get together with the other families and see what can be done. We need to do that real soon. We're a little nervous here because nobody came down on us. What doesn't look good... is that we were out of the country when all this bullshit happened and to us, it looked a little funny... Like someone's trying to set us up. The good thing is that Bobby's trusted in New York and he smoothed things over with them. We owe him for that. So welcome back. If you want out, just say the word and we'll understand."

"What's good to eat here Vinny? By the way guys,' I'm picking up the tab... You catch the tip."

"I don't got any money," Vince said. "Does anybody have any money? How about you Sonnie...Bull...Bobby?"

"Okay guys... I get it. Welcome back Petey. Pay the bill and the tip. Ha ha, very funny."

They all had a good laugh at Petey's expense... even Petey. The dinner was nice and there were some good laughs along with some quiet times too. Sonnie could see a big change in Petey even though his entrance was a little shaky. The five of them knew there were some rough times ahead but with their strong brother-like alliance, they were confident they would face their problems head on and would be a real force to be reckoned with.

CHAPTER ELEVEN

A couple of weeks passed and all was quiet...too quiet. Connie and Theresa were doing well at the bakery and despite their dilemma... they were making the best of the situation. When Vince or Sonnie would call, the girls were nice but anyone that knew them could tell it wasn't the same. Sonnie and Vince were so involved with finding Rando and the hit and attempted hit on their competition, that they didn't realize they were being ignored. Bull was doing his thing selling cars and still had his people looking in every drug hang-out for any signs of Rando. He knew how important it was to find him. It would be one less thing to worry about for Sonnie and Vince. Bull knew that the sooner Rando was taken care of, the easier it would be to concentrate on the other thing that troubled them. Bobby was busy recruiting but was having a difficult time finding the right people. Vince and Sonnie had told him that they wanted to find local talent instead of going out of town simply because it would be easier to check them out and that they felt out-of-towners may not have the respect and loyalty needed for the job. Sonnie on the other hand, was a basket case. He knew in the back of his mind, that something was in the works He was sure that they were the next ones to be hit by whomever it was trying to take control, especially if it was Maria. If anyone could pull it off, she could. She's very resilient, as any one who knows her, knows what she's capable of.

It was a rainy Sunday when Sonnie called the troops in to discuss a sit-down with the guys from New York and Philly. Bobby could set up the thing with New York but how could they get with the boys in Philly? Sonnie and Vince felt somewhat out of the loop because they always stayed in Atlantic City and didn't get involved with the other families, except when they had meetings to discuss territories and any other major problems to be solved. Now, Sonnie and Vince were wanting them to come for a meeting with them for reassurance. It was fact that they ran Atlantic City and the other organizations showed their respect. Sometimes Bobby's friends from New York would come down for a visit and Bobby would show them a good time. On the other hand, the Philly bunch for the most part, went to Vegas for a good time, especially after what happened when they tried to take over J.D.'s organization before Sonnie and Vince became partners with him. Like Sonnie's grandfather that raised him in Italy and had his own organization, they stuck to themselves and didn't have any aspirations of being in the big time. They liked to keep it simple. Now they were in a jam and were concerned about who was going to trust them in the other families. Bobby could help them with his boss in New York but how would they get the people in Philly to trust them? After all, Sonnie and Vince were the ones that helped J.D. at the expense of a couple of wise guys named Ralphie and Jake. They were the ones that came to Atlantic City and thought J.D.'s organization would be a push-over. Now it was going to come back to haunt Sonnie and Vince. Only time would tell. They would have to make it very enticing to get them to the table for this sit-down. Hopefully, someone would come up with an idea to remedy the problem.

At Sonnie's place, the troops gathered to see what they could do to get the boys from Philly to come to the sit-down. Everyone was there: Bull, looking bigger than ever, Bobby and of course Sonnie and Vince. Sonnie also invited the girls from the Clip Joint the sports-haircutting, massage and gambling parlor that Sonnie opened when he first came to Atlantic City. The girls were looking real good. There was Gina, she was the first girl to come work for Sonnie and the most loyal. She was the one Sonnie and Vince chose to run the business when they took over the organization from J.D. Then there was Claudia, an ex-show girl, Mary a hairstylist that came from another salon and Bunky, a girl on the rebound from a bad relationship with drugs. She had been straight and enjoying life ever since she went to work at the Clip Joint. Of course, Petey was a no-show. Sonnie had set up a nice buffet. He believed that a little food and wine stimulated the brain and he was right. It had been a while since everyone had gotten together and with everything that was going on, time just seemed to fly by. Everyone was hitting the wine pretty good and enjoying each others company. Sonnie kept looking at the girls, thinking something was different.

"It's been quite a while since I've seen you guys. Man... you guys look really good. Don't you think, Vince? It looks like you'nz been working out or something. Look at'em Vinny."

"I see what you're talking about," Vince replied with that shit-eating grin he gets when he's had too much wine. "I'm going to start getting my massages at the shop. They look like Victoriana's Secret Models' but better. They have more meat on their bones. Tell us what you guys been doing to look so good."

"Should we tell them? Gina asked, or let them suffer? Ah hell, I'll tell them. You know that hundred-ten-thousand we used for remodeling? Well, we all got made-over... as part of the remodeling. How we looking? Great huh?"

"You're always the smart one Gina," Sonnie nodded in approval. "Always using your head. I've been wondering why the cash flow has been so good... now I know. Tell us all about it."

"Well, Mary didn't need much, she just got boobs and a little lipo around her chin and neck. Mary, show them your new...what do you call them Sonnie, chummies?"

"That's okay," Vince interrupted, "That won't be necessary. Just get on with it."

"Claudia already had giant boobs so we just had them sort of tacked up a little, but she did get some implants in her tiny butt.

Bunky, she needed the works. How do you think everyone looks? I hope that was alright?

"Good Job." Sonnie answered as everyone clapped for the ladies. "You're a piece of work Gina. Where are the new girls or did you think they were ready for us yet? You know who I miss don't you?"

"I know Sonnie... Gayle. We've called her a couple of times and she's doing real good but she's bored."

It had been nearly three years since Gayle had done some undercover work for Sonnie and Vince and it nearly cost her, her life. Both Sonnie and Vince had regretted putting her in that position.

"How is her plastic surgery coming along?" Vince asked.

"She's all done. It took a little over seven months to complete and she claims she looks better than before, if you can believe that."

Sonnie shook his head. "I can't believe it's been that long. It seems like just a couple of months ago that all that bullshit went on. I'm so glad we took care of business, especially the way we did it, thanks to you Bull. Those dogs were great weren't they? Why don't we get her down here for a visit? Call her and suggest that. Tell her we'll fly her down and back and she won't have to worry about a thing. It'll be like old times. We'll have a blast."

"I know she would love to come for a visit. The thing I worry about Sonnie is... she won't want to go back. She asked me if she could have an opportunity to come back. I told her I would talk it over with you guys and see what you suggested."

"We would love to have her come back. Only thing, I wonder if she is stable enough mentally, to deal with being here where all that shit happened to her. I guess the only way to find out is to let her come on a temporary basis and see how she handles it. What'da you think Vinny?"

"I'm all for it but I don't think we should throw her in the mix right away. She should take it slow and see if she's really ready to get her feet wet. She can watch the desk and answer the phones... you know, that kind of stuff. Then go from there."

"What's she going to do for money and a place to stay?" asked Claudia.

"She can stay with me," suggested Mary. "We've lived together before...I don't see that as being a problem. As far as money, I don't think that will be a problem either. Gina can give her a small salary under the table and we can all pitch in from our tips, along with anything else she needs."

"You have her number with you Gina? Give her a call. We'll put her on speaker so we can all talk at once. That will freak her out."

"I know it by heart," she replies as she punched in the numbers.

. Gayle was hysterical with laughter and started packing immediately. Everyone enjoyed talking to her and was looking forward to her visit.

Just as they were ready to get down to business, Petey showed up... late as usual which didn't set too well with Sonnie.

"Where the hell you been? I guess you'll never change. What kind of bullshit excuse you have for being late or don't you think you need one because you're a married man now?"

"My wife called and wanted me to do something for her. That's why I'm late... honest. No really, I was at the bus station looking for Jumbo."

"I ought to kick your ass. Since when did you become this joker? That's all it's been since you've been back. What's gotten into you?"

"It's the lighter side of me. Something tells me, you don't like it Sonnie. Gee's, what happened to the good times? You guys can't take a joke anymore? Is it that bad? You know we can take care of any problems we have when we put our heads together."

"We have enough problems already without you being another one," Vince suggested. "Bobby have you had any success finding anybody to join our little organization?"

"I've been thinking about Angelo, Vince. Why can't we move him up? He's been with J.D. longer than I've been here with you. He's a loyal guy... he does anything we ask of him without question. You know he drove J.D. for years and knows all the routes and the people to talk to for the collections. Also, he knows what's been going on and he's been working hard on this Rando thing. I think he's ready to move up. He went nuts when Maria slipped through his fingers... he told me he didn't sleep for days. He looked everywhere for her, even went underground for a couple of days and almost got killed. He pissed off some drug people and somehow, they found out he worked for us and we were the ones that did away with Desmond. Remember that Bull? You had to go save his ass. Bull sold a lot of cars to those people. Angie knew that, so he called him and that's what saved his ass. Angie told me that when Bull and him went to this restaurant where they all hung out, they about shit."

"I never paid that much attention to him," Sonnie acknowledged. "I just thought he drove everybody around. If you think he's ready, that's alright with me. What do think Vinny?"

"That will be a little more help at the top and all we'll have to worry about is some soldiers that we can trust. Maybe he can help you with that Bobby. You know how to get in touch with him? Get him here so he can be in on what's going down. We'll eat while we're waiting for him to come over."

Bobby didn't tell him why he was wanted. It took Angelo about an hour to get there. He was always available and when anyone from the organization would call, he'd drop everything that he was doing and come right away. While the girls put away the food and made coffee, Vince had to put away the wine because everyone was getting too happy and he was afraid nothing would get accomplished if he didn't. When Angelo arrived, he was happy to see everyone but still had no clue why he was asked to come. Sonnie had wanted to initiate Angelo the "old country way." Nothing like that had ever happened there before. The ceremony took place in a private room in the basement below the kitchen. The girls, Bull, and especially Petey were left up stairs, wondering what was taking place. Sonnie, Vince, Bobby and Angelo gathered for the ceremony. It consisted of signing a paper committing him to loyalty to the family and then burning the paper in the palm of his hand. The Don… in this case was Sonnie, would kiss him on both sides of his face. The induction was then complete Angelo was now a made-man. Angelo was beside himself and was honored that they moved him up in the organization. It's something he always wanted. He was now a captain.

CHAPTER TWELVE

Vince called everyone into the large family-room to discuss what to do about the Philly connection and how they would get them to their meeting without complications. No one seemed to have a solution until Angelo spoke up.

"Can I say something, Vince?"

"Feel free to speak up. We brought you into the organization because we trust you and thought you could bring some new fresh ideas. So let's hear what you have to say."

"Well, my cousin's a priest in South Philly…"

"Why do we need a priest? You trying to tell us something?"

"Let him finish Bull." Vince interrupted. "Maybe this will go somewhere."

"He grew up with some of those guys," Angelo went on to say. "You know how it is in an Italian neighborhood. Some kids grow up good and others…you know what I mean. I could give him a call and see what the mood is around there concerning us. There's this one friend of his named Denny. I think he told me some time ago, he was pretty high up in the Philly organization."

"How'd this priest get so close to them? Are you sure he knows them well enough to talk about what we're proposing?"

"Sonnie, Denny was my cousin's best friend. This guy Denny went to the seminary with my cousin and was going to become a priest too. His temper got the best of him and one night when this faggot in the seminary came on to him. He beat him almost to death with a baseball bat. After that, they kicked him out of the seminary. He did a one-eighty after that and started hanging around with some wise guys and worked his way up. He started doing a lot of their dirty work. From what Father Mark tells me, he's a real bad ass now. If you want, I'll call him right now and see what I can arrange?"

"What makes you so sure your cousin Mark...the priest, will do this for us? He doesn't even know who we are... or does he? "

"I've always looked up to Mark. He's my older cousin and I just thought he could conquer the world. I followed him around like a little puppy when we would go for a visit. We lived about two hours away and would visit two or three times a month when I was little. Then when I got older, I would spend some time there and would hang out with him, but I never got to meet this guy Denny. Not long after he got into the seminary, he stole a car. He hadn't quiet converted yet. Well, I took the fall for him... spent three months in reform school. I think he owes me a favor or two."

"Call him... feel him out. See if he could come here for a visit, then we'll see if we're on the same page with him," Vince suggested.

Angelo made the call and returned back into the room with a smile on his face.

"You won't believe this Sonnie. Mark is on vacation at the shore and is leaving in about an hour. He said he would stop here since it's on his way. He said he always wanted a reason to come to Atlantic City, now he had a good one. You talk about good timing."

Vince was feeling a little reluctant. "We'll see about that. You didn't tell him anything over the phone did you? You never know who's listening in. I hope we didn't make a mistake doing this."

"Vince, I've been with J.D. for about eight years. I know how things work. I'm very careful when I do things, even if it don't pertain to my job. J.D. taught me never to relax and let my guard down. It only takes one brain-fart and you're dead. He used to tell me that all the time. He was a wise man although everyone who worked for him thought he was a moron. I had more fun driving him around. That guy was a real stud. Sometimes he would make three different stops on the way to the office."

"So what time did he say he would be here?" Sonnie asked. "I don't know if I like the idea of bringing him here and him not knowing what's going on."

"Don't worry Sonnie. Once he sees Gina and the rest of the girls, he'll be just fine. He might be a priest, but that's only when he has that robe on. He's pretty wide-open. Believe me, I've partied pretty hard with him plenty of times."

"So I guess we'll have to wait and see what happens. Now if we can find out something out about where that prick Rando is, we'll be getting somewhere," Sonnie went on to say. "I've about had it with him. I really never thought he would do us like that."

"Wait 'til he sees the way we're going to do him," Vince added. "Bull, you have to come up with something good. Something original. You know... be creative. Something slow and painful. I'm jumping the gun here. First we have to find the prick. We'll have a good talk... then turn him over to you."

"I'll be waiting. You know Vince, we've been everywhere looking for him and it seems like we just miss him. Everybody we talked to says, 'I just saw him yesterday or last week.' I get really pissed some time, we're so close. Boy I would've liked to have had him here and surprised you and Vince when you got back from Italy. I thought we had him that night he shot at my boys. It's probably good they didn't catch him after he tried to take them out. They probably would have cut him wide open and put his insides in the garbage. If you find him, just call first... I'll be ready."

"Sonnie, if I may?"

"What'da you want Petey? This better be good. First you come an hour late then all you've done since you've been here is eat. Do they feed you where you live? Go ahead... tell us what you got."

"I was in this hole down under the bridge and this junkie-bitch started talking to me about Rando."

"What?" Bull asked. You've been here a couple of days and got a lead and we've been looking all over God's creation and hadn't come up with nothing? I don't get it."

"I just know a different kind of lower-life people than you do... no disrespect. She didn't mention his name but she said he was throwing all kinds of money around. When he left with this skinny drugged-out stripper, a couple of guys left after him and no one seen him since."

"If no one knew his name," Bull continued, "How did your friend know it was him?"

"I don't know but you can ask her if you want. She's outside in my rental car."

With anger in his eyes, Sonnie took a step towards Petey. "Don't tell me this, you little shit. You mean you brought her to my house? What the fuck you thinking? I thought you had better sense than that. You must be nuts. Damn... I ought to kick your ass. I can't believe you sometimes. Bull, you and Angie... go out and talk to that bitch out there and then figure out what we're going to do with her."

"Sonnie don't panic," Petey uttered. "She promised she wouldn't say anything to anyone about where she's been or what she's done. All we have to do is treat her nice and give her a couple bucks and she'll forget everything."

Before Bull and Angelo could make it out the door, Sonnie stopped them. "Hold on Bull," he said and looked at Petey. "What's her name?"

Petey's attention was elsewhere "Hey Gina! You guys really look great. What happened, you guys join a health club or something? I can't believe how good you look. Come rub those big..."

"Hey shithead, I'm talking to you. You just don't get it do you." Sonnie glanced over at Vince. "I think I should have let you put him out of my misery a long time ago. All he does is irritate the shit out of me. Every time he's around, my blood pressure goes sky high. I just want to choke the life out of him." Sonnie then turned his attention back to Petey. "Now answer me you little shit."

"Damn Sonnie, why so inpatient? Take it easy... you're too uptight."

Sonnie started across the room and Petey quickly retreated behind Bull as Vince grabbed Sonnie and made him sit down. Gina and the girls got quiet because they knew that Sonnie wasn't playing. Grabbing Petey by the back on the neck with his huge hand, Bull warned Petey to settle down and instructed him to tell Sonnie what he wanted to know.

"I'm sorry Sonnie. I was just trying to be funny. Her name is Sherry. When you see her, you won't even know she's a user. She looks like a secretary for one of those big time lawyers or something like that. You know that look. She looks like she's got a lot on the ball."

"What the fuck... you in love with her or something? You better know what you're doing here, that's all I'm saying. Something happens because of her, you'll never see Jamaica again. I'm getting tired of your bullshit."

Bull and Angie went out to talk to her and ten minutes later, Bull came back in.

"Sonnie, this chick says the guy we're talking about had a tattoo of Popeye on his arm, flashing the finger. That tells me, it really was him. I asked her if she knew the guys that followed him, she said she could take me where they lived. I thought... if it's all right with you, me and Angie will go with her and see what we can dig up. Oh, there's one problem... she blew her guts out all over your car Petey. I need a wet towel or something so she can clean up a little before she gets in my Hummer."

"That bitch. I'll kill her ass. You're telling me that bitch just puked all over my car? DAMM IT!"

"You won't even know she's a user. Isn't that what you said Petey? Oh, she looks just like a secretary... yea right. She's like all the rest," Sonnie replied, teasing Petey with his own words.

Bull looked at Sonnie. *"What now?"* he thought. Vince could see the troubled look on Bull's face.

"After she shows us what we want," Bull said. "The problem will solve itself."

Gina grabbed a wet towel from the bathroom. Claudia went to her car for her overnight bag. Sherry was in pretty bad shape so they took her to the bathroom and gave her a change of clothes. Sherry turned out to be a good looking lady, a little older and maybe a little shorter than the rest of the girls, but she had all the right qualities. She looked part Porto Rican but had slanted eyes which suggested she had some oriental in her. She had a nice figure but you could tell she had been around the block a few too many times. Vince offered her something to eat and drink and Sonnie started in on her right away.

"How'd you know to talk to Petey about his friend?... And no bullshit either. We don't have any time for that."

"I heard him asking questions about your friend. I sort of knew that stripper he was hooked up with. She's a real bitch, with capital letters. Those guys that left right after he did were friends of hers. It's sort of a scam they have going on. She gets you hooked, then they steal everything you own. I know about you guys and who you are. That's why I came here. My friend told me to come to you for help but I had nothing to offer. I knew I needed to have something good for you to even listen to me. I knew if I had something like information you needed, you might help me. Now with this information maybe you'll do something for me. I need to get straight. I have a kid to raise and I can't do it in this condition."

"What do you think you know about me, and who's this friend of yours that supposed to know about my organization? Just what has your friend told you? You still haven't said anything about these people that got my guy hooked on that shit you put in your arm. It better work out... what you're telling us."

"Calm down Sonnie," Gina exclaimed. "Don't scare the poor girl. Give her a chance to say something. Be patient... settle down."

"Look Gina, we ain't got a lot of time here. I've been dealing with this shit long enough. That bastard stole from us. You know I can tolerate almost anything, but when someone steals from me... well, you know how I get. I hate that shit. There's no reason for it. Just come to me and tell me what you need and you know I'll do anything to help, if I can. Now...what's your friend's name, Sherry? Talk to me. Who's this so called friend of ours?"

"Her name is Gayle."

"Gayle! How'd you come to know her? She worked for me from the beginning, she's never mentioned you before. Gina, you ever hear her mention her name? Tell me something Sherry, this has been going on long enough. Do you know where they live or hang out? I need to know something. I need to know why that prick would do this to us after the way we treated him."

"I use to hang with the guys that took off after him, until I saw them kill a guy for some stupid reason. They beat his head in with a cement block, that's when I started staying away. From time to time, they would ask me to party with them. I only did it when I was desperate. I know where they hang and where they live. I'll be glad to take you there but let me warn you, these fuckers are nuts. They'll hurt anyone and they don't need a reason. Please let me help. This sounds real important and if I can help, maybe you can help me."

"When's the last time you saw them?" Vince asked quietly.

"I saw them with your friend and that stripper on Friday. Your friend and the stripper left together round about midnight. That's when the other guys left after them… like I said before."

"You mean that fucker's been in town all this time and you guys couldn't find him? Bull, take Bobby and go with her. Call me when you find out something. Angie, you stay here in case your friend should show up."

After they left, Sonnie had Gina get Gayle on the phone so he could ask her about what she knew about Sherry and what kind of a friend she was to her. Gayle told Sonnie that she had only known her through another girl they had met several years back. She told him Sherry wasn't really a friend and she didn't know why she would have said what she said. It had been years since she had talked to her. Gayle told Sonnie she had only been working for him a short while when she met Sherry. So how could she say anything about him to her?

"So what you're saying… she's not a friend of yours. If that's so, why is she telling me all this bullshit? Gayle, I don't need you monkey'n around with me, I need the truth."

"Sonnie, I promise. I only saw her a couple of times. I was never alone with her. I never even told her where I worked, let alone who I worked for. I don't know where that bitch came up with that story. With all you and Vince and everybody did for me, I couldn't lie to you... even if I wanted to. Please believe me Sonnie, she's nothing to me."

Sonnie could tell Gayle was starting to choke up.

"Gayle, don't get emotional on me... you know how I am. I have to check out every angle. I believe you. Finish packing and get yourself down here soon. Looking forward to seeing you and how you're doing."

Sonnie hung up the phone and motioned Vince to come to another room to relay what Gayle had said.

"You know Sonnie, something about this chick doesn't sit well with me. She didn't sound creatable and I don't think we should trust her. Besides, she's too far gone on drugs and I don't know if we could believe anything she would tell us."

"I agree with you," Sonnie replied. "Let's just play it by ear for now and see what happens."

Sonnie went into the kitchen and slapped together a salami sandwich while the rest of the troops sat in the living room waiting to hear from Bull and the arrival of the priest.

When the door bell rang, Angelo stood up but Vince motioned for Mary to answer it. Mary was speechless. There in the doorway stood a man six foot tall in Bermuda shorts and a tank top. His thick black curly hair and face looked as if it was chiseled out of granite. He had three dimples, one in each cheek and one in his chin. His dark tan and pearly white teeth made him look like a God.

Mary was speechless.

"You're a priest?" she finally asked.

"Yea...I'm Mark, Angelo's cousin."

As Angelo was introducing everyone, the phone rang and Gina answered it. It was Bull and so she handed the phone to Sonnie. Bull told him that Sherry had taken him and Bobby to the house where the guys lived. In the bedroom, they found three bodies, the two guys along with a girl Sherry said wasn't the stripper Rando was hooked up with. They all had their hands tied behind their backs and shot in the back of the head. This meant, Rando was gone and the trail was cold again. When Bull and Bobby left the house, they were alone. There were now four bodies there in the house.

Sonnie instructed Bull to return to his house and they would discuss the Rando thing later.

"Besides," he told Bull. "Angelo's priest friend just got here and I want you and Bobby here when we talk to him."

CHAPTER THIRTEEN

While Sonnie, Vince and the troops were meeting at Sonnie's house, Connie and Theresa were having a killer day at Nonna's Bakery. They sold twenty-seven cases of wine, all the seventeen different kinds of bread and rolls and almost all the pastries. The bakers will be surprised in the morning at how much work they will have to do. It was closing time and they had sent all the help home and were in the office in the back counting down all the money.

"I really love it," Theresa said as she totaled the last sales slip. "We've really turned this place around. We have so many repeat customers... what's really got me puzzled is, all the older Italian women that come in for our pastries and tell us they taste just like the ones they make."

"I know," Connie added. "That's like the biggest complement any one could give us. I don't know about you, but I'm beat. You have any plans for dinner?"

"This is going to shock you Connie, but I'm thinking about calling Vincent and inviting him over for a candle light dinner, if he's not got something to do. I really miss him. I don't know how it is for you, but I can't hold out much longer. I need him more than I ever thought I would. What they did in Italy... I've put that all behind me for now. I just want to go back to the way it was before. I know that's going against the way we were talking, but I just can't stand not being around him. Don't be mad with me."

"I know what you're saying, but I don't think I can ever put behind me what went on in Italy. I dream about it so often, it's like I relive it over and over again. It's weird but every dream is different. One time they save us and the next time they're too late and I can see us dead. I don't know if I'll ever get over it. I wish I was as strong as you. Listen Theresa, I could never be mad at you. You're my best friend. I understand that you've got to do what you think is right for you."

"I'm really glad that you do Connie. It's nothing except that I'm in love with Vince and I don't think I can survive without him, no matter how he is. You have to do what you think is right for you. I'll always stay close to you no matter where we end up. I'll always be your friend and you can count on that. We have to make a promise to stay close to each other. You know, everybody always says they will stay in touch, but then you don't hear from them for a couple of years when they have a problem or their life's screwed up. Tell me something, have you lost all your feelings for Sonnie? I don't see how you could… you guys were so close, you'nz looked like high school sweethearts, I couldn't believe how he acted around you. I don't see how that could have changed, no matter what went on in Italy."

"I'm scared of Sonnie now. What happened to us…well, I think maybe I could get over that in time. What he did and how he just killed those people without hesitation? What if he gets pissed off with me? I could end up the same way. That's what scares me. I could end up in the river or in an unmarked grave somewhere. It really worries me Theresa. I've given a lot of thought about trying it again with him but… I don't know."

"Maybe if you give it a little more time you'll have a change of heart. I don't see Sonnie that way. With you he looks secure…like he depends on you to be there. I think it would devastate him if you were to leave. What's the total for the day?"

"It's the biggest Sunday we've ever had," Connie smiled. "We took in eight-thousand seven hundred-thirty-nine dollars and change."

"That's great! We'll have to call them and tell them the good news. You want to put the money in the safe Connie?"

"I've got to go right past the bank on the way home anyway. I'll just put it in the night deposit. I don't have anything to do and it's on the way. What'da you going to do? You going to call Vince?"

"I think I will," she replied. "You go ahead, I've got some things to do so I'll lock up. I'll give you a call later and let you know what's up."

Connie left and Theresa went back into the office to straighten up a bit before leaving. She looked at the pictures of the four of them sitting on the desk and it made her think that she wanted to try and get Connie to have a change of heart about Sonnie. As Theresa went to shut the lights and lock up, she noticed that Connie had walked out and forgot the bank bag. As she reached for the phone to call her and tell her what she had discovered... two drugged-out gang-bangers walk in. One's named Dante (A.K.A. "Eyes") about five-foot-eight, black greasy hair, dark skin and had eyes the size of a fifty-cent pieces poking out of his head. He spoke broken English like he might be Latino or Puerto Rican. The other was named Jamal. His hair was in long braids but not dredge locks. He looked to be six foot-three and around two-hundred forty pounds with a long scar going from his forehead to his jaw. All the teeth in the front of his mouth had been gold capped. The stench of alcohol and marijuana permeated the air around them.

Dante pulled a switch blade while Jamal closed all the blinds and locked the door. Dante grabbed Theresa and yelled for her to get all the money that was in the place. She told him he was too late because her partner had just left to go to the bank. With that said, they asked her where the safe was.

Theresa tried to keep her composure, "I don't have the combination," she said. "I'm just the waitress here. Do you guys know who owns this place?"

"We don't give a shit...we just want the fuck'n money. You better find some money somewhere or it's going to get real bad for you bitch. Now get the combination and open the fuck'n safe. I'm not fuck'n around!"

Jamal ran over to Theresa and punched her in the face, knocking her to the floor. She hit so hard it almost knocked her out. He then grabbed her by her hair and pulled her to a chair and tied her hands behind the back of the chair.

"Look," said Theresa, "You don't know who you're mess'n with. When my boss finds out you did this... you'll pay big time."

"I'm real scared bitch. Tell me... who's this faggot I'm supposed to be scared of? He some punk that thinks he's something? I'll cut his balls off. He doesn't know who I am. He should be scared of me. I'm the badest fucker in this town. No one fucks with Jamal. If we let you live, you can tell him that."

"My boss's run this town. They names are Sonnie and Vince. Did you ever hear of a guy named Bull? He has that car lot on Seventy-Ninth Street... he's their best friend."

"Those names mean nothing to me," Jamal snarled back. "They probably suck each other off. I run this fucking town. Hey Dante, I'm supposed to be afraid of some faggot used car salesman?"

"I'm serious. You guys are asking for more trouble than you're bargaining for. If you leave now, it'll be alright. If you don't... you'll pay. When they get hold..."

"I'm tired of listening to all your bullshit," Jamal said while growing impatient with Theresa. He grabbed a rag that was on the counter and stuck it in Theresa's mouth.

Jamal turned to Dante, "What do we do now? We need to get some money somewhere. We need to have money for tonight."

"We'll look everywhere. There's got to be something in this fuck'n place. Hey Jamal, look at the tits on this bitch," he said as he reached over and tore Theresa's blouse away exposing her breasts.

Theresa screamed, but with the rag in her mouth, it did no good. Jamal smacked her again... this time busting her lip.

"If you don't shut up, I'll stick something else in your mouth and it's a lot bigger than that rag. You might choke to death if I do. You look like you might like to suck..."

"We got no time for that shit now Dante. This shits taking too long. We have to find something and get the hell out of here.

In the meantime, Connie had gotten close to the bank when she realizes she had forgotten the bank bag and turned back around. When she reaches the bakery, she noticed that the blinds were closed and thought that was strange, so she unlocked the door and went into the bakery. The first thing she saw was Theresa tied up and she just froze. Theresa tried to warn her but once again, the rag in her mouth prevented her from calling out. Connie tried to leave but wasn't quick enough and as she turned, Jamal grabbed her and threw her to the floor.

"Look-ie here. Tell me what the fuck you doing here? Who the hell are you? You have a key so you must work here. Answer me bitch," he demanded as he landed a swift kick to Connie's right leg. "If you don't say something, we're going to hurt your friend in a way you'll never forget. See those big tits? Dante would just love to cut them off and take them home with him. You better talk to me bitch."

"Okay-okay, don't hurt me anymore. I work here. I help run the place. Please don't hurt us. What do you want?"

"Do you know the combination to the safe? If you want to save your friend from Dante cutting her up, you better give us something."

"I have the combination," Connie admitted as she pulled herself up.

Theresa tried to yell again, but Jamal ran over and smacked her again. Dante grabbed Connie and pushed her to the safe.

"Open the safe and don't fuck around. Hurry up... we got to get out of here. Let me get the money out. Don't try to be sneaky bitch... just get the money."

As Connie began working the combination, she told Dante that there was a solid gold statue on the desk that she had won in a beauty contest and that it was worth a lot of money.

"Take it," she told him. "Just don't hurt us anymore."

In her heart she knew if something didn't happen real soon they were both dead. Dante's eyes lit up when he saw the statue... he walked towards the desk to get it.

"Wait...take out the money with your left hand," Dante yelled, not knowing she was left handed.

Connie reaches into the safe and pulled out a 9mm automatic.

"Here," she answered back. "Is this what you wanted?"

Just as she pulled back the hammer, Dante turned and in an instant, she put a shot right in the middle of his forehead, killing him on the spot. Connie steadied her grip with both hands and turned toward Jamal. As he started to run, a shot whizzed by his head and she ordered him to lay face down on the floor. Connie ran over and untied Theresa before returning to Jamal and sticking the gun in his face.

"Wait, don't shoot," Theresa called out to Connie as she readjusted what was left of her blouse. "Let's let Vince and the boys handle him. For now, we'll tie him up. That fucker slapped me around... He called Vince and Sonnie faggots and laughed in my face when I told him who they were. I think it's only right that they get to meet this prick. When they get done with him, there won't be enough left to feed the pigs."

Connie held the gun on Jamal while Theresa made him stand and she attempted to tie his hands behind his back. When he resisted, Connie stuck the gun in his face again.

"As far as I'm concerned," she said, "We could end it right now."

Theresa kicked him swiftly in the balls and Jamal doubled over in pain.

"That's just a little sample of what's in store for you... you bastard. Look at my face. Look what you did to me... you son-of-a-bitch!" Enraged but in control, Theresa took a paper weight from the desk and slammed it into his face. "There... maybe now you know how it feels to be slapped around a little."

Connie put her hand on Theresa's shoulder.

"That prick probably doesn't feel a thing Theresa. I heard Bull telling Bobby how they used the ovens in the bakery sometimes. Maybe we should take him back there and show him a little more hospitality. No better yet, we'll wait and let Sonnie and Vince have a little talk with him before they hand him over to Bull."

Theresa, with a half smile on her face, stuffed the same rag in his mouth that he had stuffed in hers.

"Where the hell did you learn to shoot like that?" she asked Connie. "That was awesome, I hope you don't ever get pissed at me."

"Sonnie took me to that indoor-firing-range. He always said it was good to know how to protect yourself. What do you think we should do now? I guess this makes us just like them. I never thought I could shoot anyone, but when I saw what they were doing to you…I just wanted to kill them. I see now how they do what they do. Theresa, I hate to say this but it was easy to pull the trigger on that bastard."

"I was so scared for you when you came back," Theresa replied. "I was praying Sonnie or Vince would come by and when you came in the door, my heart stopped for a second. When you pulled that gun, it stopped again. I thought we were both dead… then you shot that prick in the head. I couldn't believe my eyes!"

"Theresa, I couldn't believe how easy it was. I wanted to just keep shooting and shooting. It felt good seeing that bastard get what was coming to him for trying to hurt us. Now, I can't wait to see what the troops do to that son-of-a-bitch."

Connie walked over to Jamal and looked him straight in the eyes. "Just wait 'til we tell the guys how you treated us and that you wouldn't listen to reason, you bastard. Don't worry… you'll wish you were dead before they kill you. This will turn out to be not only the last day of your sorry life, but the most painful."

Connie looked around the corner into the office where the lifeless body of Dante lay. A small puddle of blood gathered on the floor beside his head. The look on his face was one of total surprise and Connie had to look away.

Theresa dialed Vince on her cell phone, but it wasn't for the candle-lit dinner she had been thinking about and planning all day. Now, she needed him more then ever.

CHAPTER FOURTEEN

Vince hung up the phone and looked at Sonnie and Bull.

"You ain't going to believe what just happened Sonnie. As if we don't have enough shit going on, now something like this has to happen."

"Vince what's going on?" Bull asked. "You're as white as a ghost. What the hell happened? Tell us...here sit down. Now tell us what's going on. You look like someone just died or something."

"There's no time to sit down," Vince replied. "We have to leave right away. We have to get over to the bakery. The girls...some drugged-out fuck'n bastards tried to rob'em."

"Are they all right?" Mary gasped.

"They seem like... Theresa said they were a little roughed up, but they're all right."

"You said someone tried to rob them," Gina said expressing her concern. "What's that all about? What did they get? Tell us what's going on, Vince."

"Theresa didn't tell me everything. The one thing she told me is that Connie shot this piece of shit, killed his ass. They got the other one tied up... something like that. It sounded a little confusing to me, that's why we have to get there as soon as possible. They don't know what to do. She said they were a really scared."

"What?" exclaimed Sonnie. "She killed one? I hope they didn't call the police. Connie's got more balls than I gave her credit for. She's always so quiet. I can't believe this is happening. We have to get over there and help them. Mark, I'm sorry you had to hear this but we got to go. I hope you ain't in a big hurry. I would really like to get with you about your friends in Philly. We have a lot of things to talk about, so I hope you can give us a little more time. Our meet means a lot to us... especially now with what went on while we were away. I need you to hang in there a little longer."

As Vince, Sonnie Bobby and Bull scrambled out the door to get to their cars, Father Mark followed them.

"Sonnie, I think Angie and me ought to go with you. If someone's dead, they might need last rights or something," he went on to say with a smile. "Even those who have lost their way deserve a little sympathy now and then. We'll talk business after this is all over. It's just as important to me that you understand where I'm coming from. Denny needs help and from what I see... you guys can help him. He doesn't know a thing about what he's supposed to be doing."

Sonnie stopped and turned to Vince. "Vinny, what'da you think? You think we should involve him in our business right now? He's just here for us to talk to and see what... if anything, we can work out for this meeting."

"Hell yea. I like this guy," Vince replied. "He's got a good sense of humor... he thinks like us. Come'on Mark, you can ride with me and Sonnie. We'll tell you the dilemma we're in and see if you can come up with any suggestions. We have to get something going real soon before things get out of hand and come to a head. We want to prevent that. That's why, it's important that we come to some sort of agreement as to whether Denny will be able to understand our situation. You know when you're in charge of an organization, you have to have patience and foresight. You can't stay fucked up all the time. It's a big responsibility and shouldn't be taken lightly."

Bobby driving Vince, Sonnie and Mark in one car followed by Bull and Angie in the other car, all sped over to the bakery. Of course,

Petey stayed behind with the girls, and waited by the phone. On the way to the bakery, Sonnie and Vince asked Father Mark about what happened while they were in Italy and that they didn't want anyone to think that they were the organizers of the assignations in Philly.

"Vince, I know all about what went down with Sammy G. and his bodyguards. I'll tell you… who ever did this, tried to make it look like it was a random thing. They tried to make it look like a robbery. To me… with what went on in New York, the same type of thing, someone from the outside is behind both attempts. You know, I think Sammy got too relaxed and didn't see it coming 'til it was too late. I don't think it's anyone with ties to any other organization trying to move in. Angie said he told you about Denny. He's now in control of the organization there. To tell you the truth, he doesn't have a clue what he's doing. The whole organization's falling apart. He was next in line which is not always a good thing. There's a lot of unhappy people… a lot of hot-headed young wise-guys just waiting for their chance. There's going to be a lot of trouble I think… real soon. Denny was used to taking orders, not giving them. He doesn't have the balls for the job. He's got people running all over the place trying to find out about what happened. They're so unorganized… it's like a Chinese fire drill. Anyone could move right in and take over in a second. He needs your help more than you need his cooperation. He tells everyone what to do, then goes out and drinks with these pigs he knows. He doesn't follow up on anything and in my position, I can't get that involved. I can only help from the outside but he keeps coming to me. He's lucky I can keep the peace but I don't know how long that's going to last. Someone has to step up and take control. I'm trying to keep my distance but he won't let me. Instead of going after the problem, he wants it to come to him. I've talked to him a number of times. He seems scared to me, just looks past what I say. I've done about all I can do."

Sonnie and Vince were absorbing everything the priest had to say.

"We were hoping you could organize a meeting with him and some of his associates," Vince went on to say. "I know you don't know us, but I can assure you, this is on the up and up. We have other worries. We don't need anyone thinking we're trying to take over their territory. We definitely don't need any more bullshit right now. Tell Denny he can come down and stay in a suite at the casino we just bought. Tell him he'll have a healthy credit line so he can gamble 'til his heart's content… that's after our meeting, of course. He can stay as long as he wants to."

The father rolled back his eyes. "I don't know if that's a good thing Vince. He gets carried away when he over-does it in the drinking department. If he looses at the gambling tables, then his temper comes out. He's hard to control as I said before, especially when he losses at the tables."

"What do you suggest then?" Sonnie asked. "It sounds like you know him pretty well. Tell us what you think. We want to do the right thing. We wouldn't want for anyone to get hurt or nothing like that. If he's that head strong, do you think he'll listen to you? We don't want to make trouble and we don't want anyone to get into trouble."

"Angie's talked to me about the two of you, a number of times Sonnie. From what he told me, it made me wonder what it would be like to meet the both of you. He told me you're not like a couple of cocky wise-guys that fell into a good proposition. Angie said you guys saved you're ex- boss's life. He said you were reasonable and think things over before you act, not like the person I'm telling you about. When I tell him how well you have things working, I'm sure he'll want to come down and meet with you. I'm probably the only one he takes advice from. As a matter of fact, I more or less have just as much say so in the business as he does… not by choice. I don't like being in the position. Don't get the wrong idea here, he's the head of the organization but it seems like he can't make a reasonable decision without coming to me. He's done more confessions than all the rest of the parishioners put together. So I think everything will be fine. All I want to do is hang out in my church and mind everybody's business. I have a question if you don't mind. That guy Bull… what's up with him? He's scary looking." In haste, the father made the sign of the cross before he continued. "What role does he play in your organization?" he asked.

113

"One of my guys," Sonnie explained, "Lenny… the grass looked greener on the other side, if you know what I mean. Now he's not with us anymore. He was broke down about two in the morning on the interstate and Bull pulled over to help…."

"That would be real scary," Father Mark interrupted. "I would have probably shit my pants."

"He did," Sonnie answered. They all had a good laugh. "As I was saying, he takes care of some of our hard to-handle business. His real business is dealing in exotic cars. When we get done, we'll take you down there and let you pick out something for yourself. It'll be nice driving back in a like-new dream car."

"Thanks for the offer but I'm just a modest priest. How would it look if I drove up in a Ferrari or something like that? All my people at the church…they already think I'm doing shady deals now. All they would have to do is see me in an expensive car. I can hear them now."

"Hey, these are modern times now," Sonnie continued. "You shouldn't let shit like that bother you. With all the shit you hear in the confession box, they shouldn't say a thing. Maybe you can let us in on some of the little secrets you hear in the box. I've always been curious about that gig you guys have going on. From what Angie tells me, your church is pretty financially secure. Let me just say, if everything goes well between the boys in Philly and us, it could prove to be very rewarding. We have strong connections in Italy and their connections in the church reach very high up. A good word with them…well you know what that's worth. If you don't mind me saying so, I think we're on the same page and can get something going that will benefit all parties involved. It would be good for this friend of yours, Denny… that he comes to us and hears what we have to offer. We like everything peaceful and quiet."

"I'm sure we can come up with something. Any solution you guys can suggest will be better than what's going on now? I'm just not sure that Denny has the balls to handle the situation. If it were up to me… which it's not, someone else would be in charge and Denny would handle all the rough stuff just like it was before. That's where he does his best, keeping everyone in line. Since he's not the enforcer he once was, everyone sort-of goes their own way without any organization and you know what the results of that can be. As I said, he can't do both."

Once they had gotten a half block away from the bakery, Vince called the girls and told them where they were and that they would be coming in through the office. Just as Theresa went to unlock the door to the office, Sonnie, Vince and the rest of the boys entered. Sonnie walked over to Dante's body and looked at Connie.

"Daammnn! Nice shot honey, you learned well. I was always afraid that you wouldn't be able to pull the trigger if you needed to. I see now that wasn't a problem. That's center cut."

"You know Sonnie, I didn't start shaking 'til it was all over and that son-of-a-bitch was laid out on the floor. Then we had that bastard over there to contend with. He called your organization…well he said you'nz were probably a bunch of faggots sucking each other off… especially you Bull. We told them who they were fucking with but this one over here said he was the main man in town and a bunch of faggots weren't going to tell him what to do. He said he could handle any shit you threw his way. Then, two women took him down. Connie walked over to Jamal… silent tears running down his face. "Who's the pussy now?" she taunted as she raised her foot to kick him in the face.

Sonnie grabbed her arm and held her back. "Ohhooo… calm down! Is this the same Connie that never says anything bad about anyone? You better be careful, you might start to like this stuff. Come over here honey" Connie backed away from Jamal as Vince looked on with a half smile on his face.

"Vince, I'm so mad right now. You won't believe what they were going to do to us. They said all we had to do is give them the money and they would leave us alone. When did you ever see that happen? That dead fucker over there wanted to cut off Theresa's tits. They had her tied to a chair when I came in and stripped down to the waist. They had a rag stuck in her mouth and they were humiliating her by telling her what they were going to do to her. I couldn't let that happen, she's the best friend I have."

Vince walked over to Theresa and put his arms around her.

"You alright now? How do you feel? I'm sorry we weren't around."

"I'm okay. I just wish this hadn't happened. Why did these pricks pick us to rob? Oh well, they won't have to worry anymore because they don't have any money for drugs."

Theresa noticed Mark standing beside Bull. "Who's this?" she asked Vince.

"This is a friend of Angie's from Philly. He came here to help us arrange a meeting with some people there."

"I don't understand." Theresa replied questioning his answer.

"I'll explain later about the priest. As far as that piece of shit over there, it doesn't matter what we say in front of…what's his name? It's Jamal, right? Well, you want to know who you've fucked with Jamal, you bad ass? You've fucked with a little club, you know a little bunch of guys that call themselves the Mafia. You've heard about them. If you haven't, let me introduce you to everyone. I'm Vince, one of the bosses. This is Sonnie, the other boss. This is Bobby one of our captains, this is Angelo the assassin and last but not least, this big fucker over here is Bull. You're going to get real familiar with him when you'nz leave." Vince motioned Father Mark to come over to Jamal. "I want you to meet a special person you might want to see before you and Bull leave us. His name is Father Mark… that's right, he's a priest. Is there anything you want to say to him?"

By that time, Jamal was so scared that he pissed his pants and as Vince pulled the rag out of his mouth there was a knock at the front door of the bakery. Connie went to see who was there and it was two of our local men in blue, so she opened the door and let them in.

"Please, somebody help me!" Jamal screamed.

CHAPTER FIFTEEN

"You have any cannoli or biscotti left?" One of the police officers asked. "We're having the folks over tonight and Mom's favorite is the cannoli. I wanted to get by earlier but there was another gang shooting. Those bastards aren't ever going to stop killing each other. I just wish they wouldn't do it on my shift. I hope you're not all out," he continued.

"No officer, we had an exceptional day today but I think we can fix you up."

Connie bagged up the treats and told them there was no charge.

"It looks like it got a little hectic around here," one cop uttered with sarcasm. "It doesn't look like you need us for anything so we'll be going now."

As they were about to leave, Jamal couldn't believe what he was happening and yelled for help once again.

"Did you hear something?" One of the officers asked the other.

"Not I," He answered and they left closing the door behind them.

Vince walked back over to Jamal. "I guess you figured out your chances of getting any help around here are slim and none. You should listen to people when they tell you something. You should have never picked this place to rob. Look at the mess you got you and your friend into. He's lying over there with a bullet in his head and you're begging for your life. I don't have any respect for fuckers like you that take from everyone else. How many people have you and that dead spick friend of yours beat up and just took what you wanted? That will all stop now. I ought to slit your throat right here. The only reason I don't, is that I don't want to have to clean up the mess. So what we're going to do is turn you over to Bull. Let me ask you something first. Now that you got to see Bull, does he look like a faggot to you? I think you've really hurt his feelings by calling him a name like that without really knowing him. He's really a nice guy… kind'da sensitive too. Father Mark, is there something you want to say to this bastard before Bull takes him for a ride?"

Father Mark stepped directly in front of Jamal. "When's the last time you've been to church? Don't be afraid, just answer what I ask."

"When I was little," he began. "My mother was in the choir and made me go three or four times a week. I don't know what happened. She died when I was nine… I don't know what went wrong after that. I just started hanging…"

Father Mark raised his hand for him to be quiet. "I hear the same shit from you people all the time. You're real tough when you're in control. Once your world caves in, you're all sorry and you come to me for forgiveness. You think by saying you found God when you're about to die, saves your sorry ass? Well… I got news for you. It don't work that way. Bull, do something with this piece of shit. His kind makes me sick."

Everyone looked at each other in surprise. They didn't expect Mark to handle the situation that way.

"Wait!" exclaimed Jamal. "If I give you something, can you give me a break? Maybe I could work for your organization, I always wanted to be in the Mafia. I watch all the movies about them. I'm not with any gang, but I know all the leaders. My cousin Chico, he's the head of the Silk Hats. They're the biggest gang in these parts. They control all the business, you know… chop-shops and that sort of things. They got all the hookers on the North Side and he knows when and where all the drug deals go down. It doesn't happen without him giving the okay. He's not like me... he doesn't do drugs. He just sells them and makes all the deals. He's big business," Jamal went on, trying to impress.

"Where's you cousin now?" Sonnie asked.

"He's in the islands making connections to bring in some new girls to work the streets. Like I said, he has all the hookers too. He can get you anything you want. I'll introduce him to you and tell him you're one of my good friends. Then, what ever you want, he'll provide for you. He's a pretty straight up guy."

"So he doesn't know you're here? Sonnie continued. What else can you give us?"

"The Mayor and two of his constituents use big time. They're always having drug parties at this hotel and casino on Forty-Ninth-Street. Com'on...please give me a break. Now that I'm not high anymore, I realize how much I fucked up. I didn't know who we was fuck'n with. It was all Dante's idea. I just went along with it 'cause I was high."

"First of all," Sonnie explained. "I don't care to know your cousin. He's a piece of shit and I don't need to be associated with some drugged-out fuckhead. Besides, he can't do anything for me. Second I already knew about the Mayor."

Sonnie glanced over at Bull, "I don't need to hear any more of his shit, Bull get his ass out of here."

Jamal, begging for his life broke away from Bull as he was dragging him out. Bobby ran him down and took him back to Bull. To make sure that it didn't happen again, Bull hit Jamal with a crushing blow to the head and knocked him out. Bobby and Bull threw him into the trunk and headed towards Bull's junkyard a couple hours away. About half the way there, Jamal came to. It was dark in the trunk and he felt something wet on the side of his face. Not being able to see, he put it to his lips only to realize it was blood. He began to feels around and discovered Dante, his best friend, was in the trunk with him... Jamal let out a scream.

Up front and smiling, Bull looked at Bobby... "Do you hear something? Turn the radio down. Ahhh...that fuckhead back there must have come to. Maybe it's a little too crowded in there for him. Oh well, he'll have to wait 'til we get to the junkyard."

Bobby smiled back, "He better save his voice. He's go'na have a lot of screaming to do. I wonder how he feels now? I'll bet he doesn't think he's such a big shit now. All the drugs and all the people can't put Jamal back together again."

"Good point Bobby. I wonder if he feels sorry for all the bad things he's done. You know, Mother use to say: *'When you do evil... you become evil. Then you're friends with the devil.'*

Meanwhile, back at the bakery, Vince was stewing about what Jamal said about the Mayor.

"That's the son-of-a-bitch that's holding us back from getting the go-ahead to redo the casino... and he's do'in drugs. That bastard. Who does he think he is? Sonnie, we've got to do something with that fucker. How long have you known about him do'in drugs? Why haven't you said anything? That's not like you to hold something like that from me."

"Calm down Vinny," Sonnie suggested. "I just found out myself... but I promise you, now that I have this information, we'll make good use of it."

"You shithead, I should have known better. This is a break for us in a way. Now we can go after that son-of-a-bitch and make him pay for all the unnecessary bullshit he's been putting us through. I knew in time we'd have the upper hand."

"You know Vinny, it seems to always work out that way. I don't know why it happens...I guess we're just lucky like that."

Sonnie and Vince pulled Mark aside and asked him if he could stay overnight so they could have a little more time before he went back to Philly. Father Mark told them that he thought he knew what he needed to do and that he was sure everything would go as planned. He assured Sonnie and Vince that he would have Denny in the palm of their hands and that he would come back with him so he wouldn't be uncomfortable, if that was okay . Sonnie and Vince both agreed that Father Mark's plan sounded workable. Angie took Father Mark to see the sights and to hit a few spots along the strip.

Vince and Sonnie asked the girls if they needed to go to the emergency room or if they wanted their doctor to come there to look at them.

"I'm fine," Connie replied as she walked over to Sonnie. "I need to apologize to you. I've been putting you off since we've got back from Italy and I'm sorry."

Theresa looked at Vince. "Vince, I was also doing the same thing," she said half smiling.

Vince, with a surprised look on his face glanced over to Sonnie.

"We've had so much going on," he said. "I didn't even realize you girls were doing that. I noticed a couple times I called, you were a little distant but I just though you were tired. How about you Sonnie?"

"I sort of had that feeling but I just thought it was me. You guys know how paranoid I've been. Why were you giving us the cold shoulder? What did we do that made you'nz feel like that? I thought we were treating you okay. If you didn't like what we were doing or saying, why didn't you let us know? There's always a way to work out any differences we might have."

"Well here goes," Theresa went on to say. "We always knew what you and Sonnie were into, but as long as we were never involved with any of that on-the-job stuff, we were cool with it. When that shit happened to us in Italy, we sort of realized how much you guys protect us and how safe we were after that. We were a little scared after we saw how you handled the situation at the winery. Connie and I talked about this before you got here and were trying to figure a way to tell you how sorry we are. We both know how difficult our lives would be if we were to go and do something stupid. We're not talking the stuff you guys give us. That means very little compared to the way we feel about you'nz. We want you to know how much we appreciate the trust you gave us when you let us take over the bakery. Vince, I never knew how much I love you and how hollow I would feel without you. So take me home so I can get cleaned up and see what I can do to make my face look presentable."

"You look fine, nothing that a little makeup wouldn't hide. You girls are pretty tough. I would have never thought you would handle yourselves in this way... especially you Connie. I knew Theresa was pretty tough from the way she does things. Connie, no disrespect but you always seems so skeptical about everything and so scared at the least little thing. Then you perform like this... what a surprise. Theresa, how's your head? I know you were banged around pretty good. You need some drugs or something, just for stress? You know what I mean... something from the drug store. I didn't want you to get the wrong idea."

"Love is the drug I'm thinking of," she replied as she winked at Vince. "Let's you and me get out of here. I've had enough of this place for one day. What do you think we should do about all this?" She asked. "How about if we close tomorrow, so we can clean up this mess?"

Sonnie put his arms around Connie. "I don't think we could open if we wanted to, not with all this mess in here. I think it'll take at least a couple of days to clean this up. I think you guys should take off a couple of days and go... maybe go to the mountains or somewhere. Vince and me will take care of everything. Just take as long as you want... we'll understand. You've been through a lot. It was bad enough what happened in Italy, then this shit. We're thankful everything turned out alright. It bothers me how calm you both are. Oh well... I don't know why I'm asking this, but is anyone hungry?"

"Vince and I will get something at my place, Theresa added. "I've got something to show him. Besides, we've got a lot of talking to do. It's going to be a pretty long night."

"I'll bet. How about you Connie? Tell me what I can get for you?" Sonnie asked.

"This might sound strange but I could eat a couple of bags of French fries from that place with the golden arches."

Sonnie just shook his head. He was thinking more along the lines of prime rib and lobster. Vince called the house and told Gina that Connie and Theresa were okay and that he would fill her in later. He thanked them for waiting and said to let everyone go home, making sure she locked up.

Just about the time they were leaving the bakery, Bull and Bobby had arrived at the junk-yard. Bull dragged Jamal from the trunk while Bobby removed the body of Dante and put it in the front seat of an old car waiting to be crushed. Bull shoved Jamal into the car's backseat so they could see his reactions. First, the sides of the crusher contacted the car to hold it steady while the front and back came in and started crushing the car. The trunk was pushed up to the back seat while the front was pushed back to the front side window with the motor laying in the front seat. Just before the top of the crusher came down and smashed the car into form, Bull stopped the crusher. Jamal was begging for his life.

"Is there anyone you want me to call?" Bull shouted out to Jamal but before he could answer him back, Bull just laughed and turned the crusher back on.

"That was cold," Bobby said slapping Bull on the shoulder. "You know Bull, no matter how big and bad you think you are, when you see death starring you in the face, we all piss our pants. Anyway, I'm getting hungry. Why don't we get some of that soul food you're always talking about? Or we could drive back to the strip and hit that great steak house we always go to. Com'on, I'm starving."

All was well with the troops… once again.

CHAPTER SIXTEEN

Monday morning came early, too early. It was a very long night for Sonnie and Vince but it was a night to remember. Both Connie and Theresa were very passionate about showing Sonnie and Vince their renewed love. The boys were on cloud nine. Sonnie made a few calls and got a good cleaning crew over to the bakery the first thing in the morning. Vince, not knowing this, did the same thing. Vince and Theresa arrived at the bakery the same time Sonnie and Connie did and they all had a good laugh at what they had done. At least they knew they were still on the same page. They stayed for a while to get the workers coordinated and then decided to walk a couple of blocks to a little deli and have some breakfast. Just as they were about to order...one of the ladies from the cleaning crew called Sonnie.

"There's what!" exclaimed Sonnie. "I'll be right there. Tell the driver not to go anywhere 'til I get there. Sonnie looked hard at Vince. You're not going to believe this one Vinny. There's a truck making a delivery to the bakery."

"What's wrong with that?" Theresa interrupted.

"It's a truck load of live hamsters! This must be some kind of joke or something. Maybe they got the wrong address. Yea, that's what it has to be. This is something Vince, ain't it? If it ain't one thing, it's another."

"What the hell, you telling me here? You're shitting me, right? There's got to be some mistake. Wait… girls is there something you're not telling us?" Vince asked in a joking manner. "You're not going to start serving hamster pie now are you? Hey Sonnie, you want me to go with you? I don't mind."

"No, I'll be right back."

Sonnie left mumbling to himself. When he got back to the bakery, the driver was waiting with the delivery slip in his hand. Sonnie took it from the driver, and from the look on his face he knew it had to be only one person that could have done this. That's right… they were Petey's hamsters.

"I'm going to call that little prick right now and get this thing straightened out. What the hell is he up to now? It's always something with him. Damn him, he'll be the death of me yet."

Sonnie was furious and once again, Petey had his blood boiling. As Sonnie was dialing his cell phone to call Petey, a well dressed man ran into him almost knocking him down. The man smiled and apologized and then moved on. Sonnie, concentrating on his call, just brushed it off not looking at the guy.

"Hey, no problem," he shouted as the man hurried away.

"Where the fuck are you?"

"Geeze, can't you say hello, how are you? Just where the fuck are you. That's real cold Sonnie. After all I sacrificed for you."

"I'll give you sacrifice, I'll give you a boot in the ass is what I'll give you. I'm standing here looking at a truck load of furry rats. Please tell me you didn't do this. What the fuck were you thinking? What the hell are you going to do with all these furry little fuckers? You better get your ass over here… and I mean fast. What do you expect me to do, stand here with my finger up my ass and watch these little fuckers? Look, now you've got me cussing like a sailor. I never talk like this except when you're in the picture."

"I can't come right now Sonnie. I'm on the way back to New York to see my wife…spend the day and tell her that I was going to stay here with you'se guys … because you'nz needed my help and I would see her back home whenever. That SON-OF-A-BITCH this damn car in front of me just had a blow out and almost hit the guard rail. I wonder if I should stop and help her. Ah…hell with it. Can't you do something with them 'til I get back? There's only a hundred of them. I bought them to take back home. I do some work with kids at a mission there and I thought it would be fun for them to each have a hamster to take care of. It would give them something to look forward to…you know, watching them grow and all that."

"I got news for you… you shit-head. There's over three hundred of these little fuckers running all over this guy's truck. The delivery slip says you ordered three hundred of them and when you do, they give you another fifty free. Now what? All I can say is, you better turn your bony little ass around and come do something with this shit or I'll get about a dozen cats and throw them in the back of this truck. Now you're holding up the driver. He's got better things to do than just hang out for your sorry self to get back here."

"Sonnie, I'm about a hundred miles away. Can you put them in front of your office 'til I get back from New York? I'm only going to be there two days. Com'on… help me out on this one. I'll be back before you know it. Then I'll take them off your hands, I promise. Don't mess this up for me. It means a lot to me…please."

"Man, you drive me nuts. I'll expect you back here Thursday. I'll put them in the empty space 'til then. If you're not back by then, I'll start giving them away with each cookie the girls sell. If they sell ten cookies to someone, they get ten hamsters. That's if I'm in a good mood. If not, I'll put them in a couple sacks and throw them off the nearest bridge. You got it?"

"That's cool Sonnie. You'll have to get some food for them and feed them twice a day. I'll be back by Thursday, I promise. Oh… by the way, pay the driver and I'll give it back to you when I see you…"When I get my hands on …Hello? Don't you hang up on me.. *Someday, I'm going to kill his ass."*

Sonnie asked the driver to put the hamsters in the spare room in his office space next door to the bakery but the driver told him that he was not allowed to unload the truck. It was against company policy. Sonnie offered him fifty bucks to do the unloading but he wasn't interested, so Sonnie got a couple of winos to do it. They all got bit by the hamsters several times and in the end, he offered them two cases of wine. However the wine was too high class for them so Sonnie gave them a hundred bucks. By the time Sonnie got back to the deli to join Vince and the girls, he had cooled off and it had become rather funny. Knowing Petey and the way he did things, it wasn't unusual that something like this would happen.

Vince just shook his head, "That's my boy," he said with a smirk on his face.

Since the bakery was going to be closed for the day, they decided to go for a drive to the shore. Just let everything run itself and see how the troops handled things when they weren't there to tell them what to do. They were caught up in the moment and didn't realize that Bobby was in New York talking to his boss about coming to Atlantic City for a sit-down. Angelo was with Father Mark in Philly trying to talk Denny into coming to Atlantic City also, for the sit-down. There was no one taking care of business. It wasn't until they were about two hours out of town, that Theresa asked Sonnie who was minding the store.

"The bakery was closed for the day… don't you remember?" He replied with arrogance.

"Not *that* store, numb-nuts."

"Oh shit," Vince interrupted, realizing what Theresa was getting at. "We better get our asses back home. Sorry girls."

Turning around, Vince pulled into a station to get gas and while Vince was pumping the gas, Sonnie and the girls went inside get four ice cream bars. When Sonnie reached into his pocket to get his money, he found a folded up piece of paper. *'What the hell is this? I don't remember this.'* He opened it. It was a note written in Italian:

It's been a long time since we hid behind the shop and shared a Perodi (Italian cigar) together. Looks like you have a nice set up here. You look real comfortable, maybe too comfortable. I've always respected you and valued you're opinion. We were a good team once. It's important, very important that we talk.
Please………I'll be in touch.
-M

Libero A. Tremonti

A slight smile came over Sonnie's face as he quickly folded the note and put it back into his pocket. He felt a sense of relief now that he didn't have to worry about where Maria was and what her next move might be. *'She's gotten herself in something she can't handle and needs help,'* Sonnie thought *'What a surprise. Out of nowhere, she shows up. Maybe she's been around all along. I can't believe that. She's probably got mixed up with some drug dealers and has gotten in over her head. Now she thinks she can just waltz in here and ask for my help... Maybe she can.'*

Vince finished pumping the gas and went inside to pay as the girls were getting back into the car. Sonnie and Vince paid a visit to the men's room.

"Vinny, look at this," Sonnie said as he handed him the note.

"When did you get this?" Vince wanted to know after reading the note. "Why are you just showing me this now? I told you she would show her colors. She'll always be a thorn in our side 'til we dispose of her. She'll do everything possible to cause confusion. We better find her and let Bull take care of her. I hope you're not considering... Damn it, I knew she would show her ass sooner or later. You're not going to meet her are you? You are, aren't you? I can tell by that look on you're face. Ahhhh... shit Sonnie. This can't be good. Just think real hard before you agree to anything. You know how clever that bitch can be. If she can fool Don Aldo the way she did... just be careful and don't let her suck you in. I would like to be there to make sure you don't do anything stupid. I know she wouldn't want that."

"Vinny, slow down. You're jumping the gun here. I don't have any plans to work with her or even meet her right now. I might hear what she has to say but know matter what her problem is, it can't be beneficial to us. Maybe it will be in our favor, I really don't know. Besides, we're in this thing together and I wouldn't make any decision or do anything before talking to you. As a matter a fact, I want you to be there every step of the way. We're a team you know. I don't ever do anything without talking with you first. This is no different. I'll tell you where I got this note, you're not going to believe it. While I was talking to Petey on the phone, some guy ran into me and he must have put it in my pocket then. That means she must have been watching. That bitch is closer that we think. She could have taken me out if that was her intentions... I'm glad it wasn't. We better be careful. For all we know, she might have put those druggies up to robbing the bakery."

Vince noticed a puzzled look on Sonnies face.

"What's troubling you now? I know that look, you're thinking hard about something. I don't know if I even should ask you what that's all about. Damn it, this is going to drive both of us nuts 'til someone puts an end to all this bullshit."

"You know what?" Sonnie went on. "The more I think about it, the guy that bumped into me...I wasn't paying that much attention at the time but the more I think about it, it didn't...his after shave... it smelled real sweet for a guy. I'll bet......"

"Oh shit! I see where this is going. You think now, it was Maria dressed up like a man. You're really starting to loose it. We better get the hell out of here before you start thinking the person that changes the toilet paper is her too. Man, I can't believe this. You know what? Whether or not she's trying, she's driving both of us nuts. Soon as she contacts you, you better get with her and do what you have to do, but just do something. I know you won't lose focus and do something stupid. Will you?"

"I might just shoot her dead on the spot. Then we wouldn't have to worry. You know Vinny, you're not going to want to hear this but I sort of miss her... even after all this time. I didn't realize how much she meant to me. After all, we went through a lot together."

"That's real nice Sonnie. I can't see you wacking her, especially after what you just told me. Besides, that don't always solve the problem. We better listen to what she has to say or what she comes up with. You know, she's no dummy. She probably has herself covered, so we better listen to her. I just hope she doesn't take forever. I hope she's not trying to play mind games with us. You know like I do, she hasn't been sitting on her hands all this time. We've got to stay focused, Sonnie. We've got a lot going on now with this sit-down... and where's that fucking Rando? That prick's got me puzzled. I didn't think he was that clever to be able to avoid us for this long. He's just not that smart."

"You know Vinny, drugged out people don't think out anything, they just react. They're in a panic all the time and looking over their shoulder. You know he's got to be shitting himself every time he sees a car like one of ours or he hears a backfire. Don't worry, he'll turn up and when he does... well, you know what will happen. We just have to stay focused. Now, more than ever, we've got to suck it up and keep our heads. We can't let anything get to us, like the shit that fucker Petey puts us through. He's one of a kind. Just think how dull it was when he wasn't around."

"He's different alright," Vince agreed. "But someday his tactics might get him in trouble. I hope he doesn't overstep his boundaries on this one. Look Sonnie," Vince continued, "our main concern right now has to be the sit-down. Everything evolves around it, everything we've done, and everything we're going to do, depends on this meeting being a success. The issues with Petey, Rando and even Maria will work themselves out in time."

Sonnie and Vince return to the car where Connie and Theresa were waiting. The four of them enjoyed the trip home and shared a good laugh about the hamsters.

CHAPTER SEVENTEEN

The time finally arrived for the big sit down with the bosses from Philly and New York. After what had happened there, he was still being a little cautious and the boss of the New York family didn't come. He sent in his place, a worthy representative named Johnny Rocco who was his second in command. Bobby knew him well and assured Sonnie and Vince that what ever went on at the meeting would be brought back to the big boss accurately. He told them that Johnny was a real bad ass and wouldn't hesitate to make things right.

Denny, the representative from Philly was not as much of a concern because Father Mark had talked to him prior to the meeting. Denny was a partier and they all knew that it could become a problem but Father Mark said he would come and try to keep him under control, since he was the only one Denny trusted. Sonnie was nervous and told Vince that he hoped they could convince this Johnny Rocco that they had nothing to do with the attempt on his boss's life while they were in Italy.

Father Mark and Denny were the first to arrive. Sonnie had suites set up at the hotel and casino that he and Vince had purchased. They had convinced the owner that the place would do better if they owned it. With a little bribery, they got it at a very good price. Gina and the girls from the Clip Joint, the hair cutting salon, were ready.

They had their party hats on and Sonnie was pleased. Bobby picked up Johnny Rocco at the airport. On the way from the airport, Bobby decided to show Johnny around a little, since he had never been to Atlantic City. As they were driving through one of the better sections of town, they came up on several police cars parked on the side of the street. Bobby spotted one officer that he knew and had close ties with, so he stopped the car to find out what was going on. He told Bobby that a little ten year old girl had been raped and that they had just caught the guy. He was a convicted sex offender out on parole that lived just three doors down from the girl. Most of the police officers and the crime scene investigators were in the suspects' house, searching for evidence. The officer showed Bobby the suspect sitting in the back of his squad car as he unlocked the car door and went into the house. When the police came out of the house, they found the suspect with his throat slit and no one had seen what had happened. Johnny Rocco had a niece that had been raped and felt in a way, a small sense of justice had been served.

Bobby got Johnny settled in and he was very impressed with the set up. He hoped the meeting would be as impressive. Bobby told Johnny he thought that he would get along with Sonnie and Vince because they were all business. They always looked for better ways to run their organization to make things better for everyone and stayed out of things that didn't involve them. He assured him that what ever plans Sonnie and Vince had, would be fair for everyone. The one thing they wanted was to make sure everyone involved knew that they didn't have anything to do with what went on while they were away. Bobby told Johnny that the meeting would be set for that night and after a nice dinner, the town would be theirs. He asked Johnny if he wanted any company and he declined saying that he wanted to rest for a bit but laughed when he said the night was still young.

Meanwhile, Father Mark was having a hard time keeping Denny under control. All he wanted to do was drink and gamble. He had already lost twenty-thousand at the tables and wasn't very happy. Father Mark called Angelo and alerted him of the problem and he in turn called Sonnie.

"I don't need him having an attitude coming into this meeting," Sonnie warned. He immediately put a call into the dealer at Denny's table. "From here on out, you make this a private table and make sure he wins three out of four hands 'til he gets his money back."

Sonnie sent over a couple of girls that worked the tables at the casino to bring him luck. Everything worked out and Denny was happy again.

The meeting was to start at eight sharp and Sonnie and Vince were in the special room they had set up for the meeting. Bobby showed up with Johnny and then promptly excused himself knowing that no one but the bosses were to attend this meeting. When Johnny walked into the room, Sonnie and Vince could tell that Johnny was high profile. He was wearing a light brown pin striped hand tailored suit with the sleeves cut just short enough, you could see his French cuffs and a pair of diamond cuff links that complimented the diamond stick pin in his tie. His light brown shirt, with a brown and white silk tie, went perfect with the white silk handkerchief in his suit pocket. Looking at Johnny's face, you could tell that he had been in a tussle or two. His right jaw looked as if it had been broken at one time and the same with his nose. One of his ears was messed up but that just added more character. His hair was dark with the exception of some grey on the sides and top. It was obvious he had spent a lot of time in the barber's chair. He had a mouth full of sparkling white veneers and when he opened his mouth, it was the icing on the cake, he was the complete package. He introduced himself to Sonnie and Vince and they both accepted him because they could tell that he was all business.

After twenty minutes, Father Mark came in and announced that Denny was a no-show.

"What's this?" Johnny asked. "We having confession first? This is a different twist. I didn't know someone else would be looking down on us. That's a good thing."

"This is Father Mark," Sonnie added. "He accompanied Denny here from Philly. I assume Denny's going to be late? From the calls I got, he wasn't in too good of shape."

"I don't know what we can do Sonnie. The shape he's in right now, I don't know when he'll be able to show up. No one could slow him down, not even the two babes you sent over to entertain him. He's just out of control."

"So what's the plan now?" Johnny wanted to know. "I hope I didn't come down here for nothing. If I go home with nothing to report, my boss is going to be real pissed. How often does he get like this? How can he be in charge of anything if he does this bullshit instead of taking care of business? Who does that... the business I mean? Who makes the choices for his organization?"

"I've been sort of guiding him along Johnny," Mark went on to say. "Ever since he became the head of the organization, he's gone off the deep end. I'm the only one he listens to and sometimes, I can't control him. I know I've got to do something with him but please be patience... it'll be handled."

Johnny, beginning to show his disappointment, turned to Sonnie. "You mean you knew he was like this? Who depends on a priest to run this kind of business? No offense, but what do we do now? You know he won't comply with anything that's decided here today. Who's second in command there? Who else can make something happen? I think they should have come instead of a priest. Once again no offense."

"That's the other problem he has," Father Mark tried to explain. "He hasn't done anything to organize the business to suit him. He doesn't even know the names of some of his soldiers. He wouldn't know who to put in charge under him because he doesn't trust anyone. If you don't mind, I'll sit in for him. Then when he's straight, I'll tell him what we decided here and he'll have to go along with it. What ever happens, he can't say we didn't do right by him. To tell you the truth Johnny, I know more about what goes on there than Denny does... isn't that sad."

"This seems strange to me having a priest sitting in on a meeting for our organizations," Johnny replied. "What else can we do? Something has to be done with this guy. You know, whoever is his second should be here if he can't control himself. Maybe you're his second Mark and you don't know it. He's got to get in control of his actions or something very ugly could happen to his organization. So tell me Sonnie, why are we here… what's so important? I'm sure everyone in this room knows about the attempt on my boss's life and the killing of the bosses in Philly."

"That's one of the reasons you're here, Johnny. We want to get it straight, we didn't have anything to do with that. We were away and didn't know anything until we got a call in the middle of the night from Bobby. We had problems of our own while we were in Italy."

"Don't worry Sonnie, we know you didn't have anything to do with the attempted take over. We caught one of the guys that tried to take out my boss. He was some rag-head. You know, one of those terrorists want'a-bee. What they did was so unorganized, we knew it couldn't have been another organization trying to take over ours. He said some woman recruited them to do the job. What woman could be that stupid or that desperate to hire a bunch of fuck-heads like that? The three stooges could have done a better job. Since the attempt didn't work, he said they were going to pay her back. He also said she led them to believe she would give them a lot of money for their group so they could buy weapons and explosives but she gave them nothing. Now, they're looking to do whatever it takes to get the money from her."

"Where's this rag head now?" Sonnie wanted to know. "I would like to talk to him."

"We gave him a new pair of shoes, Sonnie. Unfortunately, when he went swimming in the East River, the shoes were too heavy and he sank to the bottom. We tried to tell him not to go swimming with his shoes on but he wouldn't listen. If we had known that he was important to you Sonnie, we would have been glad to cooperate and turn him over to you. Do you think you know this person who organized this thing? If so, I think we have the right to know the name of this person."

"We do Johnny," Vince added. "But it would take too long to explain."

"Vince, we got all night. I think Father Mark would want to know… I know I do. You owe it to us to tell us all you know about this thing and why it's happening now. Does it have something to do with your visit to Italy? You said you had problems while you were over there. Vince, we need to know the reason for all this. My boss has been looking everywhere for the answer. He didn't think to ask you and Sonnie. He likes you guys and how you took in Bobby and treated him like one of your own after J.R. left. Now... if you know anything, we have the right to know. I don't care how long it takes to explain."

Sonnie went on to explain to Johnny Rocco and Father Mark, the reason he thought that Maria was the one organizing the hits. He started out by telling them how he, Vince and Maria had grown up as kids and when he was twelve, he found out that his Grandfather was the boss of a small family in his village. It was soon after that he learned a family in another village had killed his parents when he was three. Sonnie explained what had gone on with Maria's mother and the three of them made this plan and took care of the people that did this to their parents. Johnny, knowing Don Aldo and finding out that that Maria was his niece and what she had done to him, was starting to get the picture.

"Don Aldo knew all along what she was up to in Italy," Vince added, "but didn't know what to do about it. You know he's getting old and doesn't think as good as he used to. When Sonnie and me were in Italy and told him our plan... Oh, something Sonnie didn't mention, the reason we wanted Maria over here, was to stop her from smuggling drugs into the country through J.R.'s organization, which he knew nothing about. That's another story. Don Aldo had sent his grandson and two of his soldiers with Maria to the States to what he thought, was to expand the wine export business. To make a long story short, his grandson took care of the others but one of our own guys turned on us and Maria got away. We lost track of her until this happened. We're thinking that she might have something to do with all this bullshit."

"You think that's the reason no one tried to do anything to you guys? You think she's clever enough to think of something like this? I don't buy it. There's got to be something more to it than that. What was she going to do? Just march in and take over both families? I don't think so. I'm second in command, I want to think I'm a little smarter then that."

"Look Johnny." Sonnie said with a calm voice. "I know what this is starting to look like, but we think she wanted it to look like we had something to do with it. That's why she planned this to take place while we were out of the country. Not making a move on us and at the same time, might lead you to think that we had something to do with it. That's what she wanted you to believe. That's the reason for this meeting. Vince and I want to have everything out in the open. Now, you don't know anything about us and that might give you the right to be suspicious, but..."

"Sonnie"...Vince interrupts.

"Let me finish Vinny. We don't operate like that. First of all, we don't do anything behind someone's back. There's no reason to. If we have a problem to address, we take it right to them. If we wanted something like that to go down, it would have been handled in a different manor and it would have been successful. We don't operate like that anyway. There's no reason for violence. If things can't be worked out peacefully, there's always a way... we have plenty of recourses."

"You're right Sonnie, we know nothing about you and Vince. We knew Nicky in Philly and had sort of... well let me put it this way, we put up with each other. Now that he's gone, we don't know what to expect from them and what I see now, isn't very promising. This Denny has a real problem we need to do something about. If we don't come up with a solution, it could be dangerous for everyone. Don't you agree Father Mark? As far as you and Vince are concerned, I'm starting to get the picture. My boss told me to listen and to keep an open mind. I can see where you're coming from and I like how straight forward and to the point everything is with you'nz."

Father Mark reached up and took off his collar. "I've had it with this," he said. "It's starting to get the best of me. If you don't mind, just call me Mark. You were saying Johnny?"

"What do you think we should do with Denny? Just go on letting this bullshit continue? First thing you know, some hot-headed wise-guy will come marching in and all hell will break loose. Something has to be done. We don't need a war. Don't you agree Sonnie?"

"Mark, you think you could get that organization straight? Will they listen to you? I hate to ask this of you, but Johnny's right... something's got to be done. With what I'm getting ready to propose, we need stability everywhere. Mark, something's got to be done and soon. I know I'm repeating what's already been said here, but you know how it is. I know it's not your forte, but you're the only one he seems to respect. What about your church? If you think this is all happening too fast for you and you can't handle it, then Johnny and us will handle it. I know you guys grew up together but we're in sort of a jam here."

"Listening to you and Johnny talk, puts everything in perspective," Mark replied as he folded his color and put it in his pocket. "I can see how important the organization is. I only wish the church was that organized. I don't want anything to happen to Denny... he's my closest friend. However, I know where you guys are coming from. I'm glad I came to this meeting. I'm tired of beating my head against the wall with the church. They have no loyalty. It's like anything else, if you don't have some clout, your problems don't get resolved. I'm leaning towards resigning my position with the church and working with Denny to get things straightened out in the organization. I will do this immediately when I get back to Philly, if that's alright with you guys. How's that sound?"

"How do you know you won't change you're mind once you get back?" Vince asked. "How sure are you that you want to do this? It's something you can't just make a snap decision about. Once you're in... there's no turning back. Look Mark, we think Philly would be much better off if you do this. On the other hand, Denny will be all pumped up and if you decide not to do this after telling him you would, your buddy just might really go off."

"I know Vince. I've thought a lot about this over the last couple of weeks. I never knew how bad off Denny was 'til I seen him like he is now. I don't want anything to happen that I maybe could have prevented. I've thought about who would be in charge of what in the organization and I think I can pull it off. The guys there are just looking for someone they can trust to take control. Give me a little time and you'll see everything will be fine. I guarantee it... trust me. One more thing, I would like from now on to be called by my birth name, which is Marco. I changed it for the church. They thought it would sound better if I did. Now I can have it back."

They all smiled, raised their glasses and made a toast to their new partner.

Sonnie went on to explain that he thought it was time for everyone to expand. Sonnie called up to the front desk, and had a wide screen television and VCR player delivered to the room." Vince turned on the television while Sonnie put in the tape. On the screen, a map appeared of the area from New York, Philly and Atlantic City with a line drawn from New York to Philly, from Philly to Atlantic City and from Atlantic City to New York resembling a triangle. Sonnie went on to explain to Johnny and Marco that there was no reason why the three families couldn't control this area. He went on to say that there were millions of dollars of revenue out there waiting for someone to take it. There was enough for everybody and why shouldn't it be them? It would be a massive undertaking. The three families would have to have the trust in one another that when something went wrong, they would be able to sit down and get things worked out.

Vince went on to show Johnny and Marco the different territories they would control. They even had it broken down money-wise. The only thing that concerned Sonnie and Vince was manpower. They would have to be strong and wise enough to be able to move into a new place and take over without causing too much commotion. If everything went the way they had it planned, it should in place in six to nine months. That was, if everything went smooth which they all knew, was a big if.

Johnny and Marco both thought it was a great idea. As far as Marco was concerned, it was a go. Marco knew he had a big task ahead of him. He had to go back to Philly and redo the organization from the bottom to the top but was sure he could handle it. Johnny Rocco would go back to New York and try to sell it to his boss. Johnny didn't think it would be much of a problem and couldn't figure out why no one had come up with the idea before then. Vince, Sonnie, Johnny and Marco shook hands to seal the deal for now. They all knew that they had a long way to go before everything would be in place. It all sounded so easy but they knew better.

Meeting over, they all went to the suite that was set up for the special dinner Sonnie had planned for everyone. When they got there, all the troops were there: Gina and the girls from the Clip Joint: Mary, Claudia, Bunky and Gayle. Gayle had just arrived about an hour earlier and Sonnie and Vince were glad to see her. Everyone couldn't get over how great she looked. Bull, Angie, and Bobby were there and making a late appearance as usual was, Petey.

Johnny was intrigued by the combination of characters that had assembled. He wanted to know about Bull and asked Sonnie if they were an equal opportunity employer. Sonnie explained to him about Bulls heritage and told him about his special talents. Johnny was glad to know that he would be working side-by-side with them. Johnny loved the idea of the Clip Joint and how skilled the girls were that worked there. He had his eye on Gayle and Vince told him her story and the conclusion to it. Johnny was pleased how Sonnie and Vince worked together and handled things. They got the job done without fucking around. In his eyes, there wasn't time for that. When it came to Petey, Johnny couldn't believe the shit Sonnie and Vince had put up with but he told them that he could understand it because in his travels, he had known a lot of other people that had a Petey in the crowd.

"Hey Johnny, watch this," Sonnie said pointing to Petey. "Hey Petey, what did you do with those hamsters?"

"What's that all about?" Johnny wanted to know.

"Wait, you'll love it. Watch the way he thinks... the guy's a trip. You'll get a kick out of this."

Petey looked puzzled for a second, "The hamsters," he uttered. "Oh yea, SHIT! I forgot all about them. After you made me move them, I put them in a storage unit about a week ago."

"You mean you haven't gone to see if they're still alive? You know, you're a real asshole. Wait... if you're jerking my chain again, I'll let Johnny here handle you."

"No shit Sonnie. I hired someone to take care of them for me... on the square. I thought I bought a hundred and it turned out to be three hundred. Now, who knows how many there are. It seems like half of them were knocked up when I bought them. By the time I get them home, there probably will be five hundred of them. Customs might not let me back on the island with all those little furry fuckers. You'll help me out won't you? You could do what you told me you would if I didn't come back when I said I would. You know, give them away or something."

"That's not going to happen. I knew I didn't see the last of your rats and if you think I'm going to get involved with the demise of those pets of yours, you're crazy. See Johnny, you don't know the half of it. The guy's a nut case."

"Sonnie," Johnny said as he turned away from Petey. "I'd like to talk to you about something. That woman that you told me about that you think is responsible for the shit that happened. When you find her, I have the perfect solution. We have an interest in this too you know. The solution's name is Dario. He's a hit man from Brazil, the best I've ever seen. He never misses. The good thing about him is he doesn't linger. He'll fly in, get the information, do his thing and get out before the body is ever found. As you know, anything that's good isn't cheap."

"That's very interesting. I think I might like to try him out. I have some business for him that he might consider. It would be a quick thing, there's this politician that's fucking with the girls that we have to do something about. I always wanted to have another source. I think he would be just the ticket. You have to be careful who you talk to these days, with these terrorists doing the shit they're doing. You can't make a move without someone sticking their nose up your ass. How often will he come here? Do you think he will have any reservations about doing work for someone he doesn't know?"

"Just let me know when you need him and he'll be here on the first flight. This guy works on references only. Like I said, he's real good at what he does and if I recommend you to him, it won't be a problem. He's sort of old school. You know, like back in Italy. Those guys were quick and silent... he's the same. That's what I like about him. As a matter of fact, he was referred to me by some of the boys in Sicily."

The dinner was fabulous as usual. Afterwards, the troops took Johnny and Marco out on the town hitting all the casinos. There was a lot of gambling, a lot of drinking and a lot of laughter. Johnny and Gayle were getting closer as the night went on. She was taken back with him like when a groupie sees a rock star. Marco was glad he took off his collar but he couldn't forget about Denny and was wondering how he would react to what he had done. He knew he would have to do a lot to get him straight but for now, he wasn't concerned about it. Everyone ended up at Sonnie and Vince's casino. They just sat back and watched the girls operate and have a good time. They were all glad that the meeting was a success. Were they getting in over their heads? Only time would tell.

CHAPTER EIGHTEEN

It was the middle of May and everyone was glad to see that spring had finally arrived. The weather went from heavy coats and sweaters to short sleeves and shorts. The busses carrying gamblers started coming daily and business was booming. Sonnie was pleased with the casino they had purchased and planned to remodel it after the Christmas holidays. He and Vince wanted to give the big guns in town, a run for their money.

Still, there was no sign of Rando. Up until now, he'd been very careful and was staying out of sight. Maria had not been heard from either. As a matter of fact, Sonnie was wondering if that guy Johnny Rocco had told him about had found her and took care of business without his knowing it. So everyone was going about their business as if she didn't even exist. However, Sonnie found himself thinking about her quiet often and had a gut feeling that she could appear at any time. Vince on the other hand, couldn't be bothered with her. After all the shit she had put everyone through, he'd like to get her out of the picture all together.

As Vince and Sonnie were going over the books at the casino, Gina from the Clip Joint called and told Sonnie that she saw a potential problem brewing. He put her on speaker so Vince could hear the conversation. She went on to say that the Mayor's two sons had a gambling problem and it was known in all the casinos that they couldn't control their spending, especially on the baccarat tables. Sonnie wanted to know how that affected them.

"They found out we have a betting room in the back and they have been laying down some heavy bets. They don't know shit about betting on games, much less the horses. Now they want to establish a line of credit."

"Gina, give them what they want. I want them to have all the perks. Tell Mitsie to give them anything they ask for. Don't hold back, let them run up a good debt."

"That doesn't make any sense Sonnie. They're not paying any of their debts. They owe three or four hundred thousand all over town. Why would you want to mess with them? I know I'm not supposed to be asking questions like that, but it doesn't make sense to me. On the other hand, you always seem to know what the hell you're doing so, I'm sorry to question you. Everything's going so well and our profits are way up… everyone's just doing really well…"

"Gina, calm down. You're starting to sound like Petey. I know what I'm doing. I appreciate what you and the rest of the girls are doing. You have a good crew there and everyone seems to work well together. What I'm doing is something that needs doing. I'll explain later."

After hanging up with Sonnie, Gina told Mitsie and the other girls to give the brothers all the credit they needed. Two days later, they show up. Their names were Bruce and Maurice and they were identical twins, both of them just over six feet tall. Bruce had long dark hair pulled back in a pony tail unlike Maurice's hair which was clipper-cut on the sides, longer on the top, combed forward and spiked up in the front. They both had an air of arrogance about them and one could tell by looking at them, that they always got what they wanted. New cars, expensive shoes hundred dollar shirts, you get the picture. They looked like the all American rich spoiled brats with million dollar smiles and the charisma to go with it. They both drove Jaguar convertibles, one red the other black. Once they realized Pitsie and

Mitsie were twins, they couldn't stop making over them. The girls went to Gina and asked what they should do about Bruce and Maurice because the policy at the Clip Joint has always been not to mix business with pleasure. The girls were to make them comfortable and lead them to believe otherwise, but when it came to actually going out with them… that was not allowed. She talked with Sonnie and Vince and told them about the brothers having the hots for the twins. Vince wanted to know if the twins knew the ins and outs of the business and what was expected of them or if they were ready to do something for the organization. Gina assured them that they could be trusted and what ever they wanted them to do, would be done. Sonnies' big question was how they felt about drugs. He figured that with all the shit these ass-holes were into that they were probably into the drug scene as well. Gina guaranteed Sonnie that the girls knew the policy and that she was certain they had never used drugs nor would they, for the likes of those punks.

"You think you and Vince should meet with these girls before we trust them with doing this thing for us?"

"I think you're right Gina. We have to know for ourselves what they're like. They could say one thing to you and then when the party gets going get turned on by all the glamour and the hype surrounding these boys. These little punks are like rock stars. Everywhere they go, there's always something or somebody that's in their face. These ass-holes take advantage of any situation and turn it into something to benefit them. It seems from time to time, someone dies around them and their no good drugged-up father gets them out of the trouble there in. That fucking pisses me off real bad. We need to know that these girls can handle themselves. You know Gina, the mayor is the one that's blocking us expanding the hotel and casino. So it's important we have all the advantage we can get… when we have to go up against him."

"Now I can see why you were telling me to give them free reign. I can tell you that when I checked into their background, I found out the girls worked for some of the high rollers in Vegas for a while. You know… a lot of young punk rockers and movie stars. I think they will know how to handle themselves. Mitsie keeps a journal for us on customers that place bets along with their financial backgrounds. That way, they know that she knows and doesn't allow anyone to over extend their boundaries. Pitsie on the other hand, goes at it a different way. She has a way of getting everyone's life story and she spends a lot of time talking to the clients to find all this out. I'll tell you'nz, she has a way of finding out the whole story. She dresses like a whore but doesn't act like one. Just what the men like. I pay them well and believe me, they earn it."

"We haven't met these two yet. Why didn't you bring them to the meeting we had? Weren't you comfortable with them yet? Do they look as good as you'nz? Are they older? Com'on... tell me something."

"All I can say is that they definitely belong at the Clip Joint. You'll be impressed when you meet them Sonnie. As to why I didn't bring them to the meeting, I wanted to give them a little more time to get acclimated to the place and their new jobs. I didn't want them to feel uncomfortable, you know how intimating you guys can be. When you see them, you'll understand. They're sharp and they do their job well. Just trust me, they're real lookers. They work out at the club three times a week and take self defense classes two times a week. Everyone that comes in the place wants to get to know them and do the wild thing with them. They look sort of like me, Claudia and Bunky all rolled into one. I'll tell you Sonnie, they're hot... real hot and those little bastards will have met their match if they get hooked up with those two. You know how a black widow spider works... well times that by two."

"We don't want them to beat up the little punks, although they might deserve it." Sonnie turned to Vince who was listening over the speaker phone. "What'da you think Vinny? Should we meet them first or let Gina decide for us?"

"I think Gina's a good judge of character. Look who she's got for business partners. How loyal does one person have to be before you trust them? Com'on Sonnie, I think Gina knows what she sees and she sees these girls as doing just what the doctor ordered. Just tell them to keep us informed every step of the way. We have to do something to stop their father from giving us a bunch of bullshit about the casino we bought. That prick keeps sticking his nose where he shouldn't. He's trying to make it hard for us to get the property next door so we can expand. Next year we want to make the casino twice as large and we think the other big hotel owners are giving him money to stop us from doing it. We keep waiting for him to come to us and ask for a bigger pay off but it hasn't happened yet. That's why we told you to give them all the money they want to gamble. If they run the bill up, then their father will be on the hook. The other hotels write off their debt and take it as a loss, but we're not going to do that. That's why we have to be careful and not let them know what were doing. That's why the two girls have to be very willing to give their all. Discuss it with them first and make sure they understand what's at stake here. We don't need any screw-ups."

"I knew you guys were up to something," Gina replied. "Now it's all starting to make sense. That fucker came into the shop one day and started looking around. When Pitsie asked if she could help him, he wanted to see whoever was in charge, so I talked with him. He wanted to see the gambling licenses. I showed him all the licenses and everything was in order. He looked a little aggravated but he was still polite."

"Who came in," Vince wanted to know. "The Mayor... How long ago was this? Why didn't you say something to us about it?"

"Just recently. The same time the big meeting took place. That's why I didn't tell you. I first thought it was a little strange to see the Mayor and a couple of his staff checking out our records but nothing surprises me anymore. I'm sorry I didn't mention it but I got caught up in everything else at the time. It turned out okay though. You know...one of those pricks tried to put his hand on my ass while I was showing them around. I'm sure glad I listened to you and Sonnie and kept everything current. I don't know how many times you guys preached to me about keeping everything legal."

"I'm glad you listened too," Sonnie added. "That's why we put everything in your hands. We knew you were the only one that could handle it. We never worry about anything that goes on at the Clip Joint because you have good judgment. You sort of think like we do, that's one of the first things Vince noticed about you. We always knew you were the one we would put in charge. As a matter of fact, we want to make you a partner if you would like. You have all the responsibility to contend with. We just think you deserve a little more for what you do."

Sonnie's cell phone rang and he promised Gina that they would continue where they left off real soon. It was the garage where Sonnies $250,000 Aston Martin was being worked on. The owner told Sonnie it disappeared during the night but he though he had some idea who might have taken it.

Sonnie started yelling, telling the man that he better get off his ass and find the piece of shit bastard that took his car. Sonnie wanted to know why he didn't have the car in the garage and what it was doing outside. The owner told him that whoever took the car broke into the garage and that he had some guys on it but not to hold him responsible. Sonnie wanted to know if the car could run without the part that they were waiting for and he told Sonnie that they had just installed the part on the car yesterday. He was getting ready to call him as soon as they finished detailing the car. Sonnie didn't trust anyone, he put a call into Bull and another to Petey. They both said they would look into it and call him whenever they heard something.

Several hours later, Bull got a call from this repo man named David Lee. He told Bull he knew that he dealt in exotic cars and was wondering if he would be interested in a slightly damaged Aston Martin. He said he took it to a chop shop but they had referred him to Bull. For some reason, they wanted no part of it. Bull asked David Lee what was wrong with the car and he told him that it had slipped off the truck as he was taking it from where he got it. Bull asked him how much he was selling it for.

"I need to get a hundred thou' out of it. It'll take about fifty thou' to fix the damage and the rest would be yours."

"I'll take it off your hands for Sixty-five. That's a good deal and you know it. If you're interested, be here at ten o-clock tonight."

"Will you have the money then?"

"I have the money now but I have to leave and won't be back 'til later tonight. The money's good… you don't have to worry about that."

"Deal, I'll be there ten o-clock sharp, please don't be late, I've got several stops to make tonight. How will I know it's you?"

"Don't you be late. If you're two minutes late, I'll leave and you'll get shit. You don't want to be stuck with that car so you better have your ass here on time. I'm going to make arrangements for the car to be taken tonight so you better not change your mind and put me in a bind. I don't like dealing with you people anyway. When you come in the lot, come behind the office building… it's the only building there. You'll see this big Italian nigger standing there. That'll be me."

"I'll be on time." *'What's an Italian nigger look like? I guess I'll find out.'*

Bull called Sonnie and told him about the call from the repo man and wanted to know if he wanted him to handle it or would he be there at ten. Sonnie told Bull that he and Vince would be there and they wouldn't miss it for the world. Vince said he couldn't wait to see that fuckers face when he finds out whose car he stole. Sonnie and Vince got to Bull's place about nine-thirty. Bull broke out a thirty year old bottle of scotch so they could toast the last day on earth for the poor stupid bastard that stole Sonnie's car.

About ten of ten David Lee pulled up.

"This fucker must really need his money… he's ten minutes early. Let me go talk to this ignorant fuck."

"No Bull, let him wait 'til ten. Let him sweat a little. Look at that red neck fucker, he made me nuts all day. Look at him. He has snake-skin cowboy boots on and a baseball cap. Look at this shit. Ahh…com'on, he's got a shirt and tie on. Bull, he thinks the meeting's formal." They all laughed quietly.

Bull looked at Vincent, "I'm getting his car back for him and now he's going to bust my balls."

At ten, Bull opened the door and walked out into the lot. You could see the look of disbelief on the repo's face.

"You didn't lie."

"What're you talking about boy?"

"You said you were big, you weren't lying."

"You know boy, this car looks familiar to me. Looks like one I sold to a friend of mine. Get it off the truck. Let me go inside and get a flash light, I want to look at something."

"Wait, if it's not to late... I'd like to change my mind."

"What'da you mean change you're mind? You can't back out now. A deal is a deal. I told you I already had someone to take this car off my hands tonight."

"I'm not backing out, I'd like to lower the price. How about giving me fifty-thou and I'll be out of here. I got to get going... I got somewhere to be and it can't wait. I'll just take it off the truck, then leave. No questions."

"What's you're hurry boy? Just relax... why you getting nervous? I'll be right back. Just get that thing on the ground."

As David Lee was taking the car off the tow truck, he saw Bull coming back with Sonnie and Vince. *'Who's this? Maybe these are the guys that are going to buy the car from this guy. I'm starting to think this wasn't such a good idea. These guys look a little scary to me. I wonder if I should forget about the money and run for it or try to bullshit my way out of this. I think I really fucked up. Something doesn't feel right.'*

"Hey boy, I'd like you to meet someone," Bull shouted. "This is Sonnie and his cousin Vince. Sonnie is the friend I sold the car to. He wants to know what the fuck you were thinking when you took his car. He can't believe you would be so stupid to steal some ones car without finding out whose car you're stealing... especially this car. It's the only one like in the state. This particular car costs two hundred and fifty thousand dollars. Did you know what you were doing or were you high on something? Maybe you were just trying to be cute...playing a game or something. Is that it?"

David Lee's legs wanted to run away but they couldn't move. His stomach was a massive ball of fire inside of him.

"No sir. I'm sorry, please just let me go and I won't say anything. You don't have to give me a dime... I'll just go away. You can have my truck to pay for the damage I did to your car. Here... take the keys." Repo man held out the keys to Bull but Bull just ignored him and started walking around the car. "I know I really messed up but if you give me a chance, I'll make it up to you… I promise. I'll work for you for nothing 'til everything's square. Then, I promise I won't do anything like this again."

"Listen to this shit Bull?" Sonnie uttered. "You think this prick that stole something of mine deserves another chance? You think he can be trusted? He does have sort of an honest look. Maybe we can use him for something in our organization. Do you know our organization? Where you from boy?"

"I'm from the country and sir, it doesn't matter what kind of organization you're in, I'll still work off my debt. Honest mister, I realize I made an awful mistake. Please let me make it up. I'm willing to do anything you tell me to do. Please tell me you'll give me a chance."

"What'da you think? A country boy working for us? Bull, you think this kid has possibilities?"

"I don't know Sonnie. He's too red-neck for me. If you think he's worth a try well…"

Vince pulled out his gun, "Why you teasing this country fuck? This piece of shit don't get my vote…" and with that, he promptly put two shots in the side of repo man's head.

"Thanks for my new tow truck Vince," Bull smiled. "I always wanted a flat bed. Don't worry guys… I'll take care of everything."

Libero A. Tremonti

CHAPTER NIGHTEEN

     As Sonnie and Vince were driving back to the office, Sonnie called Gina and apologizes for having to hang up on her earlier. She was so excited about the offer that Sonnie and Vince had made her to be partners in the Clip Joint, she could hardly talk. Sonnie told her to give the go ahead to the twins and to make sure they keep her informed as to what was happening. Gina went on to tell him that she was just leaving to meet the twins at his new casino and wanted to know if he and Vince would like to join them. It would be a relaxed environment and she thought it would be good for Pitsie and Mitsie to finally meet them. Sonnie and Vince both agree.

     When they arrive at the casino, the girls were sitting in Sonnie and Vince's private booth. The floor boss knew Gina so he gave her the go-ahead. Gina was right. The twins were everything she said they were. They were identical so what you see in one, times it by two. They were both about five foot six and had medium length, red hair angled slightly to their faces. They had unknowingly seductive smiles and the only difference they could see was Mitzie had blue eyes, and Pitzie had green eyes. Gina had said they worked out and you could see that was true. The outfits they wore exposed a rather shapely but not too muscular body. They were sitting down so you couldn't tell how shapely they were but when they stood up, the whole place watched them walk by. Sonnie and Vince were pleased with what they saw and heard. They were twins but didn't act like it. You know, when one starts to say something and the other finishes the sentence. After a couple of drinks and some good conversation, Sonnie and Vince said their good-bys and got up to leave. The twins jumped up to give them a hug but Gina told them that was a no no and they apologized.

As Sonnie and Vince were leaving, the floor boss stopped them and told them he had a situation in the office that need their attention. When they got to the office, they saw the manager at his desk and a little old woman sitting on the sofa crying. They wanted to know what the problem was and the manager explained that her grandson had come in earlier and gambled away everything she had. All the money in the house including her savings account and then ran up a rather large marker.

"How much?" Sonnie wanted to know.

"About twenty-three-thousand," the manager replied.

"Why did they give him credit? You guys know better then that. I want to have a talk with the person that extended him credit without knowing who the hell he was."

"That was me, Sonnie. The pit boss told me he had someone coming with the money in thirty minutes. When his time was up, he bolted. He looked honest to me. He wasn't nervous or anything like that. I'm usually a good judge of character, I don't know what happened this time. I'll take the blame for that miscue."

"We'll have a little talk when all this is over. I've got to refresh your memory about some things. It seems like things are getting a little too friendly around here. So what does she want?"

"She wants to give us the title to her house to cover the debt her grandson's in."

Sonnie glanced over to Vince. "Can you believe this shit? It's the same old story. They keep giving and giving to these kids and they just keep taking. What'da you think, Vinny? We can't take this old ladies house. Help me out here."

"Where's the kid now?" Vince asked. Is he here? "We ought to be talking to him not her, Vinny. Something's not right here."

"She told me," the manager replied, "He's scared to come here because he saw in the movies what happens to people that owe money to gambling places. What should I do?"

Vince and Sonnie wanted to talk to the woman alone so they asked the manager to step out side the office and Vince closed the door. Looking at the woman, they could tell that she didn't have much. Her clothes were clean but ragged and her shoes were old and worn. It looked like she hadn't washed in days and she tried to disguise it with the heavy smell of perfume. Still, there was something about her that intrigued Vince.

"What's your name? Tell us your situation. Where's your grandson and why isn't he here with you? Vince wanted to know."

"My name is Mary. My grandson…he's all the family I have. He left town right after he told me what he did and I came here to pay with the only thing I have. I don't want him to have any trouble. He's all mixed up and I feel I have to help him."

She handed the deed to Sonnie. He took it and was looking it over while Vince continued to ask questions.

"Why should you be responsible for his problems? If he's old enough to make them, he should take care of them. How old are you Mary? Where do you work?"

"I lost my job because I didn't have transportation. You don't want to hear about my hardships. Just take the deed and I'll be on my way. I'll have to find shelter somewhere." Mary stood up. Everything she had ever worked for was gone.

"Wait," Vince pleaded. "Sit down please. Tell me what you did before you lost your job."

"It's rather complicated but since you asked, I'll tell you. I was a proud school teacher for twenty-eight years raised two sons on my own. They both lost their lives in the military. After that, their wives remarried and moved away. I had the one grandson… he chose to stay with me. I didn't object at the time. Being a little boy, I thought I could raise him properly. As he got older, he got out of control and started hanging out with the wrong people. He was selling drugs out of my house and got caught. The authorities let me keep the house but I lost my pension from teaching and they took away my social security because of it. My grandson went to jail and he got out about nine months ago. It didn't do him any good being in there... he just got worse. After he came back to live with me, he went back with those same people and doing the same things. I was cleaning houses but like I said, I lost my transportation. Actually, my grandson sold the little car I had. After that, I sort of gave up. They turned off my water," Mary continued. "I apologize for my appearance. It won't be long before they turn off the electricity. My house isn't much... a little small three bedroom house. When I could afford to take care of it, it was the nicest in the neighborhood. I kept the yard cut all the time and had flowers blooming almost year around. I loved my little house. It's paid for and I was real comfortable there. Then all this happened. It's a pity what people have to go through... you try to do the right thing. For twenty-eight years I helped children. You would think that would account for something.... I'll be going now."

"We don't want to go into the real estate business, Mary. There are other ways of getting the money. Why don't you take out a loan and pay the debt?"

"How would I ever get credit at a bank without a job and the things my grandson did in my house? I have that hanging over my head. That will never go away. Although I didn't actually do anything, I still have a record because I owned the house. I'm thankful they let me keep it but now it doesn't matter much... It's in shambles. The poor boy... when he was on drugs, he would get real violent. He would break up the furniture and put holes in the walls. I would just go in the basement 'til he left the house. I never thought he would hurt me but I was still scared. I would put my hands over my ears so I couldn't hear what he was doing upstairs."

"Mary, he doesn't know it yet but your grandson did you a huge favor. We always need people to work here at the hotel. How would you like a job?" Vince asked. "Listen to the deal first before you answer. We'll pay you twenty dollars an hour and you can live here until you get back on your feet and earn enough money to get squared up on all your bills. Then, you can move back to your house whenever you're ready... Take as long as you like. Me and Sonnie are partners in a large used car lot. I'm sure we can find you reliable transportation. Cheap…real cheap. We furnish uniforms here, so you won't have to worry about that. You can start as soon as you're ready. You can take a day or two to collect yourself. We have some friends down town and we'll see what we can do about clearing your record. Does that sound reasonable to you Mary? Oh hell, we'll wipe off the debt too. You've paid long enough for your grandson's mistakes."

Mary fought back the tears. "Why are you doing this? You don't even know who I am? I don't know what to say. I can't believe you would do this for someone you don't even know. I heard of people having one guardian angel, but it seems I have two. Of course I'll take you up on your offer, but please… tell me why. I knew the Lord wouldn't let me down."

"Everyone deserves a second chance," Vince replied. "After what you've been through, well… me and Sonnie want to help. I think we'll be getting the best of this deal. With your experiences in life, we know you'll do us right. Hopefully in time and when you recover from your problems, you might be interested in taking charge of some other areas in the hotel part. That's all in time. I'm not going to rush you."

Vince excused himself while he went to talk to the manager. He explained all the arrangements for Mary and asked him to have a room ready for her.

"Better yet," he continued. "Make it a suite, with a nice view of the strip." He figured she had gone long enough… doing without. If she was going to start fresh, why not do it up right. He instructed the manager to get someone to take her to her house so she could get her belongings but the manager said it was too late and he didn't have anyone he could send. Hearing that, Vince's eyes were like daggers hitting their mark.

"Oh, I just thought of someone… no problem," the manager said as Vince opened the door to the office.

"Mary, the manager is going to take you to your suite now."

"I'd give you guys a big hug," she replied. "But if it's okay, I'll save it for later."

Mary started down the hall to the elevator and turned back around. Oh Vince," she smiled. "It's Sonnie and I."

"Vinny, I knew we made the right decision." Sonnie added. "I like her already. This gal's going to work out just fine. She reminds me of all the women of that generation. Loving, caring and always correcting."

Sonnie and Vince left the casino and walked in the cool night air to Sonnie's car.

"What a day, Vinny. How much bullshit can happen in one day? I can't believe all this happened to us. What happened to the peaceful days when we were just nobodies? We use to laugh a lot more, go out, party and not let a thing bother us. Now, every little thing is a big thing. Where does it stop or does it ever?"

"I know Sonnie, you'd think we had that something everybody wanted…everybody has an angle. All we want to do is mind our own business and stick to ourselves. But noooo…People come sticking their noses where it doesn't belong. I'm getting like you, I'm getting tired of it. I've overlooked too many things. I'm going to take on a new attitude that's going to be: the hell with it. It's a new day and a new beginning."

As they crossed the street walking towards the parking deck where Sonnie's car was parked, they noticed a convertible sports car parked next to Sonnie's car and someone putting up the top. The car sped past them without the lights on and they had to jump out of the way.

"Hey! You crazy asshole," Vince shouted at the car as it disappeared out of sight.

When they got to Sonnie's car, they found a folded piece of paper stuck under the windshield wiper:

400-225-8739   M

"I guess she's ready to talk," Sonnie said as he put the paper in his wallet. "I've been waiting for her to come around. Now we'll do things my way."

CHAPTER TWENTY

After Sonnie dropped off Vince, he rode around thinking of a million things. His favorite jazz station was hitting on all his favorite tunes. It was a clear night and with his sunroof opened, he could see all the stars. He remembered Gramps trying to show him the big and little dipper. He could never find them without him. He needed the heat on but the air was so fresh, it felt good on his face. He was wondering how this call to Maria was going to change his life. Sonnie thought of all the times they would hide behind Gramps barbershop after it was closed and make out and all the times they ran through the village without a care in the world. *'I was a big'a shot then'* he thought as he laughed to himself. It was all different now. He had no clue as to how this would all turn out. All along he thought he knew what he had to do but now that it was time to get down to business, he wondered how it had to come to that. *'Why does it have to turn out bad? Why can't we talk this thing out? There has to be another way. There has to be a good reason she's contacting me. She says it's really important we meet. She must be in over her head with something. Maybe she really needs my help... or is she setting me up? I would like to think she really needs me. Look at me... I'm making myself crazy... Vinny's right. I'll just call her and take it from there. It's one-thirty in the morning. I wonder if she wants me to call her now, or when? Damn... I hate this shit.'*

Sonnie walked in the front door of his house, turned off the alarm and then for some reason, he turned all the lights in the house on. *'What the hell am I doing? I've never done this before. I must be going nuts or something.'* He flicked on the flood lights overlooking his backyard and scanned the perimeter before checking out the whole house. The radio which he leaves on all the time was playing soft and smooth jazz and Sonnie found it comforting. *'Everything seems normal... so what's the problem?'* He wondered.

Back in the kitchen he mixed himself a White Russian and noticed a message on his answer machine. It was Gina telling him that not five minutes after he and Vince had left the casino, the Mayor's sons came in. The girls hooked up with them and they were in for a long evening. Sonnie sat in his favorite Italian leather recliner. All this stuff going on with Maria, brought back memories of all the things that happened, and especially how he got to where he was today. He thought of how he took the money from Don Aldo's organization, which was being run by Maria at the time. It was nothing but drug money anyway. Sonnie remembered how he traveled through the Swiss Alps in the cold, with two heavy suite cases of cash and not having anyone to help him. If anyone had known what was in those suite cases, they would have surely killed him without hesitation.

Sonnie looked around his lavish but comfortable home and thought how lucky he was. It was a four bedroom, five bath split-level with imported Italian marble in all the bathrooms. Four of the five bathrooms included whirlpool tubs and separate showers. He remembered when he was growing up, taking a bath wasn't fun because he had to heat the water and then put it in a large tub. By the time he got done playing, the water would be cold and his grandfather would yell at him for being so slow. The bedrooms were large with plenty of closet space and decorated in modern Italian. The kitchen was ultra modern with all the amenities and a large island in the center. The dining room was next to the kitchen but was separated by a unique glass block wall. In the dining room was a table big enough to seat twelve comfortably. There was no china hutch or server. Instead,

Sonnie had designed a bar that circled from the dining room into the sunken great-room. The furniture was designed to fit the space which wasn't small. In the back yard there was a pool and an extra large hot tub that could seat eight people at once. Neither one got that much use anymore since he assumed his new position.

Sonnie, sitting back and with his eyes closed, relaxed and was comfortable thinking how lucky he was having Vinny there with him. Having all this and coming this far, not knowing whether or not someone would find him. After all, he took something that didn't belong to him and now, he was in business with the people he took it from.

There was a banging at the door. *'That damn Pete... I know it's him. I spent a fortune on a fancy door bell and that shit-head can't remember to use it.'* Sonnie turned on the front porch light and unlocked the door.

"Damn you Petey, when you going to get your head out of your ass and remember to push the door bell? You know how I hate you banging on the door."

As Sonnie opened the door and adjusted his eyes to the figure standing there, he was shocked and at a loss for words. It wasn't Petey after all.

"Why didn't you call me?" Maria asked.

Before Sonnie could answer, she pulled a gun out and pointed it at him. Sonnie jumped back. He ended up on the floor with his drink spilled all over him and his chair. He had dozed off and was dreaming. He was disorientated for a moment and his face glistened from breaking out in a heavy sweat. It took a couple minutes to collect his thoughts and when he did, a sense of relief came over him. *'Ain't this something? I'm really starting to lose it now. I need to keep my head straight. It's starting to get out of hand. Damn... I've got to do something... and fast. That could have really happened. I sitting back and letting her control me. That's got to change, starting right now.'*

Sonnie stood in the shower after cleaning up the mess he had made. His head was spinning in a hundred different directions after what had just happened. He thought about what he was taught from an early age. *'Keep everything in front of you, don't let feeling and memories get in the way. Make a plan, think about what's important and that you come out on top, no matter what it takes to get there.'* By this time, sleep was out of the question and Sonnie decided to ride around and look for somewhere to get an early breakfast.

While he was stopped at a red light, a car pulled next to him.

"Hey baby, what's happening?"

Sonnie knew that voice. It was Bull.

"I'm going to get some breakfast. I would ask you to join me but I see you're busy," Sonnie answered looking at the young lady sitting next to Bull.

"I was just going to drop her off at her car. Where you going to be? I'll join you. Give me about fifteen minutes… if you can wait."

"I'd like that. I'll be at that diner on Fourteenth-Street. I'll get a booth."

As Sonnie looked around, he could see that all the usual characters were there, people that had too much to drink. There were couples in the booths looking like they cared about each other. They did…'til each got what they wanted. There was a woman sitting by herself at the counter and looking all decked out for some special occasion. Sonnie wondered what her story was. At the far end of the counter was this guy that obviously had too much to drink. With his left hand, he stretched out his neck tie on the counter and with his coffee in the other hand, and using his tie he would guide the coffee to his mouth. Sonnie just smiled, *'Now I remember why I always liked to come here… there's better entertainment than in any of the casinos.'* Bull showed up about thirty minutes late and Sonnie had already ordered because he thought Bull wasn't going to make it.

"What took you so long… or should I ask? I went ahead and ordered, but I can wait… It's no big deal. I just need to get something on my stomach. I've had a fucked up night."

"Anything I can help you with?" Bull wanted to know.

"I just wish all this bullshit would disappear. Why does everything have to be so complicated? Everything was so easy when I just had the shop. All this shit started after I got involved with J.D.. Sometimes I wonder if I did the right thing going in with him and getting you, Vinny and everyone else involved."

"If I remember correctly Sonnie, you didn't have a choice. They came to you and put you in a position that you couldn't get out of. You had to protect yourself. Most people wouldn't come out on top like you did. I admire you for that. When I first met you, I wondered if you were smart enough to figure all this out... but you surprised me. Well... not really. I was sitting back watching to see how you were going to handle it. You made all the right moves when you had to. The thing that impressed me was... there was no fucking around. When it was time to act... boy did you ever. Then there's Vinny. That boy's scary. The two of you together... well, that's another story. I'm just glad to be alongside you guys."

Sonnie told Bull about what had gone on earlier with him getting Maria's phone number and the silly dream he had. He told Bull that he was confused about what to do about her. Part of him wanted to send her to sleep with the fishes but the other part wanted to hold her because he knew she was confused and scared. Bull told Sonnie that he needed to call her and make arrangements to see her to truly find out what she was up to. Until then, nothing was going to get settled. He told Sonnie not to let his feelings get in the way and not to treat her like she was weak and vulnerable right now. That was probably what she wanted Sonnie to think.

"From what you've told me in the past about her Sonnie, you better keep on your toes. You can't let your guard down for a second with someone like that. If she's the one you think was responsible for the hits on the other families, then she's like a two headed snake. If that's the case, you have to cut off both heads. I'm not meaning to tell you what to do, but sometimes it helps to hear someone else's input. It's important you stay focused. "

Sonnie had the waitress top off his coffee as he pondered Bull's words.

"Hey guys... ain't this something?" They heard from across the diner. "What'da you doing here? This is my favorite spot to eat."

"Don't it just figure?" Sonnie told Bull when he realized who it was. "I could have bet the farm his little bony ass would show up."

Petey pulled up a chair and sat at the end of the booth, knowing quite well that neither Sonnie nor Bull wanted him to sit next to them. He started to reach over and take a French fry out of Bulls plate, but then changed his mind. Sonnie called the waitress to the table and told her to get Petey whatever he wanted.

"Hey Sonnie," Petey went on to say, "I've done all the looking I can do to find Rando. All my sources tell me he's left town. One of my druggie friends, told me he went up North somewhere. The stripper he was involved with overdosed. That's probably the reason he took off. The law might even be after him. That's what I'm hearing anyway. Sorry, I know you don't want to hear that."

"That's par for the course. I never expected this to come easy. Some day he'll show himself. I'm not going to worry about it for now. Let's just eat and see what tomorrow brings."

From behind him, Sonnie heard familiar laughter and he turned around to see that it was Gina, Claudia and Bunky coming in the side door. They were taking a break from doing the town.

"Hail, hail… the gangs all here," Sonnie roared as Bull shoved some tables together, connecting them to their booth. "All we need now is for Bobby and Angelo to show up. This couldn't have happened at a better time."

"One thing Sonnie," Gina said, "and then I won't talk business. The girls are handling the situation with the Mayor's boys great. They have them eating right out of their hands. They weren't together thirty minutes tonight before they were following them around like lost puppies."

"That's what I like to hear," Sonnie agreed. "I hope they can keep it up and get them to bet a lot of money at the shop. I need them to get in real deep. Now… let's enjoy our food."

The next thing they knew, the sun was coming up and they were all wondering how long they could keep going before they crashed.

CHAPTER TWENTY-ONE

A week and a half went by and Sonnie had not called Maria yet. He had decided to let her squirm for a while. Vince wasn't happy with the way that Sonnie was handling the situation and he wanted it over with. The Mayor's boys were into the Clip Joint big time and had run up a betting tab of about two-hundred-seventy-thousand. Pitzie and Mitzie were playing them real good. Everything they told them to do, they did. You know the power of a woman when a man wants her. Mitzie would give them a not-so-good tip as to what to bet on and they would jump on it. All the while, hoping the two boys wouldn't catch on. Sonnie was beginning to think it was time to act. The sooner they took down the Mayor the sooner they could get moving on their plans for the casino. They had everything in place and all they had to do was to get the Mayor off their backs. They knew deep down, there was only one way to do that. Sonnie and Vince also knew that the Mayor would do anything for his boys. Now, all they had to do was show him that they weren't going to let him control them anymore. The Mayor knew what they wanted but because of who they were, he wasn't willing to give it to them. He wanted Sonnie and Vince to pay big money up front and a cut of the action each week. That didn't even guarantee them a license to operate a casino, just the hotel part of it. Now they had what they needed to close the deal.

Cousins II

Sonnie put a call into Vince and got no answer. *'That's not like Vince. He usually sees it's me and takes the call. He knows I'm not calling to bullshit. He knows when I call, it's about something important. I can't understand. What's going on here?'* Being in the office with the bakery next door, Sonnie went through the adjoining door and asked Theresa, when was the last time she heard from Vince?

"I haven't heard from him all day. Anything wrong?"

"I need to talk to him. It's important and he didn't tell me where he was going to be. That pisses me off."

"Calm down Sonnie," Theresa said. "I'm sure he'll get back with you. He probably doesn't have his phone turned on. You know how you guys are about that. The only time you don't have it on is when we need you."

Something wasn't right. Sonnie was dead serious and both Theresa and Connie were smiling and acting like it was no big deal.

"Okay... what's going on here? There's something you're not telling me. I can tell by the way you guys are acting. Ah hell, give me a coffee and I'll sit here a while... maybe he'll get my message. How about a couple biscotti... they fresh? Give me one with chocolate."

Sonnie sat back and watched how the girls ran the bakery and how the customers enjoyed coming to shop there. That was something he had never done before. He just looked at the figures at the end of the week and went from there. Twenty minutes went by and Sonnie was starting to get antsy. Just as he was getting ready to go back in the office to wait for Vince to call, he came barging into the bakery.

"Where you been? I've got something important to talk to you about. Let's go to the office... I need your input on something. Get something to drink... come on."

"No wait, Sonnie. Look what I've got. No shit Sonnie, you'll love it."

"Alright, what's the big deal? I knew something was up. Tell me what I'll love."

"I've made all the arrangements to go to the Canadian Jazz Festival. We'll be gone only four days. We'll fly up and I already got the rooms and the plane tickets. It'll be good for all of us. We need to get away…and, you always wanted to go there… now's our chance. What'da you think?"

"That's why you didn't answer my call. This is really important for the business that I talk to you. I appreciate this but we have to talk first. It has to do with the Mayor. I think we've finally got him by the balls. You know how important it is for us to get this resolved… then we can get started. You know these guys aren't going to wait around forever. "

"Don't be such a stick in the mud," Connie said as she rubbed Sonnie's shoulder. "You could be a little appreciative about what Vince did for you. Don't always think of business. What ever it is, it'll be there when we get back. This is something you always wanted to do. Give a little here honey. Take your head out of the sand and see the light once in a while."

"Okay, when do we leave? Damn… all I want to do is get things fixed up so we can have the best place in town."

"I was lucky," Vince answered. "The festival starts tomorrow… Thursday, I heard about it on the radio. We leave tonight at eight and we'll get there about midnight. The flight back is Monday morning and we'll be back here by noon."

"What about the bakery? Who's going to take care of it?"

"Don't worry Sonnie," Connie replied. "Theresa and I took care of everything. The bakers are going to take on a new roll for a couple of days and Bobby and Angie said they would check in on things to make sure there were no problems."

"We've taken care of everything," Vince added. "There's nothing to worry about. It's only four days, what can go wrong?"

"I remember someone saying that before we went to Italy. Alright then, I better get home to pack then... Or did you'nz do that for me too? You know, this sounds like a good thing. The more I think about it, the more I'm glad you did it."

As the men made their way back over to their office, everyone was smiling again.

"We can talk on the plane," Sonnie whispered to Vince.

The jazz festival was great and Sonnie got to see a lot of his favorite groups. A bunch of the old timers were there along with the new breed of jazz artist. Vince and Sonnie agreed that it was time to go after the Mayor. It was time to show him that they weren't to be messed with and they were tired of playing his game. Now they would show him how it was going to be. Not having the upper hand because of the trouble his boys were in, the Mayor would have to pay for his boy's mistakes and for being involved with drugs. It was time for a reckoning. Now, Sonnie and Vince would make their demands and they would make sure they were met or someone would suffer. The Mayor and his druggie friends wouldn't have a choice but to do it Sonnie and Vince's way. They were now in a position to ruin him after all the bullshit he's put them through. Now it was time to pay. Sonnie and Vince had friends in the police department and if necessary, they would expose the Mayor for his drug use, which meant he would have to step down from his position.

Libero A. Tremonti

CHAPTER TWENTY-TWO

On the way home from the airport, Vince had the limo driver go by the bakery. It was closed. For a Monday just passed noon, the place should have been buzzing with restaurant owners picking up their breads and desserts for the following week. As a matter of fact, there were a couple of business owners standing at the door, wondering why the store wasn't open for them. Sonnie had the driver to pull over in front of the bakery. Theresa, Vince and Sonnie go inside the bakery, while Connie made up an excuse for the business owners outside, as to why the bakery wasn't open. The air conditioner was on full blast and it must have been fifty degrees in there. All the display cases were empty.

"Where in the hell's everybody?" Sonnie wanted to know. "Some thing's not right here. Get Bobby on the phone, Vinny."

Theresa was puzzled. "I don't understand it." She said. "We left detailed instructions for everyone as to what was to be done. I wonder what went on here. I trusted those guys to do the right thing... now this."

"Where's all the pastries? All the cases are empty. It looks like they sold everything anyway. I'll check where I told them to put the money," Connie continued. She walked behind the counter and stooped down. "Shit, there's no money either. It looks like they really ripped us off. This isn't good," she replied with concern. "How hard could this be? It wasn't like we asked them to do something complicated." Connie looked again at the empty cases and just shook her head. We must be jinxed or something. "Every time we do something, it ends up in a disaster."

When Vince got Bobby on the phone, he told him that the bakers had been gone all weekend. Deli Dave and Kenny, the head bakers, had left a message on his cell that you and Sonnie had volunteered to do something with a charity for kids with cancer last weekend. He also said that they didn't want to let them down, so they took all the breads and pastries from the cases and gave it to the charity. They ended up working at the place all weekend and they were going to take off Monday to recuperate. Bobby went on to say that they would come in early Tuesday morning and get everything back to normal again and they hoped you'nz would understand.

"Ahhh shit Sonnie. Last weekend was that thing for the kids with cancer and I forgot all about it. The guys took all the goods and gave it to the charity. Get this, they got stuck working the place too. That's why the place is closed and there's no money or inventory. I guess they didn't desert us after all."

"Man Vinny, I thought we had another situation going on here. We'll have to thank them somehow. I need a nap... anybody interested?"

Sonnie called in Bull, Bobby and Angie for a meeting at the office. He was still a little uneasy about not having enough manpower. Of course, while the meeting was going on, Petey wondered into the bakery and asked the girls what was going on in the office. He had tried to call everybody but no one was answering their phones or returning his messages. All he wanted was to go bang on the office door but the girls told him that it wasn't such a good idea. From that point on, he paced the floor and got on everyone's nerves. Bobby informed Sonnie that while they were away, he had contacted a couple of his boys from the neighborhood and asked if they might be interested in coming for a visit. Sonnie gave him the okay to bring them down.

Vincent laid out the plan to Bull and Bobby he and Sonnie had come up with, which was to meet with the Mayor and make their demands. If the Mayor didn't respond in their favor, they would have to take other measures. They were tired of being harassed by him. He told Bobby that he and Angelo were to keep an eye on the Mayor's sons at all times and to report back what they were up to every minute of the day. Bull was to sit tight and be ready if he was needed on short notice. After the short briefing, Sonnie called the Mayor at his private number and put him on speaker so all could hear.

"You better not be jerking my chain like you did the last time," the Mayor lashed out. "You fed me a bunch of bullshit the last time we met and I don't want any of that bullshit this time. You'll either see things my way or you'll get nothing. I'm already thinking about taking away all your licenses to operate because you've been dicking me around."

"Okay Sir, there'll be no dicking around this time. My partner and I want to get things settled. We want to get started on our project and we're tired of waiting around. You'll see when we meet… we mean business."

"That's what I like…cooperation. I'm going to be out of town 'til next Tuesday. When I get back, I'll call you and we'll get things settled then. Remember, no bullshit. Just in case, I'll have all your papers there and if you don't cooperate, I'll tear them up right in front of you. You'll be up shits creek without a paddle. Like I said before, no bullshit."

"Well sir, we would like you to come to the casino so we can show you the plans for our improvements. We've been talking and decided we would like your input. After all, you're going to be like a silent partner. Doesn't that sound right? What'da you think? Com'on… we'll have a nice lunch and get things settled."

"Well, since you put it that way. This partner thing sounds good to me. I'll be back in town on Tuesday and we'll meet on Wednesday. I'll be there right at noon, don't you be late or try to stall. You know up front what the consequences will be."

Sonnie hung up the phone and gave the boys thumbs up. He asked Vince if he thought they should go to the Clip Joint and let the girls in on what was about to happen so they wouldn't be caught in a bad situation. Vince agreed. Someone banging heavily at the office door caught everyone by surprise.

"I told the girls not to bother us," Sonnie called out as Bull opened the door.

"It's not them Sonnie. Guess who?"

"You still here?" Vince asked Petey as he scurried through the door. "I thought you went back with your wife? What ever happened to those hamsters? They're probably all dead by now... the way you do things."

Out of breath, Petey found a seat and tried to regain his composure.

"I don't even want to talk about it. What's been going on here? Why is everyone here? No one told me everyone was going to be here. I was just driving by and saw everybody's car. I knew something was up. So...what's up? Com'on... somebody tell me something. I always have to be the last one to find out what's going on. I'm starting to get a complex. So what's happening? Somebody tell me something."

"Where you been hiding?" Sonnie wanted to know. "We haven't heard from you since you barged in on us at breakfast. We thought you went back to the islands. Where you been? You should tell somebody what's going on once in a while. We're here because we're going to make our move on the Mayor. You know what he's been putting us through. Now it's time to do our thing. When we get done with him, he'll either see things our way or he won't leave us no choice. Now we've got the upper hand."

"It's about time," Petey exclaimed. "If you ask me, you'nz should have wasted his ass a long time ago. You know he's into drugs big time. A friend of mine gets him all the shit he needs... he's in big time. His habit has gone from weed, to coke and now he's into that crystal shit and doing all kinds of weird shit too. Hell, half of his staff's using. They all get together and do their thing. You want pictures? I can get you any proof you want."

"Don't you just love him?" Vince looks at Sonnie with a smile. "How well do you know this drug dealer? Tell us about him... you know, where he's located, how he gets his drugs... things like that."

"His name is Chico. He's out of the North Side, Vince. He has control of most of the drug trade in town. He gets his hookers from the Islands and his drugs from Mexico. Boy, he's got some good looking honeys. I met him down there... in Jamaica. Small world isn't it?"

The name had a familiar ring to Sonnie.

"Vinny, isn't that the guy, that spick piece of shit that tried to rob the bakery, told us about? We're going to have a problem with that. Petey, Chico's cousin tried to..."

"Excuse me Sonnie, I know what went down at the bakery. Chico knows too. He knew his cousin was out of control and figured he'd end up that way. It doesn't bother him what you did to him. He knows all about you'se guys and how you feel about drugs. That's why he doesn't try to come into this part of town. He doesn't want a confrontation. Plus, the way he talks about Bull makes me think that's another reason he stays where he is. He told me he went one day and bought a car from Bull just to see what he was like. From then on, he said he would stay where it was safe. I don't think there's going to be any problem. I think he'll give us the information you want."

"How do you find a way to get in with all those low lives, Petey?" Sonnie wanted to know. "I never saw you like that, even when I first met you. You really had me fooled. Was it just an act? I thought you were worthless. I've really got to hand it to you, you finally got your shit together."

"Sonnie, when you helped me out in the alley behind your business that day, I was in some serious trouble. I appreciated what you did for me and said to myself. *Self, I've got another chance. This guy went out on a limb for me and now I've got to pay him back.* I didn't know who you were at the time, but when I found out, I sure was thankful. I knew then that you were my salvation. Then when Vince came along, I knew I was in for the duration. The two of you together...need I say more."

Petey strutted around the office like a proud peacock until Vince had to tell him to sit down.

"We want you to find out all you can from this Chico character," Vince continued. "But on the other hand, we don't want you to take any chances. If you see it's getting a little hairy, get out. You know we'll find a way to get what we want. So it's Monday... we have 'til Tuesday of next week. Let's not waste time. We have to have it all in place with no mistakes. We'll want to meet this Chico no later than Sunday...right Sonnie?

"I know what to do Vinny, I'm a little more cautious now. I've got a lot to lose now. Okay... it sounds like you'nz is starting to like me being around. Petey started singing....I Feeel Good....Da Da... Da Da...Da Da...Da... I knew that I would now."

Everyone left the meeting with their assignments. All Vince and Sonnie could do was wait for Petey to come back with the information they needed. Meanwhile, they knew the waiting would drive them nuts. Sonnie figured that this would be as good a time as any, to call the number that was left on his windshield outside the casino *'I might as well drive myself crazy with something else.'* He asked Vince to stick around while he made the call, only to find out that the number was no longer a working number.

"Can you imagine that Vinny? The number she gave me isn't any good... No longer in service or some shit like that. You think she did that on purpose? Maybe she's at the end of her rope. Maybe someone caught up with her and now she's paying for it. DAMN HER… anything to drive me nuts."

"Don't worry about it Sonnie, she's not done yet. She might be a little down but she's not out. She'll pop up when you least expect it. The bitch is just playing you, don't you get it? It has to be done her way, she's a manipulator. Don't you go and feel sorry for her and most of all don't let your guard down. I don't know when you're going to see her for what she is. Sonnie, you're starting to worry me. I don't like what I'm seeing here. You're smarter that this. I don't know what hold she has on you but you're not seeing this for what it is. Stop thinking she's a little kid and she needs your help. Think of her as what she is and what she did to Don Aldo. She almost killed the poor guy."

Vince put his arm around Sonnie, "Com'on goomba, what'da you say we go to the bakery, get a coffee and wait for the girls to get off? Then we'll go get some dinner and try to relax. We've got some serious issues going on right now and we can't afford to lose focus. Remember, make a plan, 'cause nothing works without a plan."

"Where have I heard that before?" Sonnie asked as he turned off the office lights and he and Vince lock up.

The next day, Petey went to Chico and told him what he needed. Chico agreed to help out Sonnie because the Mayor was putting the squeeze on him for free drugs and he was threatening him with jail time. Chico could see that by helping Sonnie do his thing, he'll be helping himself. He has a proposal that would benefit the both of them and wanted Petey to arrange a meeting with Sonnie and Vince.

"I don't know if they'll go for your proposal," Petey replied, "but I'll talk to them and see what I can do."

When Petey went to Sonnie and Vince with the information from Chico, Sonnie told him that was it the stupidest thing he could do, coming to him with such an idea. Vince suggested that they hear him out anyway and maybe there would be something in it for them. Sonnie set up the meeting at Bull's place because he wanted it to be to their advantage. Plus, he could tell whether or not Chico was on the level. If he squabbled about the meeting place, Sonnie would know that Chico wasn't serious and they would have to come up with another plan.

"Chico...here's the proposal from Sonnie," Petey explained. "He wants to meet at Bull's place on Sunday at noon. You can bring two with you. If you really want to get their trust, you'll come with an open mind. They might not accept your plan, so don't get pissed if they don't. They are very cautious. Let me tell you this Chico, they have the knack to see through schemes, so if you want this to happen, don't go there with something up your sleeve. I'm telling you this as a friend. I've seen the way they work. They're good...damn good. Trust me."

"What I have for them, I think they'll like. It'll take care of any drug problems they have going on around and in their casino. So in the end, it'll help them and also help me."

"I hope so buddy. So I can go to them and tell them it's a go? Who will you be bringing? I need to know so there won't be any surprises."

"I'll just be bringing Sylvia with me, she's my main girl. She goes everywhere with me. She's the only one I can trust. Besides, she'll be able to remember everything that goes down. Tell them I'll be there with bells on 'cause I want this bad. I know if this works out, it will only strengthen both our organizations. We'll both benefit by this proposal."

"No offense Chico, but it sounds like you're talking partnership here. I don't think you should go there with that idea in mind. I think all they want to do is get that bastard Mayor out of power. If you help them do that... well, that's the best you could hope for. You'll be in good shape 'cause the next person in line for Mayor is in their favor and Sonnie and Vince never forget the people that help them. Now the drug issue... that's going to be a big concern to them but as long as you stay where you are and don't try to take something that doesn't belong to you, then you'll be alright. That's the good that's going to come out of this."

Petey put the call into Sonnie and told him that it was a go for Sunday at noon. Sonnie acknowledged and reminded Petey to be on time.

Petey relayed the message to Chico, "We're on for Sunday."

All day Saturday Sonnie tried to stay busy. Friday night he tried to sleep but only tossed and turned thinking about the meeting on Sunday with Chico. Finally, he gave up on sleep and tried to do laundry, then it was cleaning the house and he even thought about cutting the grass, all of which he'd never done before. When nothing seemed to lessen his anxiety, Sonnie put a call to Vince and Theresa answered the phone.

"What's wrong Sonnie?"

"Nothing…you guys up yet? I'm bored, pacing the floor and wearing out the carpet. You know how I get before I've got something going on. I need some breakfast. How about you guys? Is it too early for you?"

"Where's Connie? I don't understand you Sonnie. When you have something troubling you… instead of having her with you, you stay by yourself. She's the best thing that's happened to you. It doesn't make any sense to me."

"You know what an asshole I can be," he tried to explain. "Why should I subject her to that? She'd never put up with that… but you're right. Why don't I call her and we'll all get some breakfast. I need some company. Ask Vince… see what he thinks. I can pick you guys up in about ten minutes."

"Sonnie we're still in bed. Call Connie. I'll wake up Vinny and get him going. Call us back and let us know what's up."

Sonnie picked up Connie and called Theresa back. On the way to Vince's, Connie asked Sonnie what was going on because she could tell something was up from the way he was acting. She'd seen him like that before… quiet and distant. It was like he was there but his mind was totally somewhere else. Sonnie wouldn't elaborate, but told her not to worry and that everything would be okay.

Theresa decided to cook for everyone and made a breakfast like Gramps used to make for Vince and Sonnie. Eggs scrambled with Gorgonzola cheese, Salami sliced thick and fried real crisp, sweet sausage, toast made in the oven, real butter, potatoes sliced thin and fried in olive oil with rosemary and dusted with a mild Garlic salt, apple juice and good strong espresso coffee. The girls tried to keep it light-hearted but from the way Sonnie and Vince were acting, they knew something big was about to go down. They just hoped it would be over soon and the guys could get back to being themselves. Connie and Theresa had to open the bakery at eleven so that left Sonnie and Vince to ponder the day away, talking about what was going to happen on Sunday. They spent most of the day making a plan and preparing for what was going to go down. By midday, they ended up on the boardwalk for a dog and a drink for lunch. This had become a ritual of sort to them. A place to open their minds and discuss business. They stood looking out over the ocean. It always gave them a sense of power and it looked so peaceful but in a second, everything could change, just like what they were about to get into. Vince called it the quiet storm. Somehow that power and the strength it possessed transferred to them. Later, they picked up the girls after work and took them for a quiet dinner and some entertainment. They knew that they wouldn't be together at all on Sunday.

Libero A. Tremonti

CHAPTER TWENTY-THREE

It was Sunday morning and Sonnie was up early and pacing the floor, which he usually did when there was serious business at hand. He put several calls in to Vince and as usual, he got the answer machine. Sonnie couldn't believe that Vince wasn't up early, and was waiting for his call. Then again, Vince was the cool one of the two and nothing ever seemed to bother him. That's what made them a good pair. Just before ten o-clock Vince finally called back.

"What the hell's going on Vinny? It's about time you got out of the rack. I'm about ready to go to Bulls' and get everything set up. What time do you want me to pick you up? Do you want to drive? What time you going to be here? I'm ready now, if you want to come and get me."

"Christ Sonnie, calm down before you have a stroke. I've already been over Bull's. He called me early and wanted to know if we wanted him to go ahead and set things up. I went over and we and moved some cars around, just in case this joker has something up his sleeve. The way we fixed everything...well, it's like a maze. If this Chico character is up to no good, at least we'll have the upper hand. I hope you didn't mind we didn't call you, but I know what condition you're in before stuff like this and thought it would be one less thing for you to worry about. We have everything taken care of so you can concentrate on the meeting. I can pick you up in about thirty minutes. You need some breakfast? We can get some on the way if you want."

"You guys think of everything. I'm glad you and Bull work so well together. Thirty minutes will be just fine. Have you heard from Bobby and Angie? I hope they're not late. We need everybody there."

"They were all there with me this morning. Bull had everyone there when I arrived. He's the one that had the idea for the maze of cars. He said he saw it once in a movie and thought it would work pretty good. Well, what about breakfast?"

"I don't think I can eat anything but I know I need too. We'll stop and get something at the diner."

While Sonnie and Vince were grabbing some breakfast, they keep noticing a little sports car that looked like the one they had seen in the parking deck. After it had passed by two or three times, Sonnie got up telling Vince to get him some more coffee and he would be right back. Vince warned him to watch himself and that it could be something more than what it looked like. As Sonnie stood on the sidewalk outside the diner, the car drove by slowly and Sonnie could see that it was Maria. She pulled around the corner, still in sight of Sonnie and as Sonnie walked towards the car, he casually looked around. *'This better not be a set up,'* he thought as he turned up the collar to his top coat and retreated his hands to his pockets where he would have easy access to a small derringer in his belt.

Maria rolled down the window.

"It's been a long time," he said when he saw her. "I tried calling the number I had, but it was out of service. What's up with that?"

"Gee, not even…I missed you babe…You can take your hands out of your pockets, I'm alone. I need you to help me Sonnie. I'm in some serious trouble. It seems I've gotten in a little over my head and don't have anyone to turn to. I know you don't want to hear this but after the things I've done to the people I'm supposed to love, well… I got caught up in that power thing. You know me. We need to meet when it's convenient… The sooner the better. I think my time's running out, if I don't do something soon…"

"I'll listen, just tell me how to find you. This time, don't give me the runaround. I'll be glad to hear about your problems but you better be on the level with me and don't feed me no bullshit. Right now, I've got something going on I can't put aside. As soon as this situation is resolved, we can meet... Then we'll see."

"Here's my number. I really need you Sonnie. It's not because I don't have anyone else to turn to, it's because I know you're the only one after all these years, I trust. I can understand why Vincent might not want you to get involved with my situation. I hope he comes with you when we talk so he'll see I'm...how does he say...on the square. Don't take too long...please."

As she handed him the paper with the name of the place she was staying and the number to reach her, her hand slid gently over Sonnies and he quickly pulled it away. Maria sped off and as Sonnie turned to go back inside, he saw Vince standing there on the sidewalk outside.

"It's getting late, we should go. I took care of everything inside."

"Don't you want to know who that was? I know, I know, I should be thinking about what's going down in about thirty minutes from now. Don't worry, I've got everything under control."

"I sure hope so," Vince agreed, "Cause if you fuck up and lose your composer, we'll be screwed. Keep your head in the game. You know this shit-head is going to come in here thinking he's got the upper hand because he's got something we want. I've seen it a million times and so have you. Let's get this out of the way... then you can see what, you know who... wants from you. Her timing's not the greatest... that sort of pisses me off. Promise me you'll concentrate on what's going on today. Of all the times for her to show up, it had to be now."

"I'm okay Vinny. Now that I talked to her, I know it's not a setup and all my questions are answered so it's all irrelevant now. I know she's on the up and up. She needs some help and I can tell she's desperate. That'll put me in control of the situation. For now, let's go meet this dope-head and see what he's got to offer. By the way, she wants you to come with me when I meet with her."

It was eleven-thirty when they arrived at Bulls' place and Sonnie liked what they had done with the set-up. Everyone was there including a couple of Bull's associates, standing at the entrance of the business. When Sonnie questioned Bull about the new faces, he told him that he knew they were short on manpower and these guys were as loyal to him, as he and Vince were to each other. Sonnie rested a little easier. When Chico arrived right at twelve, they were all surprised. They thought that he would show up in one of those hopped-up antique 1960 Chevy convertible that bounce up and down and have all the bling on them. Instead, Chico arrived in an old 1966 model Jag XKE, just he and his girl.

"Instead of a posse... he brings a pussy," Bull announced, watching from the office window. Sonnie and Vince go outside to meet Chico and notice a cab pulling in behind him.

"What the hell," Petey yelled as he jumped out of the cab. "Who did this to Bulls' place? All the cars are moved all over the place. This place is a mess. The cabby could hardly drive through it like this."

Chico stepped out of his car and went over and opened the door for his girl. Sonnie and Vince were surprised again. He didn't look like what they were expecting. They figured they would be dealing with this baggy-pant, sloppy-shirted, long haired druggie. Instead, he looked like one of those male models and resembled an actor named Antonio. His hair was long but neat and he looked Latin rather than Puerto Rican, as his name suggested. As his girl stepped out of the car, they couldn't help but notice her beauty. She was about the same height as Chico and her complexion was flawless, her hair was long and as the sun hit it, they could see the blonde highlights shining through. Her lips were full and she had a splendid figure. They were quiet a couple and you could tell by looking at them, that they spent time in the gym. Petey went over and walked them over Sonnie and Vince to introduce them.

"You didn't have to get dressed up for this meeting." Vince said as he shook Chico's hand. "We're just a relaxed bunch here. It looks like you mean business. We're not use to this. You came alone I see. Where's your guys? Is she going to sit in on our meeting? How's that work?"

"She's by my side all the time. Not only is she my lady, she's my advisor also. I value her opinion and she has a good eye for what's good for me. Petey told me about the way you guys operate. He told me I didn't have to worry. You and Sonnie are some straight-up dudes. Pete's been a great help to me... he's a cool guy. The only worry I had, was Bull. Pete told me about his position in you're organization and how he takes care of business. Where is he anyway? He's going to be here isn't he?"

With a puzzled look on their faces, Vince and Sonnie took Chico and his girl inside the office. When Chico saw Bull, the look on his face told everyone Chico didn't know what to think about him. After he was introduced to Bull and saw how different he was than the way he looked, Chico relaxed a little. They all sat at a round table in Bull's office.

"Gee...we could be the new knights of the round table," Chico added with a smile. "I came here one time to look at cars, just to see and meet you Bull, but you weren't here."

"What do you know about them... the knights?" Vince asked.

"Loyalty, responsibility, reliability, commitment and trust. That's what those guys were all about. Maybe we could have something like that if you guys would keep an open mind. I have some ideas that would help all of us, to the point that we could have complete control of the whole area, the board walk, the strip... all of it."

"Look Chico, with all due respect, all we want is to find out the scoop on the Mayor and his cronies that are involved in drugs. We told Petey to tell you that. Now if he didn't, I apologize for that, but that's all we're interested in."

"Pete's cool Vince. He told me just what you wanted him too. I think if you hear me out, please just listen... it can't hurt. Listen to what I have to say and if you don't like it, well... I'll go on my way without any hard feelings. I know how you guys feel about drugs, but that's not all I'm in to. It's a good thing for all of us. I'm telling you, with your connections and my connections, we control the whole city and the people in it. I can be a very good ally to have and from what I know of you'nz…what a team we could be. I know I keep repeating myself, but this seems to be a workable thing to me."

Vince turned to Sonnie. "What do you think, should we take up our time to hear what he has to say?"

"I don't know how this could possibly work out. We don't have anything in common with you and your organization. We don't want drugs coming into our area. I know there's drugs here now but if you come in, they will be all over the place. We just don't want drugs taking over. We want to keep the people that come to the casinos, away from being hounded by drug dealers. I grant you, some of them will be looking for them but I don't want it right under their noses. I've driven myself crazy trying to control the problem but I might as well be banging my head against the wall."

"That's where I can help you Sonnie," Chico went on to say. "What I want to propose to you is that if I control the drug part of it, I will make sure that no one comes into downtown and sells drugs. I'll take care of all that and you won't have to worry about it. I control eighty percent of everything that goes on in this town as far as drugs and girls are concerned. I even furnish some of my girls to the big places in town when they have a special thing going on. If you let me come into your space, I'll see to it that the pushers are taken off of all the corners and out of the hotels. Look… I know how all that stuff works, I can control it… trust me, it's my business. You come and move dealers out of the hotels and off the corners. Then in a day, they're right back again. I know who's doing this and I'll make sure it stops. What I'll do is, take the dealers and place them in certain areas and if someone's looking to do business with them, I'll see to it they find them. The drugs don't have to be out in the open for the business to be successful. We could work out something so you could gain financially from it. The other thing is the girls. I would like to bring in some of my girls, we could work something out about that. My girls are of the highest quality… no sluts. I have doctors that take care of them. If they don't take care of themselves, they're out in an instant. I've seen some of your girls and they are of the highest quality. Ours are just as good, plus I'll take care of all the protection for them and you won't have to worry with it."

"Why should we?" Sonnie asked. "We have all the protection we need. Plus, we have a lot of good people on our payroll. That amounts to power, and power is the answer to everything. How do we know you'll stick to the deal? I've never seen druggies stick to anything they say. Once the shit gets control of them, they're no good. We lost a good man to drugs. He betrayed us for drugs, money and some whore he got tied up with. I don't see me ever trusting anyone that uses drugs. Now he's on the run and we're out a good man and a lot of money. That's what pisses me off. People loose focus when they're on that shit… they can't see reality. They know something bad's going to happen to them, but they still let it happen. What I can't figure out…why would someone let something so dangerous control them? Besides, if you're doing so well, why would you want to bother with us? You said you controlled about eighty percent, right? Why then, would you want to take on more stuff? How can you be sure you can take care of everything? After all, you're only one person. No disrespect, but your girl there can only be but so much help to you."

"This may sound funny to you Sonnie but people like to experiment. Whether it be with drugs… or some other degenerate thing. We've seen it all as you have. I can assure you we will take care of all the drug movement and we'll do it with discretion. You won't even know it's around you. You see, Sylvia and me…we don't do drugs nor will we ever do drugs. We have too much to loose if we start using. We have to keep our heads about us at all the times. What we have is a business that's worth millions. Why should I risk all that just to get high? I get high just thinking about how much money I'm going to make every day. Do me a favor Sonnie, you and Vince just think about it?" It's a good deal. With the connections you have and the ones I have…need I say more?"

Vince and Bull were looking at each other and waiting for the fireworks to go off when Sonnie tears into Chico about this so called deal. They got a big surprise when Sonnie suggested that the deal sounded like it could work. He told Chico that he and Vince would talk it over and it was possible that things might work out for all the parties involved. He went on to say that he and Vince would look at the deal more closely and get back with him. For right now, they just wanted to get the dope on the Mayor and get him off their backs.

"Chico," Vince added. "The Mayor is our main concern right now. We asked you to come here today because Petey told us you had some issues with that prick yourself. Can you help us or not? We don't want to waste your time and I'm sure you don't want to waste ours. Now... what's it going to be?"

"Vince, just tell me what you want, I'm sure I've got something. If I don't, then I know Sylvia does."

"What we need is a timetable, like when he buys the drugs and how much he uses in ...say, for a week. Does he pick them up himself? I'm sure he's not that stupid. Who picks them up if he doesn't? Does he pay cash? Does he owe you for them? What kind of favors does he do for you? You know, shit like that."

"Well, to start off... he never picks them up. He always has some stooge pick them up for him. Sometimes we have one of our girls deliver them to him. Of course, he has to get into some perverted sex act when that happens. How much we give him depends on what he's doing at the time. Sometimes we deliver a key to him. Other times, he has these parties on this yacht. Damn thing's about as big as a battle ship. All the problems started when he began demanding because of who he was. He wanted all these favors because he's the head-man in town. He said he would take care of me and make sure nothing would happen to my people. After I agreed to that, that bastard went out and had a raid at a couple of my places and had a couple of my boys killed. Then he tells me that now, he would tell me what and where things were going to happen. I was too afraid to do anything because I don't know the right people. Seeing that you have differences with him and me having a proposed solution to a big problem of yours, maybe you would help me take care of this thorn in our sides. Honey, hand me that envelope," Chico said turning to Sylvia. "Here is something that will help us do in that son-of-a-bitch. As you can see, we've had people watching him for a long, long time. By the way, the son-of-a-bitch is into me for a half million and he told me it didn't look like I was going to see the money anytime soon. You're probably wondering why I let it go that long. I just didn't know what to do and before I knew it, it got out of control. I've heard for years that you kill police or a public figure...you could be in big trouble. That's why I didn't react to the situation. I know you'll probably want to handle this yourself, but if we can be of any help, don't hesitate. There's tapes and pictures in this envelope."

Chico passed the large envelope across the table to Vince and Sonnie. When Sonnie, Vince and Bull looked at the contents of the envelope, what they saw were pictures of the Mayor on this yacht, with some pretty high profile people. There were detailed documents telling when and where he received drugs, the quantities he received and who some of the people were he gave them to. There was also evidence that he was even making money by selling drugs to some of his friends. This was just what Sonnie and Vince were looking for. With this information, when they met with the Mayor next week, they could make the demands they needed to get him off their backs.

"I'm quite impressed with this information," Sonnie commented to Vince. "This is a lot more than we expected. Sylvia keeps good records, she did a good job...I congratulate you on that. This will help us a lot. We're meeting with the bastard on Wednesday, so you better be prepared in case something goes wrong. Have your eyes and ears open. There's no guarantee this is going to work. If it doesn't go as we plan, all hell's going to break loose... on our end and yours. We'll do everything to make it work, but you know how things go. Would you like to go up to our casino and have some lunch? We'd like to show you the place."

"Maybe another time," Chico answered. "We've got a lot to think about. Plus, we have a meeting at the art gallery with some stooge. I think he's trying to sell me a worthless painting. Let me know what happens Wednesday. If something goes wrong, I don't want to be caught with my pants down. Don't forget my offer, it'll be good for everybody."

CHAPTER TWENTY-FOUR

As Chico and Sylvia got up to leave, Sonnie offered his hand and Bull and Vince follow. Petey walked Chico and Sylvia to their car and they made their way through the maze of cars and left. Petey returned to the office to find out how thing went and Sonnie, Vince and Bull were still looking at the pictures.

"Sonnie, look at these," Vince said as they flipped through the pictures. "They're perfect. Whoever took these, knew what they were doing. All this information's perfect. Good job Petey," Vince acknowledged, as Petey stood looking over Sonnie's shoulder.

Vince shot a concerned look toward Sonnie.

"I can't believe you're even considering this deal with that drug lord. It's so unlike you to even think about something like that. At first, I thought you were just busting his balls, but the more you talked, the more serious you sounded. What's up with you?"

"It's like this Vinny, drugs are everywhere. You even said to me yourself some time ago I was beating my head against the wall, so I was willing to listen to him. The more he talked, the more I was liking what he said. What did you think about it? How about you Bull? You know, just because I listened to him, doesn't mean anything. We'll have to go over it again with him to make sure we're not being taken in. I guess I'm just getting old. What'da you say we round up everyone and go to the casino and loosen up a little?"

Vince called Connie and Theresa to close the bakery or to have someone cover for them. In the meanwhile, Sonnie called Gina and told her to round up all the girls, Bobby and Angelo. When they met at the casino, they were missing Mitsie and Pitsie. Gina told Sonnie that they were in the Grand Camen Islands with the Mayors' sons. The party went on until almost daybreak and everyone had a good time.

Luckily, the Clip Joint and the bakery were closed on Mondays except for the bakers that baked breads for the restaurants all over town. No one would have made it except maybe for Sonnie. He was up early scheming and waited patiently for everyone else to wake up from the dead. He knew Vince would be worthless all day Monday, so he left Connie in bed and went to see Bull. Sonnie told Bull he was thinking of taking out the Mayor's boys while they were in the Islands, depending on how the meeting went with the Mayor on Wednesday.

"Who you going to get to go down there?" Bull wanted to know. "How we going to get someone down there on such short notice? We don't even have anyone that's experienced for that. All my boys are local... unless you have another idea. I'm not so sure we can pull it off. However, I think it's a good move, if you know something I don't."

"That's just it. You remember Johnny Rocco, Bobby's boss from New York? He told me about this protector he knows that's for hire. Johnny says he's very reliable. He's quick and straight to the point. I'm thinking of giving him a call and see how he operates. We can keep him on ice 'til we need him. I'm sure he would like a trip to the islands. What'da you think?"

"I think it's a good idea, getting someone like that. We would have almost nothing to do with it. Everyone will be here and accounted for. No one can say anything about it. What's Vinny think about it?"

"I haven't said anything to him yet. He's still trying to rise from the dead. Last night he sure tied one on. By the way, why are you so wide awake? I know you're a big guy but sometimes the bigger they are... the harder they fall. You look pretty good."

"I have a special remedy."

"I'm afraid to ask, but here goes. What's your special thing?"
"I soak my winkie in be-ins."
"Be-ins...what kind of be-ins? I've never heard of such a thing."
"Human be-ins...Ha...Ha...Get it?"
"You're a real shit-head sometimes. Seriously, do you think Vinny will go for it? First we have to find out, what money this guy...I think his name is Dario...is looking to get. We'll probably have to send him a retainer to hold him 'til we need him. You up to going over Vince's and backing me up on this plan? I think he'll listen to you."

"Hell yea, I'll go with you. You know Vinny, it doesn't matter what anyone says, if he doesn't like it, he'll let you know. Besides, I want to see what kind of shape he's in. I remember you telling me once before that he's real ugly when he's hung over."

Sonnie let Bull drive to Vince's and on the way there, Sonnie called Johnny Rocco to get Dario's number. When they got to Vince's, they were surprised to find him up and all bright-eyed. Theresa was in the kitchen and you could tell something good was cooking. Sonnie and Bull went over the idea for the Mayors boys and Vince liked it. The only thing was the money. Vince wanted to know, what if they gave him a retainer and he wasn't needed, would it still be good for future services?

Sonnie put the call into Dario and he was very receptive, once he figured out who Sonnie was. Johnny had already talked to Dario and told him that Sonnie might be calling. Dario proceeded to give Sonnie the particulars of his fees. The retainer would be twenty-five thousand. The job would be fifty-thousand each. Sonnie informed Dario about his girls that were with them and he didn't want any harm to come to them. Dario assured Sonnie that he would make sure that they wouldn't be in any danger. The twenty-five thousand dollar retainer was just that. If the deal fell through, tough luck. To try again would cost another twenty-five. All was understood and the hire was made.

Tuesday, Sonnie and Vincent went to the Clip Joint and filled Gina in on what may be going down. They told her to get in touch with the Pitsie and Mitsie and to warn them of what may happen. She was to tell them that they wouldn't be in any danger and that they had to trust them. Hopefully, it probably wouldn't happen when they were around, so they would have to act normal so not to raise any suspensions. Afterwards, arrangements would have been made for them to come home. Gina made the call while Sonnie and Vince were with her in the office. Pitsie and Mitsie said that they understood and were looking forward to making the trip back home by themselves. The girls were getting tired of romancing those two ass-holes. They wanted to know how much longer they were going to have to put up with them, if this didn't happen. Gina told them that if everything went as planned, it wouldn't be long and to just be patient and keep their eyes open. Gina told them to be expecting her call. Everything was set and now all they could do was to wait until Wednesday.

It was long Tuesday night. Sonnie spent most of it watching sports on television. Occasionally, he would take a walk out by the pool and sit for a while and look at the stars. It was an unusually clear night out and the sky was full of stars. Sonnie would sit on a lounger and gaze upwards, trying to find all the constellations his grandfather had show him when he was a kid. He still could not find all of them. While looking at the stars, he would talk to his grandfather and ask for a sign from him and asked him to guide him in the right direction. Sonnie was unusually calm considering what was about to happen. For once, he had everything in place and he knew that he had the upper-hand going in. He was confident the Mayor would see things his way and a deal would be worked out. If not... oh well.

It was close to two-thirty. Sonnie was still by the pool when he heard a voice calling him from the other side of the fence.

"Sonnie... don't shoot. It's me... Bull. I found something you should see."

Sonnie opened the gate and there stood Bull, holding this half unconscious guy.

"What the hell's this?" Sonnie asked. "Who's this character? What the hell you doing here... it's three in the morning?"

"As I usually do when I'm out late, I ride by you and Vince's making sure everything's okay. I found this scruffy fucker, looking in one of your windows. What'da you want to do with him?"

Bull threw the man into a chair and asked him who he was and what he was doing looking in Sonnie's window. The little guy was a wreck, he told them he was lost. He said he was homeless and a bunch of teenagers had picked him up as he was trying to get on the other side of town. They drove him around for a couple of hours and then threw him out in this neighborhood. He saw the light on at Sonnie's house and was going to ask for some help, when he was jerked out of his shoes by this gorilla. Sonnie asked Bull what he thought they should do with him and to Sonnie's surprise, Bull suggested that they give him something to eat and he would take him where he wanted to go. In a way, that was good for Sonnie. It took the edge off and Sonnie thought that in a strange way, it might have been the sign he asked for from his grandfather.

Sonnie slapped together some salami sandwiches and grabbed some sodas from the fridge before returning to the back deck. As they talked to the guy, they found out that his wife of eighteen years had taken off with another man. After that, he just gave up. He lost his job and he just didn't care anymore.

Sonnie looked at Bull, "See, this shit happens all the time, they just suck the life out of you."

Bull took the guy to drop him off at the shelter and on the way, asked him what his next move was. He told Bull that he didn't have a clue but thanked him for everything. As Bull drove away, he reflected back for a minute on how he almost ended up like that. *"I'm one lucky son-of-a bitch,"* he thought.

When ten-o-clock rolled around, Sonnie called Vince to let him know that he would pick him up in thirty minutes. Vince suggested that it would be better if they drove separate cars in case something should go wrong, they shouldn't be together. Sonnie agreed. When Sonnie got to the casino, Vince was already in the restaurant having a coffee. Sonnie joined him and they started planning out their strategies. Vince thought they should work the Mayor over slowly then go at him hard with the evidence they had gotten from Chico. They both knew he wouldn't be a happy camper, once he saw all the evidence they had on him. They had to be firm, not making any threats towards him but trying to work things out. Vince and Sonnie were going to want the Mayor to step down from his position and that way, it would put their man, the vice Mayor, in his position. Then they would have the bull by the horns, since they already had the Police Chief in their pocket. How that came about, it started out quite innocently, the Chief came into the Clip Joint one day for a hair cut. It was an extremely tense day but Claudia talked him into a massage. One thing led to another and the first thing you know, he was coming weekly for his massages and the extra good things on the menu. Then he started betting on football games and he was hooked. Thanks once again to those angels at the Clip Joint, his loses outweighed his wins ten times over.

The Mayor arrived promptly at twelve noon, driving up in his own personal vehicle. Sonnie and Vince met him at the door. They first took him on a tour of the casino and showed him the changes they wanted to make. Then they took him to their office. There they showed him the blue prints so he could really get a grasp on how big the changes were going to be. The place would be about three times the size it was now. The Mayor was impressed. He told them that the bigger it was, the more it was going to cost them. That comment didn't sit well with Sonnie and Vince but they decided to just let him have his say.

"I'm going to get right to the point boys," The Mayor pointed out. "I don't have a lot of time. I hate little shit like this... it just takes up my time and I don't think I should have to put up with your kind anyway... but I'm willing to listen after you hear what I have to say. You know, you guys want to come on the strip... my strip and your kind just thinks you can do as you please. Everything that goes on here has to go through me, you hear me? Now...I think we can work something out because I know how bad you want this to go through. So this is what I'm proposing. All the plans you have for the casino will go through me. I will decide how much it will cost you with each phase that is built. Then... after the casino's finished, I'll expect a detailed financial statement each month, then I'll decide how much you'll pay me each month. If we don't do it my way or the payments are late for any reason, the work will stop and you'll never get this place done. I know what you two represent and I've handled your kind before. I knew J.D. also. He was a punk, just like all you goombas are. Now, that's the way it is and there's no room for negotiation."

Vince looks at Sonnie and could see the rage in his face.

"I thought you said you would hear us out!" Vincent shouted.
"Well Mr. Mayor, you're going to, whether you want to or not."

Sonnie throws the envelope in front of the Mayor.

" Now you'll listen to what we have to say," Vince continued. "First, we know about your drug use and all the parties you have with underage kids. We know where you get the drugs and who sells them to you. We know the other members of your staff that are involved in all this bullshit. It's all there: pictures, names... everything. Next, your boys just go around this town like they own it. They're into us for about two-hundred-fifty-thousand. We're not going to let them off the hook like everyone else does. They're going to pay one way or another. Now, Sonnie was willing to cut you in on this venture but I'm changing the rules. Since you came in here with this attitude, I want you to resign as Mayor, affective tomorrow or….."

"Or what?" The Mayor interrupted. "You'll go to the papers? Who's going to believe your kind? There's no place in this town for organized crime. I've got the only organized crime in this town. You don't have a leg to stand on. You could have had those pictures doctored up. Certainly with the good job I've done in this city in the past four years, the people are not going to believe anything like that, especially from your kind. As for my sons, they'll do as they please. They won't pay you a cent. Come tomorrow, I'm going to send the inspectors over to that place you call a hair cutting salon. It's nothing but a whore house anyway and I'm going to have it shut down. That's the way it's going to be…so you better pack your shit and leave my town. I'll expect you out by the weekend. I've had enough of your bullshit. Every time I meet with you punks, it's always the same. This is the last time I'm putting up with it."

The Mayor got up to leave but Vince pushed him back down in the chair.

"Now look you bastard, you're going to listen to what we're telling you. This is the way we say it's going to be…."

At that moment, Sonnie came up behind him and wrapped the telephone cord around his neck.

"Sonnie!" Vince yelled. "What the hell you doing? It's not supposed to go down like this. Turn him loose."

Sonnie just kept squeezing tighter and tighter as Vince tried to but couldn't pull him off the Mayor. When it was allover, Sonnie slumped down in a chair holding his head in disbelief.

"What the hell we going to do now, Sonnie?" Vince asked as he paced the floor. "I hope you thought about this before...oh what the hell, that piece of shit had it coming anyway. What a prick that bastard was. We're really in a fix now. I hope we can come up with something."

"I'll think of something. First thing, we have to get his car out of our parking lot. Call Bobby and Angie. Tell them they need to come here right away. We'll take the car to the warehouse and call Bull to dispose of it."

"What we going to do with the body? Should we let Bull take it too? I guess we better put a call in to Dario and tell him to take care of business. Damn it Sonnie, it's another fine mess you got me into. We'll call our friend at the newspaper and give this information to him. He'll put it in the paper tomorrow and it'll look like the Mayor skipped out. We can get Gina to call that news anchor at the television station that has the hots for Claudia and get the stuff to him too."

"Good thinking Vinny. I knew you could do it. I don't know what got into me. I just knew he wasn't going to budge. I guess I just snapped. Man...that was heavy. Hey Vinny, he thought he did such a good job in this town and he always liked looking over the strip, why don't we put him and his boys somewhere they can look over the whole place?"

"And where might that be? I really don't want to know but I'm sure you're going to tell me. Well go ahead, let me hear what caulk-a-mamie idea you got now. Damn Sonnie, I thought one of the rules was not to kill political figures. I can't believe this."

"Look Vinny, this bastard got what he deserved. The son-of-a-bitch just wouldn't listen to reason. You know what, I'm not sorry because I know he was going to cause us more trouble. I just wonder how many people he had taken advantage of, that miserable bastard. I just lost it. It'll be okay, I know it will. No one will ever know where him and his sons are except us. We'll get Chico to give us more pictures for the newspapers, if he has any. When he hears what happened, I guess he'll be pleased. He now owes us. We better call Gina and tell her to warn the twins."

"First, tell me your plan for the Mayor, or should I say ex-Mayor. We better call Charley and tell him what to expect. He'll need to know that his title will be changing from Vice-Mayor to Mayor. So what are we going to do with the Mayor? You know we can't have any slip-ups. He or his sons can to never be found."

"You know that five story police station that's being built at the end of the strip? Well they're working on the fifth floor now and it's almost finished. The construction company is the same one we have doing the work for us. I thought about putting the three of them in the outside wall overlooking the strip. He said it was his town, we'll let him see what he's missing. We shouldn't have any problem with getting them up there. No one will ever know the difference. What'da you think... huh... huh?"

After a couple of days, all the necessary calls were made and Dario had gotten the job done as planned, hitting the Mayor's sons. They had been sitting at an outside café and when the girls went to the power-room, all hell broke loose. They were questioned by the police and then released. Pitsie and Mitsie didn't care for the idea of coming home on a private plane with the dead bodies wrapped up in body-bags, of the one's they had been involved with over the past weeks. They had started to get close to them.

Bull got the Mayor's car taken care of by crushing it twice for good measure. The newspaper printed the pictures in a series of articles about the corruption the Mayor was involved in and his strong drug use. The names of the staff members were also exposed. The pictures said it all. After the articles were published, the Mayor wasn't even missed. Charley, the vice Mayor, took office and was accepted quietly. He promptly fired all the staff that was involved and replaced them with his own, some being hand-picked by Sonnie and Vince. Now, everything was falling into place and it could only get better. As always, when a situation was taken care of and the organization was successful, Sonnie had the troops over to his house to celebrate. Sonnie did something very out of character, he invited Chico and his girl Sylvia to his house for the celebration. They were impressed with what they saw and Chico expressed to Sonnie and Vince that he wished that they could have done business together. That was all that was said. Day turned into night, but it didn't seem to matter. Everything was going as they planned.

CHAPTER TWENTY-FIVE

With the mysterious disappearance of the Mayor and his sons and with the new Mayor and the Police Chief in their pockets, Sonnie and Vince were riding high. Except, Sonnie still had other issues he had to take care of… Maria and way in the back of his mind was Rando. He'd been gone for a while and there was no sign of him around town. They would have to wait until he screwed up and made a mistake. When he did, Sonnie and Vince would have to remind him of what it's like to betray them.

While Connie and Theresa were working in the bakery one very busy day, this extremely good looking lady came in looking around. They could tell she was Italian, especially when she spoke. She asked to sample the biscotti with almonds in them and after tasting it, she commented that she knew the recipe and thought it was from the Naples area.

"What town are you from?" Connie asked. "I don't mean to get personal or nothing like that. It's just that my "special" friend is from a small mountain village outside of Naples. Next time you're in and he's here, I'll introduce you to him. Maybe you'nz might have something in common."

With a polite smile, the woman ordered a dozen biscotti and left, never answering Connie's question. Later that evening, Connie told Sonnie of the strange visitor at the bakery that day.

"What was her name?" Sonnie wanted to know. "Where did she say she was from?"

Connie told him that she was real busy at the time waiting on three people and couldn't remember if the woman even mentioned her name. Sonnie knew who she was and that he would have to do something... and fast. She was getting a little too personal coming to the bakery like that.

Sonnie put a call into Vince and told him what went down at the bakery. Vince agreed with Sonnie that something had to be done... and soon. He asked Vince if he would come with him when he went to see Maria but Vince declined. He said that he wouldn't have the patience to deal with her and he thought it best, Sonnie handled it himself. Besides, he and Theresa were flying to Pennsylvania for a visit. They were to leave in the morning and it was only for three days.

Sonnie hung up the phone. Now he was starting to get nervous. *'What if I fuck this up? What if she sweet talks me into doing something I don't want to do because I'm feeling sorry for her... and in a moment of weakness, I do it? Damn it Vince, I need you now more than ever. I guess I'll just have to suck it up and deal with it. I'm not going to worry, I'll be a real hard ass... yea, right. I know...I'll make a plan that always works. SHIT! Why me?* Sonnie made the call to Maria and got no answer so he left a message and his number for her to call back. Five minutes later, she called back.

"Sorry I missed your call, I was in the shower. I found this new body soap. It really makes your skin soft. I never found anything like this in Italy. Did you want to meet? Just tell me where and when. Would you like to come here? It'll be alright... believe me."

"I don't think so Maria. For our first meeting, we should meet somewhere in public. I don't want to be set-up. By the way, what's the idea coming to the bakery?"

"I told you Sonnie, I'm not playing games. I'm in deep trouble and you're the only one I can turn to. Please believe me. I'll do anything you say or meet you anywhere you say. I really need your help. I know you're the only one that can help me. You're powerful enough and have all the necessary connections to do so. The bakery, oh…I went there because I knew it would piss you off and it would make you call right away. Besides, I was in the mood for some good biscotti. She seems very nice, Sonnie."

"Always curious aren't you? I don't think she should have anything to do with this. It would be in your best interests she doesn't."

"My, aren't we the protector. She is of no concern to me. I just want this problem I have to go away. Then, I can get on with my life… which I want to discuss with you."

"I'm not in the counseling business. Besides, how bad can it be? Any problem can be solved if you have the right people to solve it. You must have gotten yourself in real deep. What happened to you? I always knew you to be smarter than that. You must have been desperate."

"I'll explain all that to you when we meet. Please let it be soon. I'm always looking over my shoulder and I'm getting tired of it. I really need this Sonnie."

"There's a little restaurant on Thirty-Forth-Street named Dom's. I'll meet you there tomorrow at two. I know you… and if you're more than ten minutes late, I'm gone. You know I don't like people to be late. There's no reason for it."

"See you then, Sonnie. Looking forward to seeing you after all these years. It's been a long time."

"This isn't a reunion. I'm only doing this because Don Aldo asked me to. As for me, I've always wondered why you went the way you did. You weren't raised like that. 'Til tomorrow then."

Sonnie spent the rest of the day wondering around like some kind of homeless person. Finally, the bakery closed and the four of them went to dinner. Vince and Theresa's flight was at ten in the morning and Sonnie was going to take them to the airport. That meant Connie would be running the bakery by herself. When that happened to either of the girls, they had some part-time girls that would come in and help out. That also meant that Connie would be getting off later than usual.

The next morning Sonnie took Vince and Theresa to the airport and while Theresa was picking up the tickets, Vince asked him if he had called Maria. Sonnie told him about their conversation and about the meeting at two that afternoon. Vince reminded Sonnie to keep his head and not to get sucked in by anything she said. He also wanted to know if anyone else was going to be there to watch his back. Sonnie told him he thought he could trust her. Vince looked at him and then started to say something but then shook his head and walked over to the ticket counter where Theresa was. Sonnie waited until the plane took off and then went back to his house to get ready for his meeting with Maria. He felt he could trust her, but still strapped his twenty-two magnum pistol to his inside left ankle.

Sonnie got there at one forty-five and told the manager, which was a personal friend of his, that he was going to need privacy and to watch for Maria. He put Sonnie in the back at a corner booth which had a round table, so he could have a good view of the whole place. When Maria walked in promptly at two, all heads turned. The manager knew that she was to be escorted to Sonnie's table. As she got closer to the table, Sonnie couldn't believe how good she looked. He felt this strange feeling in his stomach, one he hadn't had before. He couldn't remember her looking like that. *'This is going to be harder than I thought. Damn she looks good,'* he thought.

"Ciao (hello) Sonnie."

"Sedere (sit)… we finally meet. Now, what's so important? All this mystery, how bad can it be?"

"I'll get to that in time, Sonnie. First, I'd like if we could just catch up a little so I can explain a few things. Look, I know I shouldn't be wanting explanations from you on why you did what you did. I know why. The thing is how you pulled it off. It was brilliant, even if you did do it to me. Where did you go and how did you get out of the country? It must have taken a long time to plan it."

"Not really. As a matter of fact, it was a spare of the moment thing. I decided to do it that morning. I just had enough of the drug thing. That and seeing everything my grandfather worked for, turn to shit because of it. So that's why I did what I did. I'll tell you… it wasn't easy. After I blew up the boat with the last rocket, I knew it would come in handy one day, I went north to Switzerland. I got to a spot that looked safe to me and beached the boat. Then I walked, it seemed like forever, carrying these two suit cases full of your money, up and down mountain after mountain. Lucky for me, I didn't come across any of those bandits that run the hills there. I couldn't get a ride, everyone looked at me like I had the plague. If they only knew what I had in those cases. Finally, a farmer hauling sheep helped me get to a village where I got a car. The rest was simple after that. All it took was money."

"Why did you pick this place to come to and how did you get a license to open a business? It was a good idea you had. What made you get into what you're into now? I mean how did you get your own family? I know I'm asking a lot of questions, but it bothered me how you left like you did. I cried for days. It wasn't about the money either, it meant nothing to me. I thought we could talk about anything. All you had to do was tell me that you were dissatisfied and we could have worked something out. I had no idea you were that unhappy with what I was doing. If you would have stayed and we talked, maybe you could have talked some sense into me and everything wouldn't have turned out like it has. I'm not saying you're the blame for me doing what I did, I was stupid. My uncle took me in and looked after me like a daughter and what did I do? I almost killed him. I regret everything."

"We all do things we regret when we're young and foolish. We all think we're invincible. Look what me, you and Vincent did. My god, we were still wet behind the ears. To come up with a plan like that and pull it off... that was amazing. You want some lunch or something to drink? You know, when Lenny shot J.D., it opened the door for me and Vince. Thanks to you in a way."

Sonnie motioned for the waiter and he brought over two glasses of wine.

"If we would have found you that day, we wouldn't be having this conservation. Things change though and maybe that won't be necessary. Enough about me... now tell me your problem. Tell me, what kind of mess have you got yourself into? Remember how the old-timers did? They didn't panic, they waited for the right time then they struck quietly and swiftly. Like a cat waiting for a mouse. So tell me."

"I know what you're saying Sonnie, we came a long way since we were young. I'm hoping we can come to some agreement before you make any decision like that. I know I'm taking a big chance getting up with you. After all, I did try to do something stupid by taking up with Sal and Lenny. I wasn't thinking straight. I was greedy and just wanted everything, I guess I was getting power hungry. What did it get me? Aldo taught me that we all learn from our mistakes. Unfortunately, I didn't listen to what he was saying. Well here goes... After what happened that day with Lenny and J.D..."

"Not to interrupt, but where the hell did you disappear to? We looked everywhere, we tore this town upside down looking for you. Tell me how you slipped past us. I have to give you a lot of credit for that."

"After the shooting happened, I hid in the storage room behind the freezer. I almost got caught while I was in there. I could here Bobby walking over to check it out. I had a can of something in my hand and was going to try to fight my way out of there when the doctor came in to attend to J.D.. After that, no one came back to look in there again. I stayed there 'til everything got quiet, it must have been four or five hours. Then I took a cab to some little town about thirty miles away and caught a bus to New York. They hid me out for a while, but then they said it would be trouble for them if I was caught there, so I had to leave. That's when I got caught up in the situation I'm in now. Once again, I'm on the run because someone wants to kill me. I'm scared... I hate being scared. These people are dangerous."

"Yea... tell me who these characters are. First I want to know something, did you have anything to do with the hit on the families in New York and Philly? If you did, why New York? I thought they were your friends. You've got a lot of explaining to do."

"A so-called friend of mine introduced me to a couple Afghan soldiers that came here working as clerks in one of those big department stores. They took me in as one of their own after my friend told them who I was. He assured them that he thought we could work together because they're big into the drug thing. Little did I know they were members of the Muslim underground. They're terrorists. There are three groups of them, two in New York and one in Philly. I was scared to death after I found that out. I tried to distance myself from them but they wouldn't let me. They figured that if they could take over the families in New York and Philly, that would give them a lot of clout. I called my friends in New York but they didn't believe me. I didn't know anyone in Philly to call, so I took off after they did the hit and I've been running ever since. That's why I came to you for help."

"What do you expect me to do? Why do you think I should do anything at all? You know they won't stop 'til they find you."

"I was hoping you might have some special people working for you that could take care of my problem. There's about fifteen members in each group. I know where their headquarters are and where the leaders live. Most of them have good paying jobs but they spend all their money on drugs, mostly heroin. They're trying to set something up. I don't know what it is but all I know, it could hurt a lot of people."

"Why didn't you go to your friends instead of calling them? Why didn't you tell them who you talked to and that he didn't believe you? I'm sure they would be reasonable. You know, it's always better to talk face to face instead of making a phone call. Tell me this… are you using? If you are… there's no deal, I can tell you that right now. I have no use for that."

"Sonnie, I may have sold drugs in the past, but I was never a user then and I'm not one now. Besides, you loose control when you use drugs. I don't care how strong you think you are, the drugs always win. You always preached that to me. As far as the people in New York, my trust in them was lost after that. I was thinking that if I went to them, they wouldn't believe an outsider, so I decided to try to get some help from you. I was hoping I would be able to explain everything to you and you would see that I'm not giving you the runaround. Besides, I would like to patch things up with my uncle. I realize that he may never trust me again, but in time, if he gives me a chance, he'll see that I can be trusted. Everyone's due another chance."

"I'm glad to hear you talking like that. Here's what I need from you. I need the location of all the places and names of these so called terrorists and who their leaders are. If I have them checked out and if everything's on the up and up, then I'll help you. Now go, get me the stuff I need so I can get working on it. Call as soon as you have everything in order."

"I have everything. What can you do against them? They have no mercy…I mean, they're brutal. They'll kill anyone, I've seen them in action. You remember that bank robbery in Manhattan when the robbers killed nine people after they gave the robbers what they wanted? That was them. They didn't have to kill them. They just did it to make a statement. You've got to be very careful. If they suspect that I'm giving you this information, they'll hunt me and you down, no matter what we do. They won't rest 'til they get revenge."

"Look, you came to me for help didn't you? Now let me take care of this. I already have a plan which I know will work. Just trust me, you'll be safe. I think I can do this without getting involved myself. If it works out, we'll all be safe."

Maria got up to leave and Sonnie watched her walk away,' *Shame on me for what I'm thinking. I wonder what the name of that body soap is. Sure did smell good. I wonder what it felt like on her skin. This isn't what she looked like when we were young. Maybe if she did… Mama Mia.*' All the while they had sat at the table Sonnie noticed this guy kept staring at them. He thought it was just someone admiring Maria's beauty but when she left, he got up and followed. Sonnie got concerned thinking about the possibilities that someone could have followed her there. He jumped up and darted out the door after him only to see the man going in a different direction. Still, Sonnie followed him and after a couple blocks, the guy met up with a woman. They hugged and got into a cab and left. False alarm.

Sonnie waited patiently for Maria to bring him the information they had discussed. In the meantime, he put in a call to Petey and asked what if anything, did he know about terrorists groups. Petey wasn't much help but said he would check things out. He told Sonnie that he knew some people around and if anything was going on with them here, they would surely know. Petey asked Sonnie why he wanted this information. Sonnie brought him up-to-date on the situation with Maria and told him that he wanted to do everything he could to help her.

"After what she did to you and her uncle?" Petey asked. "Why would you want to help her? That don't make no sense. She's not reliable... I can sense it. She'll betray you. I got bad vibes about this Sonnie, but if that's what you want to do, I'll do my best to find out what I can. You know anything about these types of people? I hope you're not going to try to take this on by yourself. Tell me you're not. What ideas do you have? Help me out here Sonnie... Tell me something. Does Vince know anything about this?"

"Calm down, she's giving me all the information she has on them: names, addresses and so forth. That will give me the upper hand. Vince is away right now. When he gets back, I'll fill him in on everything. Look, I already have a good idea of how to handle this problem, which will probably not involve us at all. I know you think I'm just doing this because she's helpless. There's more to it than that. Someday I'll explain it to you. Just help me out on this one... if you can."

Sonnie hung up from talking to Petey and as he walked across the room towards the bar, the phone rang. It was Maria. She told Sonnie that she had the information he had requested and wanted to know how soon he wanted it. Did he want her to bring it to him or what did he want her to do?

"I didn't expect you to call so soon. You in a hurry or something?"

"I told you Sonnie, I'm scared. If they find me, I'm dead. I need some protection. I don't have anybody else to turn to. You're my last chance... if you don't help me and soon, I hate to think what they'll do when they find me. I've been staying here too long and it wouldn't surprise me if they didn't already know where I am. Meet me and get this information so you can get things started. The sooner you do, the sooner I'll feel like I can breath easier."

"You know where I live, I'm sure. Bring the stuff here."

"I'd rather you meet me somewhere. That way if they're following me, they won't know who you are and where you live. I don't want to put you in danger."

"Look, at this point it doesn't matter much. If they're following you, they already know everything about me, so what does it matter?"

Maria arrives at Sonnies place and had all the information he wanted. He poured some wine and they went over all the documents and notes she had brought. Afterwards, while Maria was still there, Sonnie called Johnny Rocco in New York and Marco in Philly. Sonnie put the phone on three-way-calling and speaker so Maria could hear everything. He told them it was very important they come as soon as they could and that he had information about the murders in Philly and the attempted assignations on Johnny Rocco's bosses. They all agreed to be there Thursday. When Sonnie got off the phone, Maria told him that she was relieved and glad he was finally able to get the ball rolling.

""Look, I've been thinking," Sonnie went on to say. "Would you feel safer if you stayed here a while? You can stay in the guest suite downstairs. I'll take care of anything you need so you wouldn't have to go out."

"What about your lady-friend?" Maria asked. "What would she think about me staying here?"

Sonnie told her that Connie would understand because she trusted him and knew he wouldn't be having her there unless it pertained to business. Maria agreed to stay.

Sonnie broke out a bottle of vintage Italian wine from Italy and he and Maria sat around reliving the days when they were kids in Italy. By one-thirty in the morning, Sonnie thought it was time to turn in and so he showed Maria to her bedroom and he retreated upstairs to his master suite. A summer storm was passing overhead and the sound of the raindrops beating against the windows was almost tranquilizing. Sonnie turned out the light and settled in. Without warning, the soft rain turned into a full blown storm, pounding against the sides of the house with the wind blowing fiercely and accompanied by lightning and thunder. The lightning was coming fast and furious and the thunder was so loud, it shook the house. Sonnie turned and tossed but when he heard a noise in the room, he glanced over and saw Maria standing there. She was standing near the window and when the lightning would flash, he could see her naked silhouette.

"Sonnie, I'm still afraid of the storm. The lightning terrifies me."

Sonnie knew he shouldn't but he pulled back the covers and Maria crawled in beside of him. She felt safe in his arms. The storm lasted most of the night but Sonnie and Maria didn't hear any of it.

CHAPTER TWENTY-SIX

It was Thursday morning when Johnny Rocco and Marco arrived at the casino about the same time. Vince was still out of town, unaware of what was happening. Sonnie put a call in to him and Vince told him that whatever he did was alright with him but not to take any action if necessary, until he returned. Sonnie assured him that if it all turned out the way he thought it would they wouldn't be involved at all. That's the way they liked it, advise without compromise.

As usual, there was a nice spread of food and various wines in the conference room where they were to meet.

"Okay Sonnie, what's this information that's so important that we had to come here immediately?" Johnny asked. "What's it pertaining to? Does it have anything to do with the attempts on my boss?"

"I called you and Marco here just for that reason," Sonnie replied. "What I have to show you, will clear up all the questions we had as to who and why this all happened. I got this information from a real reliable source and I can depend on whatever this person says. What you do with this information is up to you. It will be your responsibility to take care of the problem. That's not to say, if we are needed we won't be by your side because we will. That's the way we work. I'd expect the same from you. I was taught if we all have involvement, we should all share the rewards. We don't want anything special. What I'm giving you is in good faith. If we don't watch out for each other, we don't have a chance of succeeding with what we want to do. If we're to keep control of all we have, we have to make a strong statement every time we make a move. We have to learn from the past. The way the old-timers… the mustache Pete's, the way they handled things. We should have learned from them. We've all had good teachers. You know… those who do not learn from history are doomed."

"Now what my informant has given me," Sonnie went on to say, "will help both organizations get to the bottom of why, what and who did this. Johnny, what we're dealing with here is a couple groups of Muslim radicals. Three groups, two in New York, and one in Philly. There's approximately fifteen men in each group. What they're doing is what the Russians and others have tried to do. Take from us what we have worked so hard to build. Our people before us took all the necessary steps and made a lot of sacrifices to get everything the way it is today. We need to make a statement to these people and others that try to take away what we have. Once they get a little bit of confidence, they'll try to get control of everything. What they want to do is, take over what we have, then do harm to this country and make it look like we had something to do with it. If they get this accomplished, it won't be safe for the Italian people in this country. I think we have to act fast and make examples of these Muslims or whatever they call themselves. The papers I'm giving you will tell you all their names and places where they work and live. I'm confident that when you understand this information I have for you, you'll want to act on it quickly."

Sonnie handed out the information to Johnny and Marco and after looking it over, Marco wanted to know how Sonnie came about getting this information. Sonnie told them that it was an old friend from Italy that came to him with it. Sonnie explained that he had grown up with this person and put his faith in whatever this person had to say.

Johnny scanned over the papers and listened intensely.

"Sonnie, the first time I met you and we talked, I sensed you did some things the way our predecessors did to some extent and that impressed me. The way you talked about family and what you learned growing up in the old country, makes me believe in you. I actually think you could run the whole deal if you wanted to. You know, be the head of all the families. They need a younger man with new ideas. As strong willed and with the wisdom you've acquired over the years, I think you're needed somewhere else other than here. We could use a strong leader and I'm going to put you in front of the commission. You're just what we need up there, new blood without any ties to anyone else. Oh, by the way... Gayle said to tell you hello. She can't say enough about you. You don't know how many times she refers to you in our conversations. It makes me jealous sometimes but I know she says those things out of respect for you, nothing else. She really appreciates what you've done for her."

"She's a good girl. She's been through a lot. We think a lot of her...she was a little rough around the edges when she first came to work for me. She's come a long way, I wouldn't want anything to happen to her. Gina and the girls love her. It took her a long time to come back after what happened to her."

"I know Sonnie... she told me the whole story. I've gained a lot of respect for you myself. You have a small crew but a loyal one. I see now, why Bobby doesn't want to come back with us. There's a lot to be learned from that."

"I have a lot of people working for me that don't even know they're working for me, if that makes any sense. I don't like to let everyone know who the boss really is. That way, they just do their jobs without wanting something in return. Me and Vince didn't want to be in the position we're in, but since we are, we'll make the best of it. We've learned to watch our friends sometimes even closer than we watch our enemies."

"Oh, you learned that from that movie about thirty years ago. You know the one with Brando in it."

"No, I learned it from my grandfather when I was a kid. By the way Johnny, no thanks to that offer. I'm not looking to complicate my life any more than it is right now. I appreciate the accolades Johnny, but what me and Vince have going on here, is all I need. I just want it to be peaceful for all of us. We've worked hard to get what we have and no son-of-a-bitch'n foreigners are going to come waltzing in here and just take it away. They don't know who they're fuck'n with. So what's it going to be guys?"

"I'm going back to Philly and look into this stuff you gave me," Marco answered. "We'll keep you informed as to what goes on. We'll handle this as soon as possible. It won't take us long to get to the bottom of this. They will pay for what they did to my cousins. That's right, two of the people they killed were my relatives. Now it's personal."

"Now don't get crazy Marco," Sonnie replied. "It's important you keep your head and don't do something stupid. Don't let Denny fly off the handle. We want to keep this as quiet as possible. Act swiftly, be precise and get the job done. Call me if you need anything."

With the meeting over, Johnny and Marco left to go back to their own situations. Sonnie felt confident that everything would be taken care of in the very near future. Johnny got back to New York and started right away rounding up the people that were on the list. Johnny's boss was grateful for what Sonnie had done for him. He called him to personally guarantee that everything would be handled without hesitation after they were thoroughly questioned as to what their purpose was. Marco on the other hand, was not interested nor did he care why they were here. He started immediately eliminating them one by one. First, there were four brothers found hanging in the basement of an abandoned house in the projects. In Marco's organization, one of his boys was an expert with a high-powered rifle and systematically took out five more. Marco's contact in the police department put out a bulletin to the newspapers saying they were racial shootings, so the city would not think there was a sniper going around shooting people at random. The others were eliminated in various ways. One shot to death while sitting in his car and another was run over while crossing the street. Down by the side of the river, two of the last four were found with their throats slit. The other two died from poison put in their drinks by two of the hookers on Marco's payroll.

While all this was going on, Sonnie called Don Aldo in Italy and informed him as to what had transpired when he met with Maria. He told Don Aldo that she wanted to make amends and wanted to return to Italy with him to make a fresh start. Sonnie asked Don Aldo if he thought there was any chance that he would take her back. It was the only thing she wanted, Sonnie told him. Sonnie also said that he had spent a great deal of time with her and he was certain she was remorseful.

"She confessed to me," Sonnie continued, "that the way she acted was all for power and she now realized it was wrong. She wants to make it up by standing by your side… if you'll have her… and work to make the family better. She also said she understood that when young Aldo got old enough, that he would be your choice to take over. Maria said she would work with him in everyway to make sure he didn't make the same mistake she did. I asked her if she was looking to get her old position in the family back, but she said, she wanted no part of that again. She knew that it wasn't the direction she wanted to go anymore. She said to betray the family is unholy."

"So," Don Aldo asked, "What do you think I should do Sonnie? What would your grandfather do? If you say you would take her back, tell me one good reason I should. You know what she did to me. Not only did she try to poison me and make it look like I lost my mind, but she tried to turn my family and everybody in the organization against me. It took me a long time and cost me a great deal of respect for letting that happen. It made me look weak. Luckily there were enough people left on my side so I could take back control." He paused for a moment, "How does she look?"

"Oddly enough Don Aldo, for some reason I thought she would look intimidating, but she look quite the opposite. She was very humble. I didn't get the impression she was willing, at any cost, to get what she wanted. She just said her piece and asked if I would talk to you. One reason for her acting this way, she's gotten herself in a pretty rough situation. She got herself involved with some characters that she thought she could control. They took what information she gave them and instead of them doing what she wanted, they turned on her and tried to take over the families in New York and Philly. They didn't succeed but it hurt the families here and she got scared and ran. Now these Muslims are after her. That's how she came back to me. I know what you're probably thinking, why would I be helping her. I don't know, just say I have a weak spot for her, I always did. We go back a long way. You know what we were involved in when we were young. Besides, she's your niece. That's the reason you should consider taking her back. She's family and sometimes they, no matter what they've done, deserve another chance. She's on borrowed time... if I can't get you to change your mind, I'll have to come up with another way. You can keep a close watch on her to make sure she's on the up-and-up. You know, give her six months. Just let her come to you and then you can judge for yourself, how far you can trust her. Let Little Aldo handle her. He's very wise for his age and she's pretty beat down right now. You've got to explain to him what she is and what she's done so he'll be on his toes while around her."

"It sounds like you've made my decision for me Sonnie...I think you're a good judge of character so I'm going to go with what you propose. I'm only going to tell you this... if she doesn't seem to me like she's willing to go with what I say, then other measures might have to be taken. I can't afford to let something bad happen again. Everyone will be watching closely. I cleaned up the organization after she left and I have it the way I want it now. I hope she realizes that all her old friends aren't here anymore. I'll talk to Little Aldo and see if he'll be willing to come to America and bring her back."

"Better yet Don Aldo, you've said you wanted to come for a visit. Why don't you come with him? You're well enough to make the trip now, besides... I would be honored for you to come. The weather here is perfect for a visit. I can show you around. You know, show you what we're doing with all that wine we're buying from you. Who knows, you might want to retire here some day. What'da you say?"

"I like that idea. Give me a week. I'm sure I can get everything taken care of by then. How's that sound? Little Aldo and I and a couple of my most trusted boys. We'll come by my plane."

"Great, I'll make all the arrangements for you to stay at the casino. You'll really be able to see the good life from there. I'll have everything ready. I'll see you then next week. Arrivederci Don Aldo."

Sonnie hung up the phone and chuckled, *'I hope he doesn't use the same pilots that flew us back. He'll be a basket case by the time he gets here. I wonder if those guys ever solved their problem.'*

When Vince arrives back home, Sonnie filled him in on everything that happened while he was away. Vince agreed with most everything Sonnie had done except he was disappointed that Sonnie had slept with Maria. Eventually, Vince told him that he understood and it was something that happened at the spare of the moment and was out of their control.

As Sonnie waited for Don Aldo's visit, he told Maria that he thought she should move into the casino instead of staying at his house. There, she wouldn't have to worry about her safety because there would be a lot of people looking out for her as opposed to staying at his house alone. The main thing was her safety but Maria refused saying she had just rented a little house and it had a very good security system and she felt safe there. Meanwhile, Johnny Rocco called Sonnie and told him that they had gotten all the people on the list, except they were having trouble finding two of them, the ones that were supposed to be the leaders of the group. Johnny went on to say that they had tried every way possible to convince their captors to give up the last two but said they just wouldn't budge, no matter what they did to them. Johnny concluded by telling Sonnie that they were all put still alive, into a container on the docks and buried so deep, it would take twenty years to find them.

CHAPTER TWENTY-SEVEN

Thursday came very fast and Don Aldo, young Aldo and two of young Aldo's older cousins Donato and Renato arrived safely. Vince and Sonnie were there to greet them at the airport. As they were getting off the plane, Don Aldo was shaking his head and cussing in Italian. Vince and Sonnie were laughing because they knew what all the cussing was about.

"Some ride huh, Don Aldo?" Sonnie asked as Don Aldo made his way off the plane. He reached out and steadied the aging Don as he reached the bottom of the stairs.

"I swore I would never ride with them again after the last time. The son-of-a-bitches are crazy," he replied as he hugged Sonnie and then Vince.

"Did they ever straighten out that thing about the pregnant daughter?"

"No, they're still arguing about it. It's almost committing suicide riding with them. I told them to go back home...we'd take a damn boat. Now get me out of here. I'm a wreck."

Sonnie and Vince had come to pick them up at the airport in a twelve passenger stretch limo. Don Aldo had never seen such a thing and he wanted to know all about it. He was amazed at all the things inside, television, telephone, bar, all the plush carpet and the leather upholstery. He especially liked the Italian music playing on the surround-sound.

It was about noon when they arrived at the casino. Don Aldo kept running into people because he was so busy looking around at all the glamour. When they got up to the penthouse, he was really in ah. The size alone was too much for him to imagine, plus the way it was decorated with the sunken living room and floor to ceiling glass windows on two sides. Don Aldo thought he was in Hollywood with the view of the city and all the signs lit up, he wanted to know why they wasted so much electricity. Sonnie told Don Aldo that after he had rested up a little and had something to eat, they would take him and show him around.

"Who needs to rest? I want to eat in that good restaurant down stairs and then see those girls in that dancing show young Aldo told me about."

The day was long and everyone was dragging except Don Aldo. It was like letting a person with a sweet tooth, loose in a chocolate factory. They finally got him back to his room about two in the morning and for a man of seventy plus years, he sure showed up the young guns. He laughed at them for being so pooped out.

The next morning at six-o-clock sharp, Don Aldo was banging on the adjoining door of young Aldo's bedroom trying to find some espresso. When young Aldo didn't answer, he decided to go to the restaurant himself but when he opened the door of his suite to go downstairs, there stood a man so big that he took up the whole doorway, guarding the door.

"What the hell you doing at my door? Movimento, movimento. (Move, move)"

When the guard just looked at him and stood his ground, Don Aldo slammed the door and went back inside. This time without knocking, he went back to young Aldo's room and shook him until he woke up.

"What the hell's going on?" young Aldo said angrily. "Oh, it's you Gramps."

"There's someone in front of the door and he won't let me get by."

Cousins II

"Where you going at this hour, Gramps? The man out front was put there by Sonnie. He's one of Bull's men. He won't hurt you... he's there to protect you. Why didn't you call me if you wanted something? You know I know my way around here. Why you up so early?"

"Why all the questions? I'm hungry, at home I can get something to eat anytime I want. I don't know if I like this place. All I want is some salami and eggs and some espresso. What's so hard about that? I don't understand, help me Son."

That was the first time he had called young Aldo son, and he didn't know how to answer.

"Let me call down to the restaurant and have them bring up something for you." he replied.

"No, I want to eat there so I can see all the people."

Little Aldo hurried to get dressed so he could take Don Aldo to the restaurant for breakfast and the guard followed them, just as Sonnie instructed.

All day Friday and Saturday, Sonnie and Vince were busy taking Don Aldo to all the places where they did business and he was very impressed how they ran their organization. He especially liked being in the bakery because it reminded him of home with the old world décor and he was pleasantly surprised how good the pastries were. Friday night, young Aldo had taken his grandfather to see the show girls he had told him about when they were in Italy. He wouldn't stay in his seat and kept walking towards the stage. Young Aldo had to put him in his seat several times. Don Aldo insisted on returning to the show again on Saturday. Sonnie and Vince arranged to have all the troops over to Sonnie's house on Sunday. That's when Sonnie was going to bring Maria to Don Aldo. He thought that if everyone was there having a good time, it wouldn't be as tense for either of them.

Meanwhile, Johnny Rocco was still trying to find the missing two militants and was having no luck. When he called Sonnie and told him that he thought they had left New York, Sonnie in turn called Chico and told him of the situation. He told him to be on the look out for anyone that fit that profile trying to by drugs... especially heroin. Chico put the word out on the streets but there was no one fitting that description that Sonnie had given him. He assured Sonnie that he would talk to the other dealers and warn them what the consequences would be if they didn't let him know if any strangers were inquiring to buy heroin. Sonnie didn't say anything to Maria about the two missing militants because he didn't want to alarm her... if it wasn't absolutely necessary.

Sunday rolled around and it was a beautiful day with a bright blue sky and pearly white clouds that almost seemed to stand still. The slight breeze made the seventy-five degree temperature seem cooled that it really was. Sonnie was up bright and early because it was a very important day. It was the day Maria would be reunited with her uncle. It was the first time in a long time, Sonnie stopped in front of a set of rosary beads hanging in his hallway. He knelt down and made the sigh of the cross and he said part of a prayer that he learned when he was a small child and his grandmother would take him to church. Sonnie wanted this day to be perfect but he knew that if it was, it wouldn't be because of his prayers.

The caterers arrived at ten o'clock and the troops were to begin showing up about twelve. Vince was to get Don Aldo at noon. Once he got to Sonnie's house and introduced to everyone, Sonnie would go and pick Maria. Everything was going as planned. Don Aldo remembered Connie and Theresa from being in Italy and was glad to see they were alright. Although he didn't have to, he apologized to them for what had happened while they were staying at his home. He loved Gina and all the girls that worked at the Clip Joint. He told them he would like to spend the day there before he went back home and everyone laughed.

"You Italian men are all alike," Gina replied.

Sonnie's cell phone rang... it was Chico. He told Sonnie he had gotten a call from a connection he had with some outlaw-bikers. He went on to say that they had sold some H to a couple of funny looking guys and thought they might be the ones they were looking for. Sonnie turned to Vince and told him about the call and that he was going to get Maria, just in case they were the missing militants. Sonnie asked Connie to go with him, but she declined and suggested he take someone else. Just as Sonnie was about to ask Little Aldo, Connie grabbed him by the arm and said she had changed her mind and wanted to go.

'If he wants me to go with him, he must have told me the truth when he said they were just friends. This is the first time I feel like he really cares about me,' Connie thought. Sonnie called Maria and told her that he and Connie would be there in about thirty minutes to pick her up. Maria felt a little hesitant about Connie coming but she understood that the night of the storm was just something that happened.

When Sonnie and Connie arrived at the house Maria was renting, they could hear what sounded like a struggle going on inside. Sonnie tried to open the door but it was locked.

"KICK IT IN!" Connie shouted.

Sonnie kicked in the door and ran inside, Connie behind him. Just off the foyer in the large living room, the two militants had Maria pinned down on the sofa, one holding her as the other was beating her. Sonnie noticed a leather bag on the table beside the sofa with what looked like a syringe sticking out of it. As Sonnie pulled his gun and yelled for them to stop, one of them turned and fired a shot towards them. Without hesitation, Sonnie fired two shots and both of the men went down. He ran over to Maria to see how badly she was hurt and as Sonnie turned to Connie for help, he saw her slumped down in a chair holding her shoulder. Sonnie left Maria and ran to her and held her in his arms. Maria made her way over to Connie. She looked at Connie's shoulder and assured her that she didn't think it was too bad. As Sonnie regained his composure and got Connie to sit up, he could see that the bullet had passed all the way through. He asked Maria if she could get him a cold rag or something to put over the wound until they could get back to his house. As Maria turned to go to the kitchen, she saw one of the men laying on the floor that Sonnie had shot, aiming his gun right at Sonnie. She yelled at Sonnie and as she stepped in front of him, he fired. In an instant, Sonnie turned… only to see Maria go down. He shot the bastard three more times and rushed to Maria's side. He gently turned her over. Maria was dead and Sonnie slumped to his knees.

When they arrived back at the house, they went to the pool area where everyone was waiting, expecting Sonnie and Connie to bring back Maria. Connie opened the gate and Sonnie walked in, carrying Maria's dead body. Claudia was the first to see them.

"OH MY GOD!!!" She screamed.

Everyone turned to see what all the commotion was about. Bull ran over and took Maria from Sonnie's arms and laid her on a lounge chair. Maria had a partial smile on her face and with the sun shining on her, it look as if she was having a pleasant dream. Don Aldo, speechless... dropped into his chair in disbelief. All the girls started crying and Gina went to Connie to see what she could do for her.

"Vince, call the doctor so he can come to take care of Connie. Those bastards got there just before us. If we were ten minutes sooner, none of this would have happened. I guess they were going to shoot her up with heroin when we broke in."

Sonnie turned to Bobby and told him to take Angelo and Bull over to Maria's house. There was some cleaning up to do and they would need to leave right away.

"I don't know...it all happened so fast. Gina how's she holding up? Damn it, I'm sorry Don Aldo. I thought I had everything under control. The next thing I know, another shot took Maria down. She stepped in front of me. I thought I killed them both the first time."

"It's alright Sonnie," Don Aldo said as he reached his hand for Sonnie's. "Don't blame yourself for this. You know what she was and the mess she got herself into. You tried...maybe too hard to make this thing work. You can't blame yourself for what's happened. Maybe it's for the best. Just take care of Connie... I will take care of the rest.

The doctor came right away. The injury to Connie's shoulder wasn't too serious after all, it seemed to be just a flesh wound. The trip for pleasure turned into one of heartache for Don Aldo. He made arrangements to take Maria back home to Italy. He would bury her next to her father. The next day, on the bottom of the front page of the newspaper was an article that read: 'Firemen responded to a house fire about two in the afternoon. The house was burned to the ground. Inside, they found two bodies that were burned beyond recondition. The cause of the fire is under investigation at this time.'

CHAPTER TWENTY-EIGHT

    For several days afterwards, Sonnie walked around like the life was taken out of him. Connie stayed by his side the whole time, knowing there was more to Sonnie and Maria's relationship then was let on. She would never know just how much they had meant to each other. Vince took care of the business while Sonnie was away. The girls went back to work at the Clip Joint and Bull put his car lot back the way it was. Business for everyone else was back to normal.

    Two weeks went by and Sonnie did nothing but hang out on the boardwalk. He'd go there every day in the morning and not come home until dark. Everyone was starting to get worried about him. When they tried to help him, he just withdrew even more, so Vince and the troops decided to continue to do business the best they could without him and let him work things out by himself. Connie was at her wits end with him, it seemed nothing was good enough. He'd put down everything she tried to do for him. Finally, she got tired of his negative attitude and decided to leave him alone and let him do what he had to do. She knew it would only be a matter of time and he would bounce back and be the same old Sonnie again.

Libero A. Tremonti

Every time Sonnie would stand at the railing and look out over the ocean, he would see Maria's face... smiling at him. *'I'm sorry for what I did and I hope everyone will forgive me."* This just haunted him, it made him feel guilty for what happened. One day, leaning over the rail in sort of a trance and starring out at the ocean, he felt something tugging at his pants. He looked down only to see a little girl about five years old with black wavy hair, big black eyes and a dark olive complexion. It looked as if she could have been Italian or Greek.

"Hey mister, you're not going to jump in the water are you? If you do, all the people that love you won't have nothing to love anymore. Please don't jump," she pleaded.

From a bench behind them, the little girl's mother called out, "Leave`a da man alone Marie... venire qui (come here)"

The little girl went skipping back to her mother and they walked away. It was just the wake-up call Sonnie needed. When he turned from the railing, he saw a flower stand with a bright red and yellow umbrella and slowly walked over to it. There were carnations and daisies, all neatly wrapped in little bunches but Sonnie was drawn to all the different roses and had never realized there were so many different colors. He told the young girl selling the flowers, he had heard once that each color of the roses stood for something but he couldn't remember what. With Maria on his mind, he bought one yellow rose for their friendship, one white rose for their innocence when they were young, and one red rose for the passion he had for her. He walked back to his spot on the boardwalk and threw them into the water, making the sigh of the cross.

"You'll always be in my thoughts, Maria." He smiled and walked away.

Sonnie was whistling as he walked into the bakery. Theresa was taking inventory at the wine section and Sonnie playfully smacked her on the butt. He then walked over to Connie who was waiting on Mrs. O'delli, picked Connie up and gave her a big kiss.

"My... my... aren't you the lucky one," Mrs O'deli smiled as she paid for her order.

Vince hearing all the commotion from the office came to see what all the noise was. Sonnie walked over to him and gave him a big hug.

"I'm glad to see him back," Connie told Theresa as the men walked back to the office.

Vince was relieved also, even though he could handle everything without him, it was nice having the other half of the team back.

"Tell me what I've missed Vinny. What's been going on? Everybody, okay?"

"Everything's fine Sonnie. Business is going rather smoothly... no glitches. Everyone was wondering when you were going to snap out of the funk you were in. You were starting to give us some concerns. Don Aldo called a couple times to see how you were holding up. He's the one that told us to quit trying to make you see you weren't the blame and to leave you alone. So we took his advice and it worked. I guess he knew what he was saying. He said they buried Maria next to her father and would see to it that her place was taken care of because he knew you would want it that way. Johnny Rocco sent his condolences and Marco wanted to know if he should come down."

"How did they know what the hell was going on here? This is our business... nothing that concerned them. Is there something here I'm missing Vinny?"

"Don't be so touchy, coump (friend), I guess word gets around. I don't see any harm in that. Its better they're concerned than not giving-a-shit. I think it's a good thing. I think things are different now. People are different now. To keep our triangle in tact, we have to care about what's going on... it affects all of us. How can we keep control when we don't know anything? We don't want to be left in the dark about things anymore... do we? I expect they don't either."

"I guess you're right Vinny. I guess I'm still a little touchy. I appreciate everything you've done while I was fucked-up in the head. I always knew I would have nothing to worry about. I know a lot of times, you sit there and don't say what you're thinking, I know you do it out of respect. I'm your little cousin and I know I started this thing but from now on, you have just as much right to things as I have."

"Since you brought that up Sonnie, I've been thinking about something. When you get back to normal, we'll talk about it."

"I'm okay... let's talk about it now. I want to know what you're thinking. Any changes will be good for the organization if it makes things run smoother. I've been wanting to turn more of the responsibility to you... if you'll have it. I trust you Vinny more than anything in the world. After all this stuff that's been going on, I've been thinking of stepping back a little. With your help, I'll be able to do this. I've got to start taking more time for myself and not let all this bullshit get to me. I don't want you to hold back anymore, whether you think I'm going to like it or not. What'da you think? How's that sound?"

"It's about time. You've been killing yourself trying to take care of all this bullshit, as you put it. Just let me help you. When I first came here, I didn't know how you would act... me giving you my ideas. Not that I would have done things too much differently. Sonnie, I'm your blood. Nothing should come before that."

"Okay paisano, tell me your idea."

"Well, that meeting you had with everyone from the other organizations. I think it was a great idea. I also think... if we could organize a meeting like that once a month, just to keep up on things, it would be good for all parties concerned. Have it in a different place each time. They come here, we go there...you know, that kind of stuff."

"That's a great idea but if it were up to me, I would have them come here every time. That way, we would have the upper hand and we wouldn't have to worry about someone setting us up. You know, all there has to be is one crazy wise guy and the whole thing goes up in smoke. We're in no position to just go out there and trust everyone. By that I mean... we don't have enough people to go around spying on all the other people concerned. We've got to be very careful if we're going to be involved in something like that. When all's said and done, I think it's something worth considering. I have a question for you Vinny, what about this thing with Chico? What do you think we should do? Should we get involved with that or pass?"

"Well Sonnie, I see it this way. The drug thing is here to stay. We can't fight it anymore. This a great opportunity for us to be involved with it, while not being involved directly, if you know what I mean. He called me the other day while you were away and suggested that we should have another talk. Chico said he thought we would have the city virtually wrapped up. He said they have the La Hermandad (the brotherhood) and we have the La Famiglia (the family). Working together, we could have it all. Bull said it reminded him of something his mother taught him. When the Romans united, they became invincible. You know Sonnie, the thing I've been concerned about is, what you were saying about us being such a small group. It's unheard of... doing all we're doing. We have to watch everything going on around us... we can't relax. With Chico controlling that part of it, it'll be one thing we don't have to be concerned about anymore. He has no interest in gambling and wants us to take control of the whole strip so he won't have to worry about anyone coming for him because of the drugs. The drugs will be out of our area and you know how it goes, out of sight out of mind. The only thing that worries me about the whole thing is... if we can trust him."

"We'll have to take our chances but I think we should give it some time to see if it'll work. If it doesn't, we'll have to deal with that at a later time. I don't believe I'm saying this Vinny, after I drove myself crazy all these years trying to destroy anybody that had anything to do with drugs. Now I'm going to team up with someone that's a drug lord, so to speak. I'm glad I finally got over this shit with Maria and everything is going smoothly, thanks to you. Man, my head was really screwed up. Let's try to live it up a little. Fuck Rando... if he turns up, we'll deal with it then. I'm going to put him out of my mind and concentrate on making everything run smoothly around here. I think I owe Connie an explanation about what happened with Maria. After all, she's been through a lot between what happened in Italy, shooting that piece-of-shit in the bakery and being shot herself. I don't know how she's handling all of it. I need to just be with her alone for a while. You think you can handle everything? That was a stupid question. Now why did I even ask that? I think I'm really losing it. It'll be only for a couple more days while I take her somewhere. What'da you think Vinny?"

"Great idea. Everything's quiet and under control. You take her and take as long as you like. Hell, marry her… no on the other hand…don't do that, I want to be there when that goes down. Don't make any plans, don't pack anything, just grab her and go. Well, what are you waiting for? Go, the troops are here and everything's secure. Check this out Sonnie before you go. You know Petey had those damn hamsters right? Well, when he went to that storage place where he had them, he opened the door and they ran out all over the place. He could only find about half of them. He was a wreck for about a week after that. He went back to Jamaica with his tail between his legs. Oh…do you want me to talk to Chico or wait till you get back?"

"Whatever you feel comfortable with. I'll only be gone for a couple of days. If you think it's that urgent to get this thing done, go ahead. I have no problem with you handling it. That Petey is a mess. I wondered what happened to those little rats. If everything's cool, I'm out of here. Arrivederci (good-bye)."

Sonnie gave Vince a hug and returned to the bakery where Connie was stacking the pastry case.

"Take off your apron. We're getting out of here for a couple of days."

As Connie laid her apron on the counter and she and Sonnie were walking out, Theresa noticed Vince standing at the office door. He winked at Theresa and she knew everything was going to be okay.

"What's this all about?" Connie wanted to know. "Where we going? I can't leave Theresa to take care of the bakery by herself. What's going on Sonnie?"

"Don't worry honey, everything's been taken care of. Vince is going to stay with Theresa and make sure she has everything she needs. She'll be fine. We're going to get away for a day or two. We need it…I need it. I need to talk with you about some things and it would be better if we're somewhere that we can relax and see things with a clear head. We're just going. We're not going to pack anything or even go to our places before we leave. We're just going."

Sonnie called ahead and reserved a suite at one of the hotels right on the ocean. When they arrive at the hotel, it was extremely crowded because it was the first weekend that the temperatures were going to be in the mid-seventies to high eighties. That didn't bother Sonnie because he had his mind made up he was going to convince Connie in no uncertain terms, what she meant to him. Before checking in, they stopped at a little diner for some lunch. It was very noise there and seemed like every family had two or three little kids, running wild. Sonnie remarked to Connie how cute they were and that he couldn't believe how anyone could hurt such innocent little creatures. No matter what they did, spill their drinks, run around the tables or hit each other, it didn't bother Sonnie. Connie thought that was strange because Sonnie was always on edge. Normally, he would have gotten up and walked away from all the commotion... but he just smiled. After they ate, Sonnie wanted to walk on the beach. They took off their shoes and frolicking in the surf like two children without a care in the world. Connie couldn't believe how relaxed he was, and how he was like a different person.

"What's this all about Sonnie?" Connie asked looking him straight in the eye. "Why all the sudden turn-around?"

"We're here because there are some things I need to get straighten out with you."

"Tell me Sonnie, is something wrong? Have I done something I don't know about? Let me know and I'll correct it."

"It's not about you, it's me. I want to tell you about Maria and our relationship. You see..."

"You don't have to explain anything about that to me. I've put all that out of my mind. It's over... so just let it disappear."

"I want you to tell you everything from the beginning. I think you should know. It'll help our relationship be stronger. I know you're wondering about some things. If it were reversed, I wouldn't rest 'til I knew everything."

"That's where we're different. Sonnie, I love you. I think you already know that. That thing with her...it's over now. She's gone and out of our life. As far as I'm concerned, she didn't even exist, so if we can leave it at that, it would be fine with me."

"You mean, there isn't anything that's bothering you about what happened? I'd have all kinds of questions for you to answer. There's got to be something bothering you. I can't believe there isn't."

"Since you won't shut up about this... and I can tell you're not satisfied with what I've said, there is one question I have. Here goes. When she spent those last days before the shooting at your house, did anything happen between you and her? I want the truth. I can handle the truth. I know you were with her sometime in your life. After all, you grew up together and hung out as kids and I know how that can be. Like I said, she doesn't even exist to me. So don't lie, just tell me in one word, you don't have to go into detail."

"What are you asking me? You asking me if we slept together? What...once, twice? I don't get it. One minute you say it doesn't matter, now you're giving me the third degree."

"Hold on here! You're the one that kept asking me if there was anything I wanted to know. So I ask and what happens? You get you ass in an uproar. I don't know what you want from me. Just forget about it.... No, don't forget about it. You brought it up... so answer me."

Sonnie calmed down and took a deep breath. "Look Connie, I brought you here because I thought you would want to know some things. Apparently I was wrong. I want our relationship to become more involved. I told Vincent I was going to cut back and divide the time for the business between the two of us from now on. That way, we can have more time to be together. I want that... I've wasted too much time as it is."

"That sounds good to me, you already know how I feel about us. When we came back from Italy, I was ready to end it for us but I just couldn't get myself to go. What happened there scared me. Then what happened in the bakery... well, I don't know what to say about that. I guess I just reacted. So let's just wipe the slate clean and start over. You don't have to tell me a damn thing if you don't want to. It's your choice."

"I'll tell you anyway. I'll give you the answer in one word, as you asked. NO... the answer is NO."

They spent the rest of that day and night in the suite. They showed their love for each other many times over. Sonnie believed Connie trusted him fully. In the back of her mind, Connie was convinced that he had only given her the answer he thought she wanted to hear.

CHAPTER TWENTY-NINE

Sonnie and Connie returned home from their trip to the shore. Sonnie had done everything he could think of, to show how Connie he felt about her but Connie on the other hand, had her doubts. Still, she felt she had to stay just to see how everything was going to work out. When Connie talked to Theresa, she told her what a wonderful time they had at the beach, what little time they saw of it. She told Theresa how romantic Sonnie had tried to be but she knew at times, his mind was somewhere else. Connie told Theresa that she was going to stay for the long haul. Theresa was excited to hear that and told Connie that she and Vince had celebrated his connecting with Sonnie and hoped it would make things run smoother. Sonnie leveled with Vince telling him although he went away with Connie to get rid of Maria's memory, he couldn't do anything without thinking about her.

"How long do you think this is going to go on Vinny? I can't go on this way. I think I'll go nuts. I'm just leading Connie on and not being truthful with her. What do I do? I tried the best I could not to let it show, but at times I know Connie knew my mind was somewhere else. She did all she could not to show it but I could sense she knew. After all she's been through because of me, I go and treat her like this."

Cousins II

"Look Sonnie... that's bullshit, she's no dummy. Connie's a lot smarter than any of us give her credit for. She knows the score. I think if she didn't want to be with you, she would have been gone a long time ago. The same with Theresa. They're tough broads... they can handle it. What we've got to do is concentrate on business. I think all this bullshit that happened, happened for a reason. It happened to make us stronger and I think it did for the most part. If you don't mind me saying so Sonnie, I think you're focusing on all the wrong things. You better get your mind back on business and not worry about Connie. That shit will take care of it's self. If you need more time to get yourself together... take it. Otherwise, get your head out of your ass and start thinking straight."

"You don't understand Vinny."

"Understand my ass. Maria comes over here to kill you. When that doesn't work, she gets involved with... as Bull puts it, some sand-niggers. They try to wipe out the other families so she could get her power back. That's all it was about with her and you know it. She fucks that up, then she comes crying on your shoulder and you take her back with open arms. Gramps probably flipped over in his grave. Where's your head?"

"She saved my life Vinny. She took the bullet that was meant for me. Am I just supposed to forget about that? I can't... I won't."

"Well then, remember what I'm telling you. If you don't snap out of it and concentrate on what's in front of you, you're going to get your ass jammed up. It only takes one mistake. I shouldn't have to tell you that. You're always preaching that to everyone else. Why don't you take your own advice? You know what we need? We need to go out with the boys and get shit-faced. I mean tie one on that we won't forget. What'da you say? Should I call the boys or what? "

"Do it Vinny, I think you're right. I have to start thinking straight again. I've lost focus. I've never been so mixed up. Emotional problems...they'll wear your ass out. I've got to get back to where I was before all this shit with Maria happened... and by the way, I appreciate your honesty."

Bobby, Angelo, Bull, Vince and Sonnie paint the town red. They hit every casino and strip joint in town. They were asked to leave several of them and did so without incident. The whole night, Bull kept watching for the drug dealers on the strip. He remarked to Vince that he couldn't see anyone selling or trying to sell. Sonnie was curious about that until Vince told him he had talked with Chico about what they discussed before he and Connie had left for the beach and Chico had already started the ball rolling. Sonnie wanted to know what their cut was going to be.

"Now that's the Sonnie I know," Vince remarked with relief.

As the night wore on, it seemed like in almost every casino they went to, in would walk this pimp character with his entourage of ladies. After asking around, they learned his name was Rico, a real throw-back from the nineteen-seventies, Miami. He had a ruddy completion and blonde-graying hair wore a loud printed shirt half unbuttoned and gold chains hanging around his neck. He topped off the look with white pants and white shoes. He had two large Samoan bodyguards with him that looked pretty rough. They were about six-two, three hundred pounds with hair pulled back in a knot and looked as if they had never smiled in their life. Bull wanted to have a little talk with Rico but Vince told him it wasn't their problem anymore and put a call into Chico to tell him what they were seeing. The troops continued having a good time and wondered how Chico was going to handle the situation. This would be a good test for him and if he handled it the right way, Sonnie and Vince would know they made the right choice.

The next day, Bobby read in the paper where the bodies of the two Samoans were found in an alley off the strip with three bullets each to the head. There was no mention of their boss and there were no leads at the time.

It was around noon when Sonnie and Vince arrived at the office. Bobby showed them the article in the paper and they knew then, Chico meant business. They liked it that way. Sonnie walked into the bakery and asked if there was any fresh coffee. Connie told him to take the pot and go back in his office before he scared the customers.

Sonnie smiled as he grabbed the fresh pot of coffee, "I love you too."

Back in the office, Bobby, Vince and Sonnie had the blueprints for the casino project laid out on the desk. When the phone rang, Bobby answered it and immediately handed the phone to Sonnie.

"It's J.D.'s wife," he whispered. "She sounds a little upset."

"How's everything there? We haven't heard from you in a while. How's J.D.? Is he there?"

"He's not doing well at all, it's all your fault. If you didn't send that guy out here, he wouldn't be in the trouble he's in. You better come out here and take care of the damage you did to my husband."

"Wait... hold on," Sonnie replied as he pressed the phone's speaker button. "What are you talking about? What guy? What kind of trouble is he in?"

"He wouldn't tell me the guy's name, but ever since he came here, J.D.'s been spending like crazy. He takes money everyday from our stash and I'm afraid he's going to blow it all. He's gotten into drugs and you know how he's always felt about that. He stays out for days at a time and comes home when I'm not here and leaves before I get back. I've took all the money we had in the bank and hid it so he won't blow it away at the tables. He even hit me once when I questioned him about what was going on. I'm sorry I called but I don't know what to do. His hip's hurting him so bad, I don't know how he's doing what he's doing. I didn't have anyone else to turn to. We don't have any friends any more. They all stay away because of the way he treats them. He's mean to everybody."

"How long has this been going on?"

"About a month. I'm afraid after all our money is gone, this guy will leave us high and dry. All he wants to do is party, gamble and play with the girls. He really has J.D. snowed... J.D. thinks he's cool."

"You don't know who this guy is?" Vince asked. "Who told you we sent him?"

"J.D. told me he worked for you and was sent out here to lay low for a while. That didn't make any sense to me. Why would he be running wild like that if he was to lay low? He said you told him to tell J.D. to give him anything he wanted and you would take care of it later. I told J.D. from what I remembered about you, you don't operate that way but he told me not to question anything this guy said. Tell me what to do, please... before it's too late."

"Stay right there, I'll call you right back."

Sonnie hung up the phone. "It's got to be that bastard Rando. Who else would have the balls to do that? I knew he would show himself sooner than later. What'da you think Vinny?"

"I think we better get our asses out there and see for ourselves if it's him or not. If it is, it'll be our lucky day."

Sonnie and Vince asked Bobby if he and Angelo would be able to take care of things 'til they got back, if they went to Vegas. Bobby assured them that with Angie and Bull being there for emergencies, he thought everything would be fine. They called Theresa and Connie into the office and told them what was going on and that they wouldn't be going with them to Vegas. Both of the girls agreed that they would be better off staying and looking after things at the bakery. Deep down, they both knew if it was going to be anything like their trip to Italy, they definitely didn't care about making the trip to Vegas. Sonnie called J.D.'s wife back and told her they would be there in the morning and not to tell J.D. they were coming. When she asked why she couldn't tell him, Sonnie told her he would explain everything when they got there and for her to trust him.

The girls quickly got on the phone to book the flights for Sonnie and Vince, but tell them the only flight they could get with such short notice, was to Los Angeles leaving the next day at noon. This frustrated Sonnie because he wanted to leave right away and he had already told J.D.'s wife they'd be there in the morning.

"This thing can't wait 'til tomorrow," Sonnie explained. "Why don't we look into getting a private jet so we can leave right away?"

"Hold on a minute Sonnie," Vince told him. "I think it's a good idea to take the flight to L.A. The drive to Vegas is only about two hours. That way, we could work out our strategy so that when we get there, we won't be caught with our pants down around our ankles. Another thing, remember me telling you when I was in Canada and found out about the cousin we have out there? Well I think this would be the perfect time to look Jimmy up."

"I thought we were going out there on business, not a social call. You know I'm anxious to see the expression on Rando's face when he sees us."

"Will you lighten up a little? I thought you were going to be more open minded and not take everything so serious. I think we know what's going to take place when we see that bastard. We'll take care of him real quick and straighten out J.D. while we're there. It's real simple what we need to do."

"Nothing's ever simple where we're concerned. Every time we set out to do one thing, ten other things pop up. You know that's the way it is. What makes you think this time it'll be any different? We just have to be ready to deal with what ever comes along. If you want to try to find this Jimmy, if it's so important to you... we'll give it a shot, but don't make it a long drawn out process. Promise me that."

"I think that's fair. We'll call him, see if he's even interested in talking with us. Who knows, he might not want any part of getting together with us. His grandfather might not have been like ours. We'll have to play it by ear and see what happens. I promise I won't drag this thing out. We told J.D.'s wife we would be there as soon as we could. I'll call her back and give her an idea of about what time we'll be there. I'll remind her, how important it is that she doesn't say anything. I'll stress to her that it'll ruin what we're trying to accomplish by going out there. I only hope she can listen for a change. We don't need her blabbing all over Vegas that we're coming out there. Better yet... maybe I won't call her. What'da you think Sonnie about that?"

"That's a better idea."

The flight to L.A. wasn't as bad as their flight home from Italy. The weather was nice and the sky had this heavenly blue look, all the way there. There was no turbulence so the flight was a smooth one. Sonnie and Vince sat in first class and the flight wasn't crowded so they had a lot of room to stretch out. The stewardess was very friendly and seemed to be catering to the two of them. They liked that... it made the flight more pleasant. Everything was fine until about halfway through the flight, Sonnie thought he would get up and stretch his legs. When he got back to his seat, he seemed to be real agitated about something because he just sat there with a blank look on his face. Vince could tell something wasn't right so he asked him what was going on.

"I was alright, minding my own business... you know. Then I see these Muslins sitting in the back of the plane. That's when it all came back and I started thinking about things I wasn't supposed to."

Vince was just about to read him the riot act when this little girl about six years old, came running down the aisle and crawled over them and hid in the seat next to Vince.

"Why you hiding?" Vince asked. "You shouldn't be playing games on the airplane. Don't you know your mommy will be worried when she can't find you? You better go find her."

"I'm not worried...I'm hiding from my brother...He told me he was going to throw me off the plane and I'm scared. He told me if I didn't stop crying about Daddy, that was what he was going to do."

"Why you crying for your daddy?" Vince wanted to know.

"He went to heaven and I miss him. We have to move to Grandma's and live in Daddy's old house. I don't want to go there. I just want my Daddy to come home so everything can be the same."

"See my friend sitting there? His mother and father both went to heaven when he was smaller than you. He went to live with his grandma and grandpa and had a great time. Your grandma will love you and take care of you just like your daddy would have. She'll teach you all the things she learned while she was growing up and she'll be able to tell you all about your father and what he did when he was little, just like you. Now you go back there and tell your big brother you're not afraid and for him to leave you alone."

"Can I sit here some more before I go back?"

"Just a little while... then you have to go. Your mommy will be worried about you."

"Okay could you put your arm around me for a minute... like my Daddy did?"

Sonnie could only smile at Vince knowing this was an awkward moment for him. After the little girl returned to her seat, Sonnie and Vince relaxed and watched one of the godfather mafia movies. Vince agreed when Sonnie suggested that this Mario guy must have had relatives in their village.

When the plane touched down, they couldn't feel a thing, unlike the flight from Italy. It was a beautiful day and the temperature was about twenty degrees warmer than it was back east. The air smelt fresh and they wondered what all the hype was about L.A. being full of smog. They made their way to where they were to pick up their luggage and surprisingly, it was waiting for them. Sonnie suggested to Vince they call their new found cousin from the airport to see if he was interested in meeting with them before they went on this wild goose chase trying to find him. Vince took his advice, only to find Jimmy didn't own the business anymore and had sold his interest to invest in a hotel in Vegas. Vince got the name of the hotel, called and made reservations from the airport using their Italian names which were Vincenzo and Santino. They made their way to the car rental office and rented a sleek sports car convertible and took off for Vegas. All the way there, Sonnie was saying how nice it was to be free from all the bullshit they were always involved in. They were like a couple of kids out joy-riding with the top down and the music blasting.

"I think we've got company," Vince said as he looked in the mirror and saw a car speeding towards them.

The car behind them turned on red flashing lights and Vince pulled over, when he noticed two female officers getting out of the patrol car, he started unbuttoning the three top buttons of his shirt.

"What the hell you doing?" Sonnie wanted to know.

"You always see girls doing it on T.V. and it always works for them. I thought I would give it a try."

"They'll either die laughing or arrest you for indecent exposure. Com'on Vinny, stop fuck'n around. We don't know what sense of humor they have around here. It's not like back home, I hear these people are serious out here."

The officers walked up to the car, one on each side with one hand resting on their guns.

"Where you gentlemen going in such a hurry?" one officer asked.

"We're on our way to Vegas." Vince explained. "It's our first time out here. We were talking business and you know, with such an open road… we just didn't pay attention to our speed officer."

"Where you coming from?"

"We're out here from Atlantic city. We want to see how much better the gambling is out here and a few other things. You get the picture."

"You realize you were going ninety-five in a seventy-five? I'm not going to spoil your vacation, so I'll just give you a warning this time. I'm going to take your plate number and if I see you got a ticket somewhere else, I'll issue you one too. Oh, and one more thing... You better button your shirt back up before you get a bad sunburn. The sun's hotter than you think, out here."

"Thanks officer, we really appreciate this," Sonnie smiled as he handed the officer standing on his side of the car, a card from their casino.

"If you're ever in Atlantic City, look us up and we'll make your visit a pleasant one."

Vince and Sonnie watched in delight as the two female officers returned to their car and sped off in a cloud of dust.

"Now you watch what she said," Sonnie warned. "No telling what those two would do to us once they got us in handcuffs."

They both enjoyed a good laugh knowing inside that what was waiting for them in Vegas, would be no laughing matter. Whatever happened, they would be together and things would work out... or would they?

CHAPTER THIRTY

When Vince and Sonnie drove into Vegas, they were amazed at the scope of things and they couldn't believe how everything changed from the last time they were there. It had been only a couple of years but everything was different from what they remembered. The hotels, restaurants and what amazed them the most, were the signs, they couldn't believe the size of them. They didn't know what to expect but were quite pleased when they found Jimmy's hotel and casino. It was one of the nicest places on the strip and it was twice as big as the one they owned in Atlantic City. Thirty stories high, with glass windows all around and a sign that covered a third of the building, gave it a real modern look compared to theirs.

As they walked into the lobby, they couldn't believe the size of it. It was about the size of a football field and just about as wide, with slot machines all over the place and all in use. The ceiling must have been three stories high. The music of Sinatra and the rat pack was blaring over the speaker systems. Sonnie told Vince they better get busy and change the design of their place... a lot. Their suites were some of the best they'd ever seen. There was a bar completely stocked with the finest whiskeys and wines in the country. The view of the strip was breathtaking. Sonnie wasn't sure he was ready for all the bright lights shining in the room but when he drew the drapes, it made the room more relaxing. They could tell whomever decorated the suites, knew what they were doing. The walls were painted in a textured soft taupe that complimented the fawn colored carpet. There was a sunken living room with big wrap-around leather sofas and a big screen television with surround sound. In the master suite was a California king size bed with modern furniture and a lot of glass and chrome. The pictures on the walls were illusions of different Hollywood movies. Vince's suite was the same size but decorated differently, still in the same style.

After they got settled in, Sonnie wanted to call J.D.'s wife to let her know they were in town but Vince thought otherwise. He thought they should look around a little and see what the place was all about first. He explained to Sonnie, if they knew a little more about the place and got their bearings first, it would be easier for them to take care of their business. Vince stressed to Sonnie that they should get done with what they had to do and get back home as soon as possible. Sonnie agreed. After relaxing a while, Sonnie and Vince met for dinner. As they passed the front desk, Vince told the man behind the reception desk if Mr. Jimmy G. was in, he was to tell him that his cousins were having dinner in his restaurant.

"Mr. J. is in now," the man replied with an English accent. "Should I give him the message now?"

"What do you think?" Vinny nodded as he and Sonnie turned and walked away.

When they entered the restaurant, they weren't surprised by the size of it. Like everything else in Vegas, it was huge and had two entrances. As usual, they requested a table where Sonnie could see the back door and Vince could see the front. It was a practice they always had in public places, you cover my back and I'll cover yours. After receiving their drinks, they settled down to talk business and try to plan their strategy. They were on their own and had no one in Vegas to help with their situation. As they talked, Vince noticed a well dressed guy talking to the manager and the manager was pointing at him and Sonnie. He assumed this was their cousin Jimmy. Vince touched Sonnie on the arm and motioned for him to look towards the door. As the guy walked towards them, neither of them knew what to expect. Sonnie and Vince thought he might look a little like them but if this was Jimmy, he didn't look like a relative, not even a distant one. Jimmy had that Vegas look. You know, grey tailored silk mohair suit with a light blue pin stripe and dark blue shirt with matching tie and hankie in the suit pocket. His initialed cuffs exposed big diamond cuff links. He was approximately five-eleven, slender built with medium brown hair that was cut with precision unlike Sonnie and Vince who were big framed and had dark wavy hair. He walked with authority as he greeted the people while walking towards their table. He had a big smile but you could tell it was a tired smile. Sonnie and Vince knew Jimmy lead a different life-style than they did. Once Jimmy, or Mr. J as he was known in Vegas, got to the table, he asked them if they were the ones claiming to be his cousins. Vince invites him to join them and Jimmy pulled out a chair and sat down. Sonnie instructed the waiter to bring him whatever he normally drinks.

"I don't drink while I'm working," Jimmy went on to say. "So tell me, how do you think we're related? Who gave you that story? I know of no relatives except the ones I have back home in Brazil. I've only seen them a couple times since my father and I moved to the states. You know, in my position... I have to be careful. Someone's always trying something."

"First, I'm Vincent and this is Sonnie," Vince explained as he extended his hand to Jimmy and. Sonnie did the same. "You know our last name because it's the same as yours. We didn't know about you either. When I lived in Canada, this friend of mine was into genealogy and she's the one that tracked you down. Our Grandfathers were brothers. Did you know anything about them?"

"You tell me about them. There's a lot of kooks out there, making a lot of claims. Like I said, I don't know who to trust. Everyone's got a story, I've got to be careful. Just because we have the same last name, doesn't mean anything to me."

"Is that what you think... this is a scam? You're way off base here. If you think we're here to..."

"Hold on Sonnie," Vince interrupted. "I don't think he means anything. I can understand where he's coming from..."

Before they could continue their conversation, the manager came over and told Jimmy someone was there from New York and needed to talk with. Jimmy told the manager to seat them and he would be with them as soon as he could.

"I didn't mean it like it sounded," Jimmy apologized to Sonnie. "I've had some unpleasant experiences with people trying to get one up on me since I moved out here. I never knew people were as devious as they are. I'm almost sorry I took this place. I thought there were some back-stabbers in L.A. but they're worse here. In L.A., they hide and you have to look for them. Here, they come right up to you and tell you to have a nice day, while planning to do you in. So don't be upset if I'm a little leery about things. I have to keep on my toes."

Again, the manager interrupted and motioned to Jimmy that he had a phone call but Jimmy just waves him off.

"I've got an idea," Sonnie suggested. "Why don't you take care of business and we'll get together later? We have some business to attend to that's going to take a little time and some luck, so... say we meet after you finish up here. Just let me say this to you about your grandfather and you can think on it. He and my grandfather, his name was Quadrio, were brothers... like I said. They were from this town in the mountains north of Naples called Abbate. You know all those little towns are controlled by one organization or another. Some of them get along and some don't. Well, Genaro and Quadrio controlled the organization in Abbate. Your grandmother's name was Regina and your mother's name was Lenetta. She died the day you were born."

The manager motioned to Jimmy again about the phone.

"This sounds like something I've heard before," Jimmy said. "Why don't you take care of business and call me in a couple of hours. I'll be able to get away then. Here's my card with my private number... call me. I should be free from all this mess around ten or ten-thirty."

As Jimmy was about to leave the table and take his phone call, Sonnie and Vince heard this winery voice.

"Hey Jimmy where you been? "

Coming straight to the table, was this odd-looking character walking fast like he was tying to get away from someone. He was

Cousins II

roughly five-foot-five with power blue tightly tapered to the ankle pants that looked like they were from the fifties. He had on a purple and green striped shirt with the collar turned up. The shirt was opened in the front exposing an undershirt and had a raw hide shoe lace around his neck with some kind of symbol hanging from it. You could tell that he was a heavy smoker because you could smell it ten feet away. He was constantly looking around like he was expecting something to happen. His face was full of wrinkles and he looked old but it was probably from his lifestyle. His head was shaved and he had extremely small ears that looked as if someone had taped them back when he was a kid. Another thing they noticed, he was constantly blinking his eyes as if there was something in them.

"I've been looking for you. I'm broke again... how about a marker for a couple grand? I feel hot, I know my luck's changing... I can feel it. How about we go to the track tomorrow? You always tell me we're going but we never do. You're not busy are you? Who's these guys? Do I know them? Where you going? Wait... hold on Jimmy."

Sonnie looked at Vince, "He's got one too."

They both laughed and Jimmy glanced at them with a puzzled look.

"I'll explain later," Sonnie uttered to Jimmy as he scurried away.

Jimmy left to take his phone call with this character that was all too familiar to Sonnie and Vince, trailing behind him. While eating their dinner, Sonnie and Vince were trying to put together some kind of a plan on how to handle the situation when they find J.D. and this person that they expect to be Rando. They elected not to call J.D.'s wife just yet. They wanted to locate J.D. and find out what was going on, so they thought they would start by looking in some of the casinos J.D.'s wife told them about. Sonnie and Vince searched the different casinos with no luck. They decided to go back to the hotel and tomorrow, would stake out J.D.'s house. If he showed up there and was alone, they would follow him and hopefully he would lead them to Rando. When they got back to the hotel, there was a message from

Jimmy saying he was available and for them to give him a call as soon as they got the message… he'd be waiting.

When they got up to Vince's suite, it was going on eleven-thirty and they called Jimmy. Jimmy was free to talk to them if it wasn't too late and invited them to his penthouse. When they got there, Sonnie and Vince were in aw at the way it looked. Jimmy had taken two of the penthouses and made them into one. Before he had come to Vegas, Jimmy had traveled all over the world, so his place was decorated with pieces from everywhere. Europe, China, Japan, Vietnam, you name a country and there was probably a piece of furniture or something hanging on the wall from there. The great-room took up one whole side of the top floor. Sonnie couldn't get over the size of it. Jimmy showed them to the bar and fixed them all a drink. Jimmy told them he was curious about what they had told him earlier about his family. He went on to say that he made a call back to Brazil and asked one of his relatives, who he hadn't talked to in years, some questions. She told Jimmy something similar to what Sonnie had told him. Now he was interested in hearing more, so Sonnie told him everything. He started by mentioning again that Jimmy's grandfather Genaro and his brother Quadrio, ran the organization in Abbate. He told him that there was a politician and a police chief that was trying to put them out of business. Against Quadrio's wishes, Genaro and two of his friends, killed them both. That was the reason he had to go to Brazil. Vince told Jimmy that his grandfather came back fifteen years later but it wasn't the same between him and Quadrio so he went back to Brazil where he later died of cancer. Jimmy, after many more questions, sounded convinced.

"I guess that makes us cousins after all. You'll have to forgive me for what I said earlier but you know how things are in this world today. You can't trust anybody. By the way, you haven't told me anything about yourselves. You seem to know a lot about me but I know nothing about you. Tell me… besides seeing me, why are you in Vegas? You said you had some business to take care of. If you need anything, let me know. I have some connections."

"We have a bakery and wine distribution business in Atlantic City," Sonnie told Jimmy. "Vince and I… like you, are in the hotel and casino business also. We just recently purchased it. It isn't as large as yours but it'll do for now. We have some big plans for it later down the road."

"No offense... but you guys don't look like bakers to me. How's the hotel business there? Is it as hectic as it is here? Sometimes I get pretty fed up with it. I didn't realize how demanding it was. I'm used to doing my own thing and sometimes, I can't move because of this place."

"Back east, we get a break when the weather gets bad... everything slows down. That gives us time to revamp and make any necessary changes. We also have a haircutting salon there."

"Hair cutting salon? You don't look like barbers either. What's up with you guys? This gets more interesting by the minute. What other surprises do you guys have up your sleeves? Or do I want to know?"

"That's how all this started," Sonnie went on to say. "Quadrio was a barber back home in Italy and we learned the trade there. When he died, I inherited the business along with the organization. Things went crazy after that and I came to America. As to why we're here, we're looking for someone. We have an associate from back east living out here and we have reason to believe that the person we're looking for, may be here also. It's very important we find him. We haven't contacted our associate yet, we don't want him to know we're here. He'll find out soon enough."

"If I may ask, who's your associate? Does he have a business here? I might know him," Jimmy replied.

"We took over his business and he retired here. He owned the bakery and wine importing business and it got to be too much for him. His name is Joe Dolfino, he goes by J.D. His wife's been telling us he's having some problems with gambling. She said he's running up tabs all over town since this other person showed up."

"I know who you're talking about, he's into me for about forty-grand. He was here last night. Every time we talk to him about it, he tells us we don't know who he is and if we don't treat him right, he'll call back east and they'll come and straighten everything out. Are you the ones he was going to call? I'm beginning to see some things going on here. Did you come out here to help him get straight because if you did, you got a lot of straightening out to do? He's in trouble all over this town and you better be careful. Some people are real pissed at him."

Sonnie and Vince went on to tell Jimmy about what happened to J.D. and why they took over the business.

"So what you're telling me is… you guys, my cousins that I just found out I had, are in organized crime. You're the Mafia. Don't that just figure?"

"We don't like that word and we're not here to get you involved with anything that's going on with us. It bugged me that we had a cousin that we didn't know and wanted to find out about him… That's all. For all we know, we're the last ones in the family. Don't think we came to you for help, it's not like that. Besides, we can take care of our own business."

"Look Vince, I understand what you're telling me. I know where you're coming from but you don't know the trouble these guys have been causing. This guy J.D., he's a little punk. He tries to throw his weight around and he doesn't have any. The guy you're talking about, he showed up about a month or six weeks ago. Since then, they've been going crazy. I don't know where they're getting all the money they're throwing around. This J.D. won't settle any of his debits but he just goes at it real hard. I think they're doing heroin or some kind of drug. They always have that look about them. Everyone's getting real tired of the bullshit they're putting people through. When the money runs out, it'll only be a matter of time before someone makes them pay for all the shit that he's putting people through."

"Have you seen this other guy with J.D.? What's he look like? Sonnie asked."

"He's average, nothing special. When he gets drunk, he starts talking like Pop Eye and showing off his tattoo. He thinks its real funny. That's the only thing I can tell you about him."

Jimmy's description of J.D.'s partner has Sonnie and Vince convinced that it is indeed Rando.

"We've gone this far," Vince told Sonnie. "Go ahead and tell Jimmy why we're here."

"This bastard that's with J.D... his name is Rando and we've been looking for him about four or five months. We were in Italy on some business... that's when he ripped us off to the tune of about a quarter-mill. Some of that money he's spending is ours, that's why we're here. You know what has to be done. Just tell us... where's the local landfill?"

"That's the last place you want to go. I know a better place. Besides, some of your friends have stayed here in my hotel. They're the ones that gave me the idea."

"What are you talking about?"

"The DeMarco brothers from Boston, Jimmy Catolo from Detroit, he was here last month for the first time and Eugene Cappazolli from Jersey. Those are the heavy-hitters that stayed here. I try to keep the wise guys out of the place, all they do is tear things up. I have certain limitations. All you guys know each other... right?"

"We know some of them but we try to keep a low profile, if you know what I mean. I'm glad you're familiar with our lifestyle. That makes our business here a little easier for you to understand. We're not here to get you involved. Just give us a little information and we'll do the rest."

"Hey, what's family for if you can't help one another? I live in Vegas... I've seen a lot since I moved here. Let me make a few calls. I'll get Wormy, he's that little ass-hole that bothered me when we were talking earlier. I apologize for that. By the way, why did you guys laugh when he showed up? Was it the way he dresses?"

"No, that's not it," Sonnie laughed. "We have a guy back home... his name is Petey... they could be twins. He's a great guy but what a pain in the ass sometime. If we want to know anything, we call him. He knows all the shit that's going on in town. We hate to admit sometime how important he is to us, but he is."

"Worm's the same way. Once I tell him what we want, he'll be able to find out everything about them including what time they take a shit. That's why I put up with his bullshit. Why don't you guys turn in and I'll get with you tomorrow and maybe I'll have some answers.

Then we can take care of business. You guys need anything before you turn in, you know… like something to hug up to?"

As Sonnie and Vince got up to leave, Vince smiled, "We're good."

It was about one-thirty and Sonnie went up to his suite. Meanwhile, Vince was feeling lucky and went down to give it a try. He could have had a lot of luck with the ladies but the tables were cold.

CHAPTER THIRTY-ONE

    Once again, Sonnie spent another restless night. He spent most of it standing on the balcony and watching the hundreds of people walking the streets. He couldn't believe what he was seeing. *'How do they handle it?'* he thought. Vince called the next morning at eight-thirty and told him he was on his way over. When he got there, he looked a wreck. Sonnie wanted to know what the hell he'd been doing.

    "You look like you been up all night. You look terrible. Go do something with yourself. I haven't slept either... I should have come with you. I would have had a better time that sitting here all night. What did you do all night?"

    "Sonnie, you can't believe how easy it is to get laid out here. All you have to do is stand there with a bunch of chips in your hand. It's like having a hand full of bird seed. All the pigeons just flock to you. They're wide open out here. I walked the whole strip and looked to see how we could handle this problem of ours. It's not going to be so easy to take care of business out here. There's all kinds of security around. We might have to call Dario and let him handle things. I can't see any other way."

    "There's got to be something we can do. I hate that maybe we wasted a trip out here for nothing. Let's not be too hasty. It might take a little longer but we'll find a way. Let's wait and see what Jimmy comes up with and go from there. I'm going to try and lay down for a while, maybe I'll be able to get some rest. Why don't you do the same and we'll get together later and go hunting."

Vince agreed and went back to his suite and Sonnie finally got to sleep around ten. When his cell phone rang, he knew it had to be someone from back home. He told Bobby and Angelo not to call him unless it was something very important. *'What the hell's going on back there? Something's wrong, I can sense it. This is all I need.'*

"Talk to me," Sonnie said harshly as he answered the phone.

"Hi honey, I've been thinking about you and just wanted to tell you so. You sound like something's wrong. You okay?"

"I'm sorry, I thought it might be Bobby telling me something I didn't want to hear. I'm glad you called. This place is really crazy out here. It's wide open twenty-four hours a day. I couldn't handle it."

"Everything's fine here. Don't worry about anything. The place is in good hands. I know it's only been two days but I just had to hear your voice. It's pretty lonely without you. My bed is cold. How long is it going to take you to get everything straightened out there?"

"I can't tell you that but I don't think we'll be very long. Just let Bobby or Bull know if you have a problem that can't wait 'til we get back. That's what they're there for. Don't try to do anything by yourself. I'll get back as soon as I can."

"Be careful honey. I miss you."

Connie hung up the phone and no sooner Sonnie had put his cell phone down, it rang again.

"What the hell's going on? Talk to me."

"Hey Sonnie, it's Bobby. Sorry to bother you… I've got something interesting to tell you. I don't know if you want to hear it but I thought you should know before you come back. You don't need this surprise."

"Is anything wrong? Does it have anything to do with Rando? Have we got trouble?"

"Nothing like that. You'll never believe it. Guess whose moving back here?"

"Let me stop you right there. It's not what use to be my worse nightmare is it?"

"You got it. Pete's wife doesn't want to live in the islands anymore and she wants to move here in Atlantic City because she says his friends are all here. You might think I'm crazy but I'm a little excited."

"He's changed... just a little. I think I can put up with him a little better now. Vinny will be glad to hear it...Yea right. I'm glad that's the only thing you were calling me about and we haven't had any major malfunctions."

"Everything's going real smooth... don't worry. Angie's been a big help. See you after you take care of business. Oh by the way, he's looking at a house just down the street from you." With that said, Bobby hung up.

Sonnie called Vincent and asked him if he was ready to get some work done. Vince told him he would be over in fifteen minutes and they would talk and get a bite to eat. While at the restaurant, Jimmy showed up and told them that Wormy had been successful in finding out the information they needed.

"Last night after you guys left, I put in a call to Wormy. He called me back just a little while ago and said he had caught up with Rando shortly after we talked last night but J.D. wasn't with him. I told Wormy to tell him there was a high-dollar game tonight in my private game room about ten-thirty. He said Rando would be there with lots of money. Wormy didn't say whether or not J.D. would be with him."

"You sure you want to get involved with this bullshit? Vince asked. "We can find another way. We don't want anything to come down on you if anything goes wrong. We'll find a way to take care of the problem ourselves. We're not just going to slap him on the wrists and send him on his way. You understand what's going to go down here."

"Vince, this guy J.D.'s been a pain in everyone's asses since he's come to Vegas. I've already talked to some of the big casino people and they're willing to forget about the money he owes them, just so he disappears. He's been such a pain in the ass, some of the bosses were trying to find a way to get rid of him themselves. Now with this other character around, it's twice as bad."

"Maybe we should let them take care of it Sonnie. What'da you think?"

"Not on your life Vinny. I want that bastard for what he's done to us. I can't let someone else have the pleasure of doing away with him. Besides, they would be too easy on him. I want the bastard to suffer. Jimmy, if you're in this with us... you have to understand what ever happens, you can't ever let anyone know what went down."

"If I'm going to be involved in this Sonnie, you can rest assured it's going to be our little secret. I even have a plan... now listen. Wormy will get him here for the card game. He'll take him to the bar for a couple of hours first and get him all liquored up. We'll watch from the surveillance room. Then between ten and ten-thirty, I'll go to the game room and wait for Wormy to get him there. When he ask where all the other players are, I'll tell him they're running a shade late and send Wormy to find them and bring them to the game. That's when you and Vinny come in. Under all these casinos, there's a big sewer system that runs under ground for about fifty miles and empties into a water purifying system for the whole city, so you know how large it is. When anything's dumped in there, it's never found again. Every night from four to six A.M., all the casinos flush out their systems. If anything's in those sewer lines...you can figure out the rest. A lot of things disappear... if you get my drift."

"Sounds like you've been thinking about this for quite a while," Vince replied. "It sounds good to me. What about it, Sonnie?"

"Sounds good to me, Vinny. The only thing that bothers me, well... it's really two things. How do we get him down there without causing a scene? You know we're going to have a fight on our hands. The other thing is, what about J.D.? What do you want to do about him? He really hasn't given us any reason for him to pay the price, he's just a little out of control. Maybe if we have a talk with him before we go back east, he'll be alright. What'da you think?"

"That's fine with me Sonnie but what if he's with Rando? What do we do then? Personally, I think he's too far gone. I don't think he can be reasoned with. He was like this even before that prick showed up, but I'll do whatever you want to do with him. As for Rando, I think I can handle him without any trouble. All the drugs and booze he's been into, he's not going to be in the shape he once was. That shit takes a toll on you fast. So Jimmy, it looks like a plan. Sonnie, we've got all day to ponder about this, you going to be okay? You know how you get."

"Sonnie... to answer your question, after you and Vinny get done with him, we'll take him down the freight elevator. That leads straight to the maintenance area. Then we're home free. Besides, no one questions what I do here. If I may make a suggestion, there's a lot of neat places here. Why don't you guys do some sight-seeing while you have nothing to do? I can point you in the right direction. Better yet, why don't you let my limo take you? That way, you won't get lost."

So, away Sonnie and Vince go on their sight-seeing tour. The limo took them all over Vegas. Frankly, if you've seen one casino you've seen them all. They didn't care for the museums and the historical places but it took their mind off the events that were about to happen that night. They got back at six-thirty and went to the restaurant to eat but didn't have much of an appetite. They both went to their suites to try and get some rest but that didn't work either. Sonnie called Vince and told him he was going to take a steam bath and get a massage hoping it would make him feel better. Vince joined him. These Vegas masseuse didn't hold a candle to the girls back home. Jimmy caught up with them at eight-thirty that evening. They went to Jimmy's penthouse where there was a buffet table set up and they all watched a basketball game on the big screen television but had to leave before the game was over.

They went to the surveillance room and when Wormy and Rando walked in, Sonnie and Vince couldn't even recognize Rando. He had changed so much from the drugs and all the other shit he was into. He used to be clean-cut and walked with confidence. Now, he was hunched over and his hair was long and stringy. Sonnie and Vince said it would, in time catch up with him. Now, they see it did just that. J.D. wasn't with them at the time but joined them an hour later. They were drinking like it was their last day on earth... little did they know. All the hookers were around them because they knew they were an easy mark. By ten, Wormy suggested they go to the private game that was to take place at ten-thirty. It took a little while but he finally got Rando and J.R. away from the bar and the girls. When Wormy, Rando and J.D. arrived at the game room, the only one there was Jimmy. Jimmy told Wormy to go get the other players. Wormy left and five minutes later, Sonnie and Vince entered the room.

"What the hell you doing here?" Rando shouted. "God damn J.D., we've got to get the hell out of here!"

As Rando tried to make a break for the door, Vince grabbed him and threw him over a table.

"What's going on here?" J.D. yelled as he braced himself against the wall.

"This prick never told you what he did… did he? This prick, who we trusted with everything, stole from us. Not only did he steal from us, he used us and you know how we are about that. Where do you think he got all that money he's been spending around here J.D.? It's the money he took from us."

"That isn't what he told me. He told me he was broke and you and Sonnie sent him out here for me to take care of. That's my money he's been spending. He told me you were going to pay me back. You mean he lied to me? You guys didn't…man, I don't know what to say. If I would have known Sonnie, I would have called you and told you what was going on. He's got me in so much god damn trouble with all the casino people here, I'll have to leave town. I ought to kill that bastard."

"What did you do with all that money you took from…no stole from us? Where is it?" Vince asked as he smashed a hard right hand across Rando's face.

"It's gone. That bitch I was with spent it all on drugs. She got me hooked. I lost all focus… once I got in, I couldn't get out. When she over-dosed … that's when I came out here."

"Didn't you think we would find you?" Vince asked. "You knew what would happen if we did. You worked for us a long time… You know how we operate. What do you think we should do with you? You think we should give you another chance? That's not going to happen."

"I think you should make him pay for what he did to you and me," J.D. added, pointing his finger at Rando. "How am I going to get along now? Everything's gone, I didn't realize what he was doing to me."

"Yea... you were too busy having a good time," Sonnie shot back. "You've treated your wife like shit... fucking around on her with all those fancy girls. Gambling all night, doing drugs and getting in deeper and deeper. Any one your age should know better. We should be pissed at you too J.D. We took care of you because we respected you for what you did for us... how you trusted us and worked with us. We owed you for that but not for this. This is disgraceful. You've gone back on everything you've stood for. What do you think we should do with him Vinny?"

"Sonnie, he told me he didn't care about the money," Rando admitted. "He knew you would be giving him more. He said you would do anything he said because you owed him. I know what's in store for me, but don't listen to him."

Vince tied Rando to a chair while Jimmy went to check to see if the coast was clear. Jimmy returned about thirty minutes later and told Sonnie and Vince that everything was set up. They hustled Rando and J.D. to the freight elevator and down to the maintenance room. It was now about two-thirty. Jimmy got a couple of chairs and they tied Rando and J.D. there until the magic hour. J.D. was begging for them to spare his life asking them not to let him die like this. Sonnie and Vince ignored him for the most part but Jimmy was getting aggravated with his begging and put a gag in his mouth. They waited, pacing back and forth looking at their watches. It was a long hour and a half, but four A.M. finally arrived. They walked Rando and J.D. to the edge of the waste canal and waited. Soon, they could hear the systems start to open up and the waste spewing through the canal. Sonnie shoved Rando into the waste canal and let him lay there. They expected more resistance from him but he knew it was useless to beg. J.D. on the other hand, sank to his knees and lay lifeless on the floor. As the waste swept Rando away, they cut J.D. loose and took the gag out of his mouth. J.D. was clutching Sonnie's hand and thanking him for letting him live. As Sonnie and Vince turned to walk away, Jimmy got caught up in the moment and shoved J.D. into the waste canal. Jimmy joined Sonnie and Vince and the three cousins walked away.

"What'da you say we get something to eat," Jimmy suggested.

"Good idea…I'm starving," Sonnie replied. "I need to wash my hands. I touched some shit and they stink."

While they were eating, Sonnie told Jimmy they were leaving in the morning.

"If you ever get tired of this rat race, we need someone to take care of our casino. We've got into the business not knowing anything about it and now, it's consuming too much of our time. We have other obligations and this casino's becoming a pain in the ass. Life's much simpler there. You won't be sorry."

"I'll second that," Vince added.

"You make it sound very inviting. Let me have some time to think this thing out."

They lifted their glasses and toasted their new relationship. The next day bright and early, Sonnie and Vince left for Atlantic City.

EIGHTEEN MONTHS LATER…

The remodeling of Sonnie and Vince's casino was complete. The weather in Atlantic City can sometimes be unpredictable but Sonnie still insisted on a cookout at his house, Sunday the day before the grand opening, for all the troops.

Petey, his wife and new baby moved into a large house just down the street from Sonnie and brought several trays of island cuisine.

Bull was there and brought a tub of barbeque ribs he had cooked himself.

Chico and his girl brought numerous Latin dishes along with Latin music.

Gina and all the girls from the Clip Joint brought salad and fruit trays while Theresa and Connie provided goodies from the bakery.

Bobby and Angie brought to the celebration a whole cow and had it dressed and delivered the day before.

Jimmy arrived a week earlier after getting the invitation for the grand opening. He didn't tell Sonnie or Vince he was in Atlantic City until the day of the cookout because he wanted to look around at his own leisure. He cautiously checked out Sonnie and Vince, along with their Casino, and found it to be a very workable situation. The casino was smaller than the one in Vegas but Jimmy liked that. He could see great potential… him being there.

When Jimmy arrived at the cookout, Sonnie and Vince were surprised to see him. Jimmy immediately blended in with all the different characters and really seemed to hit it off well with Gina. Even Sonnie and Vince noticed how the two of them were carrying on like old friends. After a couple of hours, Jimmy asked Sonnie if there was a place that the three of them could talk in private. They went inside to Sonnie's office and after thirty minutes, the three of them returned to the party.

"Everyone… our cousin Jimmy here, has an announcement to make. Take it away Jimmy."

"I've decided to accept the offer of Sonnie and Vince, my two long-lost cousins, to become partners with them in their new casino."

There was a hardy round of applause from everyone.

"This deserves a toast," Gina exclaimed as she raised her glass and everyone followed.

"This…right here," Vince added, "is the true meaning of family."

"Salute"

EPILOGUE

For three years, things at the casino/hotel along with Sonnie and Vince's organization were going smoothly. Jimmy worked his way into the family easily with the approval of his two cousins. His knowledge of running the casino and his alliance with Sonnie and Vince proved more beneficial than first anticipated. It all seemed too easy.

However, it wasn't going as well for Johnny Rocco and the organizations in New York. There was a turf war that had been going on for two years which all started over a territory dispute. It seemed like none of the bosses could make up their minds as to who owned what, so all the heads of the families got together but nothing was accomplished. Johnny Rocco suggested to his boss they needed a good negotiator, someone that was impartial. He knew just the guy…Sonnie.

At the same time in Philly, Marco and Denny were having some differences. Actually, they had a major falling-out and Denny put a hit out on Marco. With the help of some wise guys that wanted to step up in the organization, Marco stopped the attempt and turned the tables on Denny and he was killed. In the process, Marco was wounded several times and ended up in a wheel chair.

Sonnie, Vince and Jimmy had the only organization with any stability. Therefore, all the families in New York at Johnny Rocco's suggestion… contacted Sonnie for help. All the while, Marco was doing the same. Sonnie had a plan, so he met with Vince and Jimmy. The plan was for him to go to New York and become the boss of all the bosses. Vince was to go to Philly and get in with Marco and eventually take over the organization.

Jimmy would stay in Atlantic City and handle things there. Bull, Bobby and Angelo stayed in Atlantic City and worked for Jimmy.

Petey, now the father of three, had settled down and took a position at the casino with Jimmy.

Gina and the girls at the Clip Joint remained together and their business flourished.

Theresa followed Vince to Philly and opened up a little boutique selling high-end fashions and accessories for women.

After a lot of thought, Connie chose not to follow Sonnie to New York and stayed to run the bakery. She gave up her apartment and moved into Sonnie's house.

Sonnie's triangle of power was now complete and the Cousins were in complete control.